JASON'S PLACE
Leon Dennis

◆

Historical Fiction

JASON'S PLACE

CONTENTS

THE RELEASE.. 1
EVACUATION 3
COME TO REST 18
UNFAMILIAR REGIONS.. 28
THE GUNNS.. 39
FIRST CHRISTMAS.. 51
THE THANKSGIVING 62
THE BEREAVEMENT 73
AN EFFORT OF WILL... 85
LEGALITY... 99
NEW ARRIVALS 105
PROPOSALS 112
STRIPES & COLOURED PATCHES 131
TRAGEDY 139
PLANS AND VERDICT.. 148
NIGHT OF TERROR... 156
PREPARATIONS... 164
THE WEDDING 171
IN A NUTSHELL 179
THE WILL.. 191
BAD NEWS 200
A FRUGAL CHRISTMAS... 208
CHANGES 218
NO RESPITE 229
A NEW UNDERSTANDING.. 236
THE ENIGMA SOLVED... 247
FAIR GAME OR FAIR PLAY... 258
OPENING OF LETTERS 265
THE MOVE & ALLIED LANDINGS 272

HANS 'S REPLY.. 278

RAMIFICATIONS... 283

HANS & LAURA 293

HENRY & MADGE... 302

Dedications

I would like to acknowledge the following people for their help, advice and support. Sue Gibbons, Joan Edmond, Diny van Kleeff, Tony Flood and Anderida Writers.

PROLOGUE

Fascism would fight imperialism, the discontent among certain factions stretching from Albania to the south and as far north to the Polish boarders. France and Britain were feeling threatened inasmuch, as Britain would send an expeditionary force to strengthen the borders of the Low Countries.

Bert Kneally, who had recently joined the territorials, had to undergo his military training in his spare time. His detachment were under the command and attached to the Royal Fusiliers. From time to time, Bert and his comrades would journey to Colchester barracks to be taught how to fight hand-to-hand combat and throw grenades, shoot at moving targets and use a machine gun.

The detachment made many a journey over a period of months from 1936 onwards. He found the company full of exuberance and enthusiasm, and lively debates would follow as to when the unrest in Germany would boil over and another war begin.

Nineteen thirty nine arrived with the song "Lambeth Walk" ringing in the ears of the East Ender. A young female singer was making a name for herself on the radio with leading orchestras, and people humming and whistling the tunes she sang.

Mary and Bert Kneally were happy in the electrical shop they owned. Their son Henry was progressing well in his lessons at school, Aunt Lillian who taught at the school, would eventually take him under her wing. She had recognised Henry as being a born artist.

The clouds of war descended over Europe. It would engulf all the land in flames and destruction.

CHAPTER ONE

THE RELEASE

Bert Kneally received the call one morning for him and his comrades to assemble at the drill hall in Old Road. His wife Mary only had time to kiss and embrace him on the doorstep of the little shop. His last words, "give Henry a hug for me" and with her eyes watering, he was suddenly gone.

The troops joined others at Dover docks, and the British expeditionary force set sail across the Channel to France to defend democracy and the motherland. Bert and his company fought a bitter rear-guard action to the last man.

The Stuka dived, screaming, and released two bombs aimed at the thin column of unprotected British soldiers. An order from an officer of the Royal Fusiliers echoed along the line. "Get down!" the flotilla off shore waited impatiently, and rescuers held their breath as the bombs exploded. An aftermath of carnage and outright slaughter was inflicted on the retreating army, and yet a piper in the distance could be heard piping a tune of glory.

Beads of sweat and blood ran down Bert's face, he lay horizontal to the receding tide. Bert raised his face to the morning sun and lapsed into an unconscious state.

The flotilla moved in haste with its cargo of injured and worn out troops. The beaches of Dunkirk ran red with the blood of the expeditionary force. They were no match against the German onslaught. Over three hundred thousand men were snatched to safety, and Bert would see the white cliffs of Dover again. As the soldiers disembarked on to the quay at Dover, there was love and laughter.

Bert was carried on a make shift stretcher, he regained consciousness on the homeward journey. Shipmates handed round Willy-woodbines and Players Medium, and steaming mugs of tea. Red Cross carers and Royal Alexandra nurses tended his wounds. Never in his life was so much compassion given by so few. Who cares a bugger, though; it was all over. After every soldier was counted, Bert and his mates were ordered in convoy to a rehabilitation compound ninety miles away to the outskirts of Leighton Buzzard. Nearing the town, but on a notorious bend at Eggington, Bert's wagon swung violently out of control, overturned and crashed upside down into a deep ditch.

Three of his comrades and he were killed outright. This was pure injustice, to survive Dunkirk, only to be killed on home soil was something Mary could not comprehend. Her heart heavy with the loss of Bert, she mourned for months.

CHAPTER TWO

EVACUATION

Before Bert Kneally volunteered to join the Territorial's an inheritance of the electrical shop bequeathed by his father Joseph, gave his family, Mary and son Henry, a decent sort of living. They had no competition in Old Street Shoreditch, which made life very busy. As Mary came to terms with her loss, she turned more and more to Bert's sister Aunt Lillian who to Henry was a surrogate mother. The shop she could manage, but Henry's welfare above all else presented a dilemma. Nights of intermittent bombing worried Mary. In earlier days with Bert and herself, they coped well with the shop. Henry lived mostly with Aunt Lillian.

Aunt Lillian, who lived in a small terraced cottage two streets from where she taught the juniors at Old Street Primary, also taught Henry after his infant days came to an end; Aunt Lillian laid the foundations to developing Henry's passion for his gift of drawing and painting, giving him every encouragement after school hours. One morning, after another night of sustained bombing Aunt Lillian confronted Mary about whether Henry should be evacuated.

Aunt Lillian explained. "I have heard through the headmaster that the L.C.C. are about to send a second batch of evacuees to the Home Counties. Do you think it would be in our best interest to send Henry, knowing he could be much safer away from here?"

"I have thought long and hard, and you are right, I suppose I was living in cloud cuckoo land hoping the bombs would stop" Mary replied.

"So you've decided, Henry will go, the second wave is due to leave in a week's time" Aunt Lillian revealed the letter to Mary.

Two days later for reasons, unknown L.C.C. cancelled the evacuation. Mary, her aspirations for Henry to be somewhere safe, and being of strong resolve, would carry on regardless of the situation.

Aunt Lillian suggested the three of them would use Old street tube station for protection from the air raids at night and a routine plan was quickly conceived. Each teatime she would wrap some food in greaseproof together with a thermos of dark rich cocoa, and pack them into a brown paper bag. As Aunt Lillian had left earlier from the juniors, she waited for Henry to call at the terraced cottage on his way home from secondary school. She would prepare a snack for him saving Mary the job before closing the shop.

London's traffic had lost its impetus. Every night among the scarred and beleaguered city Aunt Lillian and Henry would time their walk to coincide with Mary locking the shop and they would walk the half mile to Old street tube station. Even before the decent into the now familiar white tiled voluminous orifice, the atmosphere and acrid fumes wafted on a stream of warm air drifting into their nostrils. Their senses being guided by the now familiar sound of an accordion being played by an old gent, the melody reverberating along with hundreds of murmuring voices to Vera Lynn's "Well Meet Again".

Mary and Aunt Lillian hummed the tune, a resilience, a touch of defiance; that was what was needed. Henry's gate strode in time with the tune near enough to see the old gent's smiling face; they camped beside him and sang their hearts out, the night wears thin after a time.

A settling came down as bombs exploded; a fitful night ensued for Mary Aunt Lillian and Henry, snatching what little sleep the night noise allowed them.

Raising their heads wearily after what seemed a very long night, the three of them packed their belongings and made their way slowly up the long narrow stairway. A blast of cold air filled with an acidic magnesium smell, chilled their throats.

"Incendiaries" Aunt Lillian whispered. Everywhere was ablaze it was more than the fire service could cope with. Smouldering heaps of rubble lay strewn across Old street making it difficult to make their way through, as they did so Mary stopped abruptly and clutched Aunt Lillian's sleeve, "what's up mum?" Henry's voice broke the silence between them. "The shop" Mary replied.

Aunt Lillian cupped her hand over her mouth and held her breath. The shop was no more; it was wasted to the ground. A direct hit had pulverised the building. Mary was overcome with absolute despair.

"Where are we going to live now mum?" Henry shouted above the noise.

Aunt Lillian took charge of the crisis that had overtaken them, "well, let's see if my cottage is alright" she said.

They walked disconsolately on, turning in to Ashford Street where Aunt Lillian lived. An unbelievable sight met their eyes, all houses were intact, just a few slates and tiles scattered about "all the same "Aunt Lillian said, "We have a roof". They also learnt from a few soles that Old street School had survived and was serviceable for classes as usual.

***

Aunt Lillian's job at the primary school ended when all the juniors were evacuated earlier in the year. However, being seconded to teach at Old street secondary modern her art class proved very popular with 11-12 year olds. Henry came in the latter group. It was in one of these classes that a knock on the classroom door startled Aunt Lillian. Mr Shaunessy, the head, apologised for his intrusion,

"May I interpose on your class for a few moments, Lillian?"

"Certainly" she said.

He carried on. "This morning I received notification that this school will be closed down in three days' time, I have just received a telegram informing me and my staff that those who are willing to be evacuated may do so by giving an answer tomorrow morning at assembly, after consulting with your parents. I need a note stating yes or no, and a signature, is this clear, any questions?"

Henry raised his arm. "Please sir, where are we to be evacuated to?"

"Good question, as I understand you will be evacuated to the home counties".

Murmurings echoed around the classroom. "Yes" he continued "I know what you are thinking, where's the Home Counties. Well its forty miles north to the county of Bedfordshire, the class if all agree will be found suitable accommodation in a country town and surrounding villages. We will decide tomorrow who goes with who, and stays at what is proposed".

There is so much to attend to, she said to herself. "Listen everybody, tomorrow will be your last day before we embark on the journey, the third day being Friday, so be prepared" she said before dismissing the class.

Instructions were given as to what belongings to pack,

and times to board the bus.

The excuse the government gave for the cancellation of the earlier evacuation confused some, but as Mr Churchill sais" every child in London deserves the right to life for this country's future generations" Aunt Lillian's persuasiveness assured Mary that sending Henry was the sensible thing to do.

Mary read the note Aunt Lillian gave her, Henry needed a change of clothes, enough to fill a small suitcase, a gas mask and a label with his name on it pinned to the lapel of his coat.

"Henry" Mary called from the bottom of the stairs, the teas ready and on the table. Henry had raced upstairs to pencil in the finishing touches to a drawing of Old Street. A collection of other sketches would travel with him "Alright, I'm coming down." Henry pulled the chair to the small kitchen table and they ate baked beans on toast and a jam sandwich for sweet.

"Aunt Lillian thinks we should forego the tube tonight and chance the raids. It might be wrong but we'll take the risk." Mary dreaded Friday morning arriving, another parting; she thought of Bert, remembering the way he died on that fateful journey to rehab.

"I am sure once you get to know the people life might be good for you." She said.

"Do you know who I will be staying with?"

"No but you must be aware that guardians who will accompany you will assure you which station you and the four brothers need to exit the train." Aunt Lillian consulted the note "Yes here it is the station to listen for is called Stanbridge. Somebody, I don't know who will transport you to the village school in the village of Eggington where your accommodation will be allocated to you."

Mary slid her arm round Henry's shoulder "I know it will be strange at first, try and stick together and stand up for yourself, above all be strong."

As they bedded down for the night in Aunt Lillian's lounge, God's mighty will came down on their side; the rain never ceased until the day of evacuation. No German bombers flew.

A red London bus driven by a cheeky cockney with Henry's classmates aboard, steered expertly through rubble strewn streets to St Pancras station, filled with pensive children and yet there was an air of excitement for the journey they were about to undertake. Aunt Lillian reminded Henry that he and four close pals would be together on the train leaving St Pancras between nine and ten o'clock, to arrive at Luton by eleven a m, the train would divert there to a branch line out to the countryside over the hills and far away from the madness in London.

At St Pancras, it was smoke stained and filled with excited kids shouting for parents and parents shouting for kids. As the bus approached the station a guardian named Miss Mills tried to explain." If you can be quiet for a moment, the train on your left standing at platform three is the train we shall be joining, have your belongings about you and check that nothing remains behind, follow in line to the waiting area.

Earlier at 8am they had boarded the bus at Old Street School. Mary and Aunt Lillian took a cab and waited at the ticket barrier. Each evacuee was given a pass and all were waved through. Henry's class filled the first two compartments of the train as they would be first to alight at Standbridge, the train would continue on to deposit children at Leighton and further on into the mid-shires. Mary, her eyes moist with tears, waved, Aunt Lillian waved, and children through open windows waved.

Steam and smoke belched upwards to obliterate the opaque inner configuration of the end skylights, a seemingly short au revoir. The last carriage disappeared among other trains arriving, the exodus left Mary, and Aunt Lillian bereft of any emotional reactions, just emptiness. As the wheels on the bogies settled to a rhythmical beat, broken only every now and again over a set of points, anticipation set in amongst the five classmates. They swapped views as to where and who they would be accommodated with, the grim reality being that it could not be any worse from what they were leaving behind. Henry remained silent, he would be the odd one out when the time came the two sets of brothers should not be separated. Henry's only hope was that a kind spinster or a family of aristocrats might take pity. For his own interest, houses and tenements were being replaced by large open parks; he could see the horizon for the first time in his small but confined and crowded life.

As the train gathered speed, the semi-detached houses gave way to acres and acres of fields and hedgerows as far as the eye could see. A parliament of rooks rose up from a copse close to the railway line. Henry figured at least two hundred. The classmates argued five hundred.

"Well did you count them?" Henry answered back.

By now, the train was speeding through a very dark tunnel and all talk ceased. The guardian assured them it was not that long and that in a few minutes they would be passing through St. Albans.

"How far then to wherever we are going?" Henry asked.

The guardian checked her wristwatch. "About another hour or so." The guardian appointed by the G.L.C. followed her instructions to the book. Her compliment consisted of two carriages in her charge.

"Can I have your attention please?" she announced, and each compartment in turn were given clear orders. "As the train nears Luton it will leave the main line and divert to a branch line; here we will take a short stop as beverages will be provided by the local W.V.S, a pre-arranged assignation to allow us guardians to compare notes on how the journey is progressing. Any other food you have packed will be a bonus. Any questions?" Henry's arm shot up.

"How long a time before we reach our station?"

"We should arrive somewhere between eleven thirty and twelve, the answer to your question is three quarters of an hour by my watch."

The boys settled back into their seats aware that the train's gradual movement signalled they were at last on their final leg of the journey. As the boys peered out of the carriage windows a huge camouflage, draped building met their eyes.

"I wonder what's inside there," Henry said aloud.

As they stared and continued to wonder the train, now picking up speed began to pass row upon row of cradled armoured tanks on low bogies demurraged on sidings. No need to wonder anymore. It was clear what was being manufactured inside the large building. This was the first time they had seen anything remotely connected to warfare. The train continued its journey through the outskirts of Luton, the railway following a line of steep hills; sheep were grazing all over the chalk downs and Henry memorised these. Tanks, sheep-what next? He closed his eyes and thought of mum and Aunty Lillian.

When he opened his eyes, the train had slowed to a crawl. It was the tallest chimney he had ever seen. The boys crowded the window straining to look up.

White smoke billowed out of the top, they swore it

reached the clouds, and again row after row of cement waggons rolled past enroute to god knows where, as if they should care.

The train juddered to a halt, the carriage overlooking a very important main road.

"Why have we stopped here?" Henry asked. The guardian came along and said that for a mile from this point onward there is a very steep incline. The guard is checking the breaks before our descent to Standbridge. Gather your belongings we are but ten minutes away from our destination.

The boys were really excited. The train moved, couplings snagged as it took up the slack, pulling against the partly applied break housed in the guard's box-van at the rear, the wheels pinched against the rails, and the train eased forward ready to descend to the unknown. The carriages moved with a forward and backward motion, the hedgerows completely enveloping the side of the carriage. The boy's excited chatter caught Miss Mills's attention.

"What's the matter in there?" she asked. Henry and his pals wanted to know what the large berries that were scraping the side of the carriage were.

"They are what they are," she said "and you will have plenty of blackberry and apple pie where you are going I'm sure of that."

What little time they had left was spent peering out the window; country life was about to be thrust upon them in more ways than they could imagine.

***

Tom Goodright, station master of Standbridge, pulled the leaver to signal the train " clear track" Adjusting his L.M.S. cap, he hastened to the downline platform, as the train levelled with all breaks off and puffed at a steady twenty to arrive at eleven thirty five.

The train screeched to a halt amidst steam and smoke, Henry, and his four pals made ready to exit. Miss Mills assured the boys there would be someone at the station to meet them. Tom Goodright touched his cap to Miss Mills, seeing as he thought she was in charge." You have something to tell me?" she said.

"Yes ma'am, there's bin a bit of a hiccup in the arrangements regarding the transport" Tom swallowed hard. Suffering a shortness of breath over the years after smoking Willie woodbines, made life a bit difficult at times like these.

The end of the shift could not come quickly enough for a pint of ale before dinnertime. The guard leaned out of the rear box van to see what the holdup was, while the driver of the locomotive leaned on the side rail, also impatient to be away; all wondered what was being said. Tom shuffled around and explained how Gertrude Wilson-Green would be collecting the boys and delivering them to Eggington School but she hadn't arrived.

"I can give my upmost care and attention, the lads will be alright, don't worry" Tom said, and gave her a nod of assurance. Suffice to say Miss Mills agreed as there was no more time to waste and with that, she stepped aboard, and the train was given the green flag to go ahead, puffing its way deep into the Mid-Shires. The boys stood around a bit nonplussed. Tom lit a Willie woodbine looked at the boys.

"What's your name son?" Henry was about to say when the station office telephone rang, "Well I'll be blowed, its bin a busy old day" Tom shuffled to the wall- mounted phone. "Hullo, Standbridge Station"

The boys gathered in the doorway looking very bemused. "Yes, right, I got you." Tom clonked the phone back onto the cradle and turned to the five boys bow wedged in the doorframe.

"Well it looks like you're gonna have to walk a bit, you don't mind do yur?" He shuffled towards them; they backed away. "Look, I'll point you in the right direction. Just follow the road over the crossing; it's two miles to eggertun. But listen, the call on the phone was from Gertrude Wilson-Green who should have picked you up, unfortunately, she's otherwise engaged, but she has organised Jason Smith, a farmer, to collect you with his tractor and trailer. Ok?"

As the boys were at the mercy of all and sundry who had organised their lives this day, they accepted the challenge without any complaint. So they began to walk, Tom called out "Jason will meet you along the way, it's a pity though, you would have travelled in a Rolls-Royce, never mind, ay?" the boys shrugged their shoulders and bunched together, hiding their disappointment, and started to walk, waving goodbye to Tom.

They elected Henry as leader and spokesman for the group, should any incidents occur on the way. The four brothers marched in file behind as he led the way.

"I'm glad the weather is fine, those clouds look threatening to the west"

"Which direction are we walking then?" Billy asked, thinking he could be second in command."

Henry replied, "North, I believe"

The fresh air revived their senses. Practically a mile had been achieved, when Billy said," Christ what's that smell?" Then a piercing shriek hit their ears. It came from some low structured buildings inside a field, and a human voice, threatening, gruff, and swearing, stopped them in their tracks the smell became overwhelming. "Let's fit our gasmasks on." Henry ordered.

"Could be a gas attack" Roddy butted in.

"Follow me and keep close," said Henry.

There was no gate to the yard, bent low and creeping quietly, the five boys made an entry along the side of the stone pens. The swearing continued and the shrieking grew louder. There were six pens in the block. The loud shrieking came from the last in the row. All the pens had half doors. As they approached Henry signalled to stand up, the five crowded in front of the half door to witness the funniest sight of their young lives. They stared down on Shuffer Tody sleeping off and dreaming, from the last dregs of a pint bottle of methylated spirits. He lay between two of the largest hogs the boys had ever seen. Shuffer was in one hell of a dream, effing this and effing that. He opened one sleepless eye and saw a five headed, black-snouted saddleback peering over the door. Jumping up, groggy and shaky, Shuffer lunged to the half door, the boys took fright and scattered all over the yard.

"By Christ, they um piglets!" he yelled, swaying and swaggering and still clutching the bottle. He bumped into Jason Smith, who by this time had pulled up, seeing the five small sized suitcases left by the verge and guessed they were his charges he'd come for.

"What's up Shuffer, seen a ghost?"

"Aye, a five headed one." He scuffled off along the road; the boys by this time, still wearing their gasmasks, appeared gingerly out of the yard.

Henry slipped off his mask, "Has he gone?" he asked "Yea, that'll teach the old sot to sleep wi my pigs."

Jason turned the tractor and trailer round in the small holding yard "get your belongings, and hop into the trailer, lads"

The boys hoisted themselves over the side of the trailer on to a bed of straw, glad to be riding in something again.

Jason was full of apologies. "I'm instructed by the welcome committee to get you to the village school for an arrangement." Jason moved the tractor off.

Henry and his inner thoughts remembered his mothers' philosophy; stick together if possible. Another mile of trees, hedges, and acres of fields slipped by, and one heavily overgrown meadow. A sign on the dilapidated pavilion showed "last man out-22" the figures hanging at acute angles on the now defunct scoreboard, was the last match played, now a forgotten memory of the halcyon summer days before the war. They passed the congregational chapel, a row of cottages, a church, and a school. On the other side nestled together Town Farm and the vicarage, plus a few more cottages made for a compact community. Double British Summertime made for a very long day. Henry's thoughts were on the morning and leaving London. They were now entering a new phase of their lives; this was Eggington, their home to be.

The five boys were ushered into the primary school to form a line in front of a set and guarded open fireplace; the introduction to a few villagers who had awaited their arrival since eleven o'clock, took place and Gertrude Wilson-Green greeted the boys. Sandwiches of cheese and homemade pickle were handed round, as was Dotty Oddbins rock cakes.

"The boys look a bit undernourished," was a comment made by the village idiot.

"Well, now," Gertrude clasped her hands together, "are we ready to assess which boy you would like to join you in your homes, now is the time to make your choice?"

This was the moment Henry and his pals dreaded, their own feelings weren't considered at all, only that the peering eyes and minds were engaged in a somewhat bizarre sort of I-don't-want-to-choose-the-wrong-one attitude, but before any choice was made, Henry raised his voice and concern to Gertrude. "Mam you have two sets of brothers here." Henry introduced Roddy and Checker Burnett and Billy and Micky Spillman "and mam they must all be together, not parted."

"And your name?" she asked.

"Henry Kneally, mam," he replied.

"Well, that presents a new consideration on things, I don't think any of the village people are capable or have enough room to accommodate this many." She made a snap decision; "I will be responsible for the billeting of the brothers." The other onlookers turned away and left, leaving Henry on his own.

"What about me?" Henry was by now bereft of any home to go to and feeling very vulnerable, and lonely. That's when Jason Smith intervened. He had quietly stood back and watched the proceedings. His own affairs at the farm needed someone like Henry.

"You come with me to Claridge Farm," he said with a firm but friendly manner. Claridge farm; Henry thought to himself.

"You'll see, get yur things, and jump on the trailer. Henry turned his head just in time to wave to his pals as the Rolls Royce sped off in the opposite direction with the brothers heads bobbing around through the rear window.

Jason Smith drove the tractor at a steady pace through the village to Claridge Farm, which was situated a mile or so from the village school; its isolation made it all the more appealing to Henry.

As the tractor and trailer swung into the gravel drive leading to the farmyard, a black- and- white collie dog bound out to meet them, running alongside the trailer and yapping at the boy who had entered her domain. Jason drove the tractor straight inside a hovel, which housed an old Rover sixteen saloon car, a hay-rake, a seed drill, and some hens scratching about on the earth floor, for a second or two Henry remained sitting half frightened of the dog. Jason called, she won't hurt yur, call her Gyp."

CHAPTER THREE

COME TO REST

"Jump out, you'll be alright, in fact, yur should feel 'onoured, she usually stands 'er ground by the farmhouse door."

Henry's suspicion about the dog diminished as he catapulted himself over the side of the trailer. Immediately Gyp fussed around his stocking legs and licked his hands, while he patted and stroked Gyp's head.

"Looks like you've made a friend already." Jason's face beamed with delight. C'mon, come and meet Kathy, my wife. Who greeted them all warmly.

Henry realised there was no need to be afraid and he gently stroked the collie's head, who in turn licked his hand and wagged her tail incessantly against his legs.

Kathy Smith with her brightly coloured apron about her waist, and her arms folded, ordered Gyp to stop fussing and stand guard." Good dog "she said.

Jason introduced Henry to his wife; her features were that of a woman who had seen better days, and her blue eyes a little tired. Her voice was warm and friendly, just what Henry would have imagined, if told earlier. Together they stood at the open door and exchanged pleasantries, and then an aroma that Henry had never before encountered, drifting out the kitchen door, hit them. "By golly, Henry, we're in for a treat tonight, that beef stew if I know my senses"

"C'mon, sit yur self-down, yur must be all in after the

journey you've just made." Jason scraped a chair out for Henry, while Kathy made her way over to the sink to draw some water into the copper kettle. The black range stove had aged somewhat, but somehow managed to keep doing what it was supposed to, boil kettles and cook beef stew.

"I'll make us a cup of tea, and then show you round the house and you can choose which bedroom you would like."

"Crikey!" Henry chirped, "You mean I have a choice?"

"You certainly do" Kathy said proudly.

Jason apologised, "I must get on, and I've cows to milk and pigs to feed and bed down and hens to feed before locking up tonight. I'll see you later" He strode off across the yard while while Henry sipped his tea and Kathy studied the boy. His clothes were a bit crumpled but clean. A tidy boy, she thought. Gyp crept in and sat beside Henry, "go out Gyp" Kathy said firmly. Henry wanted her to stay; Kathy saw this in Henry's eyes "Oh just this once but her place is in the yard." While Henry fussed with Gyp he and Kathy exchanged views and lots of questions and answers about themselves, he about London and she about the farm.

"We always eat dinner late here, six thirty, so if you like bring your suitcase and we'll go and choose your room."

As they climbed the stairs, she told Henry the farmhouse was over two hundred years old, built in the reign of William the forth in around 1831 and the manor next-door to the farm was built even earlier in 1820, when George the fourth reigned. "We have a lot of history here." As they walked together along the aged corridor, Kathy showed him two bedrooms.

"Now which one do you think you would be most comfortable in?"

Henry noticed one was large, and one much smaller. This one had a nice little alcove, and the window looked out on a lovely view of the fields and beyond. Henry liked this one and said so.

"Right" she said, "I hope you will be happy here, you deserve to have something going for you." The aroma of the stew overwhelmed him though.

Kathy, Jason, and Henry sat in the farm kitchen to a beef stew dinner. Henry could not restrain himself; he was famished. Although Kathy and Jason were not religious, Jason whose parents had taught him that whatever was eaten, god had provided offered a few words of thanks.

Henry felt humbled, Henry felt warmth, Henry felt secure, and Henry thanked the Smiths.

Every night before retiring Jason would walk with Gyp around the outer buildings just for safe measure and peace of mind" I know it's been a long day for yur Henry, just a brief walk to lock up, as we call it.

Before they left Kathy asked, "Does your mother or anyone possess a telephone, Henry?"

"Well we had one in the shop but it got blitzed"

"I just thought she might."

Jason cut her short. "He can write a letter tomorrow, and you could walk to the post office in the village. He'll get to know the locals, C'mon lad, or the sunset will beat us. Kathy was left to wash the dinner plates.

They walked into the small orchard to the side of the farm where apples were still waiting to be harvested, and at the far end of the orchard were four separate wooden arks where hens were already roosting on the perches. Each housed forty laying Rhode-Island Reds, free range eggs were collected and washed every day and packed to send to the Egg Marketing Board for distribution. Jason locked each ark, and took one last glance around the orchard, satisfied every hen was inside, "Can't take any chances, old Reynard might visit."

"Who's Reynard?"

"He's the local fox, do a lot of damage, can ill afford to lose any of this lot." Henry was perplexed.

Jason noticed Henry Yawning. Poor chappie, he thought, must be dog tired. "C'mon, time for cocoa and bed. Yur'll be allowed to lay in tomorrow morning, and then we'll talk about yourself and our situation."

As they walked to the other side of the farm to lock the main gate the elevated end of Claridge manor presented its self-silhouetted against the fading light. "Who lives there?" Henry asked.

"The Gunn brothers, yur'll meet them all in good time.

The patchy rain that had persisted into the afternoon cleared, leaving a watery setting sun. Still the air remained mild for the end of September. The Widdup Grandfather clock standing at the end of the hallway chimed the second quarter past nine. Kathy stood by the antiquated kitchen range. Even in the warm weather the coke fire had to be lighted, always hot water at all times just in case, ready for the birth of a calf, perhaps, or when the vet called, or the sows started to give birth. Henry in his first four hours of being in the house realised how important the kitchen was to running the farm.

Awakened by a completely different sound, as Henry only knew the London sound, his first morning in the country was a concoction of animal noises. He would not know where the sound actually came from, only the cows bellowing at Sweet acre Gate knew this, waiting for Jason to let them into the milking parlour. The Widdup Grandfather clock standing ornate at the end of the hallway chimed; he counted five times before the tone faded away. Muffled voiced and movement along the landing alerted Henry that it was a new day, a new beginning, and a yearning to do something different. Henry raised himself from the bedcovers and leaned against the wooden headrest, realising the loneliness and how isolated one could be. The fields and hedgerows stretched as far as the eye could see, and not one living soul in sight.

He pulled the covers tighter, remembering how he left Mum and Aunt Lillian standing waving. How were they coping now? He slid down under the covers and slept for what seemed to be eternity, until a knock on the bedroom door startled him.

"Henry, its Kathy, are you awake?"

He did not answer; he lay cocooned under the sheets. What do I say, "yes Mrs Smith" or "Okay, I will get up straight away" or what do I do! He heard the latch lift and popped his head out of the covers.

"Hello, Mrs Smith"

Kathy craned her head round the door. "You are awake, and please its Kathy from now on, and Mr Smith will be known as Jason. Makes it more familiar. Breakfast in half an hour."

Henry pulled on his pants and singlet top and hopped along to the outdated bathroom. It was fundamentally simple; wash basin, long pull chain loo, and a solid cast iron bath. Still, it was much better than some properties in London.

Jason wasn't all that punctilious, but a ubiquitous man, as Henry would find out. Jason removed his wellington boots, on the guard pull outside the kitchen door; he knew he wouldn't receive the wrath of Kathy's tongue.

As Henry took his place at the table, Jason remarked, with a grin larger than a split pumpkin, "take note, Henry, don't mess up the kitchen" Gyp looked on with ears cocked, her eyes following Henry's every move. The three of them sat down to fried bread, tomatoes, and dried egg. Henry, for the first time, took note of the solid oak refectory table and chairs, bright clean curtains and copper pans. Copper pipes gleamed from the black range fireplace, which led to the radiators that heated the house in wintertime.

Without trying to impose themselves on Henry so soon, Kathy and Jason knew they had to know what sort of child they had invited into their domain. So many stories of unruly behaviour and no respect, had reached their ears of earlier arrivals, but their fears were soon dispelled as Henry briefly described his upbringing. The shop, his love for his mum and Aunt Lillian, and sadness when his dad nearly died on the beaches of Dunkirk and the injustice of him dying and finding that his death was so near to where he was right now. It was pure coincidence. He was grateful, too, to the Smiths for allowing him to stay at Claridge Farm.

Gyp reminded them of someone approaching. It was Alec, the livewire part-timer septuagenarian. Gyp's bark was of pure pleasure rather than a warning. Jason explained to Henry how his mother had died early in his life, leaving him and his father to cope with the farm, and a big helping hand from Alec, later when his father passed on Dotty Oddbin assisted as home help, before Jason met Kath, and what a wedding day it turned out to be, A thunder storm had erupted with fury, the rain and lightning and hailstones bounced off the church roof, something they never forgot.

"He loves to reminisce, but we must get on," Kathy said, also giving a reminder to Jason and Alec to get on with their duties.

"Right Henry, while I wash and tidy the breakfast things away, do you want to write a letter to your mum? I think you should give her peace of mind. You can use the drawing room-cum-study. Jason does the accounts there. You'll find a writing pad and envelopes in the bureau. Help yourself."

Henry sat and wrote his letter.

Dear Mum.

Our arrival at Eggington had its moments, I'll explain at a later date. My Guardians are Mr and Mrs Smith who own a farm. I have borrowed their writing paper for this letter. Don't worry about me; I'm sure I shall be very well looked after here. Hope you and Aunt Lillian are keeping safe. Please send writing paper, if not I will endeavour to purchase some from the village shop, Mrs Smith seems a very caring person, I know I shall be well cared for so don't worry.

Henry signed off "*loving son*" and wrote the address.

Kathy was busy about the house and passed the drawing room once or twice. "When you're ready, we'll walk to the post office, which serves as a shop as well! You can post you're letter while I buy a few things for the larder."

She hummed a tune as she went about her chores. "By the way," Henry, she called, "it being the weekend, only basic work on the farm will be carried out, meaning milking, feeding, and locking up. It means no cleaning out of sheds. We do observe the Sabbath by listening to the radio evensong on home service"

Henry completed his letter, raced upstairs, pulled on his grey cardigan, and presented himself to Kathy who waited at the kitchen door, wicker basket in hand and umbrella ready. "We will call at the dairy just to let them know we're off," she said.

The extension phone rang in the kitchen, "Oh drat" She lifted the receiver "Hello, Claridge farm" Henry waited at the door; whoever it was calling relegated Kathy to staccato voice. "Yes-yes-yes! I understand, yes, goodbye." She replaced the receiver with a clonk. "That was Gertrude; it seems that you could be starting at Beaudesert School Leighton, in two weeks' time. She's prepared to drive you and your friends, the brothers, sometime next week for you to all register at the school. How does that sound?"

"Well, at least we'll be together." Henry couldn't contain his excitement.

"Right, we'll be on our way," Kathy had a quick word with Jason and said she'd explain more when she returned home.

Kathy had walked to the village post office many times before, people recognised her, men doffed their caps, women passed the time of day with a cheery "hello", another lady who Henry learned later was another farmers wife, promptly held a conversation with Kathy over her concern about Land Army girls being recruited, and German and Italian prisoners of war to work on the farms in the country.

"What will they think of next?" most indignant she was.

"I don't take her too seriously, though she has a point," Kathy said, as they entered the shop. "It may spell trouble; we shall keep a steady eye on the situation, if it happens, Henry."

Words of belligerence were being broadcast by the Nazi propaganda war machine; Lord Haw-Haw proclaimed that England was facing an invasion by the might of the German panzer divisions. Tom Gunn, his big blue eyes saddened by the very thought of Germans inhabiting the village, found the report repulsive. He said so to the grey haired lady, Ma Leech, squatting on a high chair behind the counter, who listened intently to his comments on how the Germans were winning the war of words. He tuned into the shortwave wireless every night; the programme intended to lower the esprit-de-corps of the British people.

Unbeknown to them, Kathy and Henry had walked in on

their conversation. Henry could see him through the gaps in the shelves. He was a stout man, shirt sleeves rolled up to his biceps, a strong man. Henry noticed he stroked a very long silver-waxed moustache; his hands were large, though he spoke with a rather squeaky voice for a big man.

"I think we startled them," Kathy said quietly

He turned. His eyes settled on Henry. "Well now, who have we here?"

Kathy introduced Henry to Tom and the old lady behind the counter.

"So you and I are neighbours"

Henry nodded, Tom carried on paying for his goods, spilling the silver and coppers onto the pinewood counter. Henry was impressed by Tom Gunn's friendly nature, something Henry would learn as the weeks went by that everybody in the village knew everybody in the village, not like London, where nobody knew anyone even living along the same street. Here, villagers gossiped, told the time, patted themselves on the back, a good job done. As Tom Gunn cycled past Kathy and Henry, he called out "if the lad gets bored, send him to the manor to see the pictures, that's if he's interested!"

"What does he mean see the pictures?"

"He's an artist, you know, one who sketches, draws. He paints mostly in water colours."

"I could compare my artwork with his; it's something to look forward to."

"Do you draw then?"

"All the time, I'll show you my drawings when we get home"

Gyp was first to greet them as they walked into the farmyard. She raced across to lick Henry's hand and trot by his side. While Kathy and Henry had visited the shop, Jason had set the Fordson tractor outside the end hovel, the drive-belt flapping through a small opening power driving a horizontal saw. This operation Henry had to see for himself, there were so many things to distract his mind in the short period since his arrival. Henry's attraction to the country way of life as the days went by took away all thoughts of London, and mum and Aunt Lillian appeared to diminish into a far off haze. It was hard to focus on the London scene.

Kathy laid the tablecloth, a break at mid-day brought Jason and Alec into the kitchen for a beverage, Jason and Alec settled with a mug off tea, and a cheese sandwich.

"Where's the boy, then?" Alec enquired.

"Gone upstairs, wants to show us something, Kathy raised her eyebrows. Met Tom Gunn in the shop, looks as though they both have something in common."

"Arh, drawing, I'll bet a wager" Jason said.

CHAPTER FOUR

UNFAMILIAR REGIONS

Henry sat down next to Kathy and placed a foolscap of artwork on the table. Jason, Alec, and Kathy, with Gyp sitting in the doorway, watched Henry, anxious as to what subject matter he drew. The kettle whistled on the hob, the Widdup Grandfather clock struck the first quarter past twelve, and the first picture, a street scene of blitzed London was handed around. Each in turn looked horrified at what Henry had captured in his creative young mind. They were far beyond his years. Stunned, even the laymen of the farm knew a masterpiece when they saw one. Each in turn studied Henry's other sketches, and Jason knew in his heart that Henry's talent must be nurtured and developed for his own kith and kin's sake, and he knew he could only allow Henry to help on the farm inasmuch not to interfere with his studies and education. Here was a boy that personified everything that he himself would have loved to be, a success as a youngster in the love of natural history. His meeting with the head and employment officer would have gained him a place at college, perhaps, but that was all dashed when his mum died, and his father needed him more than ever to manage and keep the farm producing. Such was the urgency, then, that he forfeited that place and left school a year earlier than anticipated, Jason knew that Henry should never go down that road, he would get all the encouragement that he and Kathy would give in order that his gift would not be hindered in any way at all.

The day neared for all the evacuees to attend Beaudesert School, Leighton. Jason was busy repairing a fence in the outer yard with Alec. Henry sat in the tiny alcove sketching a country scene, and Kathy as always was drying the remains of the breakfast cutlery, Gyp gave her the usual warning a the postman rode into the yard on his red tradesman's bicycle. Kathy wiped her hands as she took in the mail and thanked the postman. Sorting through the mail, she called from the bottom of the stairs, "a letter for you Henry!" the rest were bills, which she put to one side for Jason.

Quickly, Henry ran down the stairs and opened the letter. Kathy knew from his expression that the letter he had waited for with anticipation over the last few days had come from his mother.

"Everything alright?" Kathy asked.

"Well, yes in a way, I suppose. Mum's got a new job as a clippie on the bus, says she does the early shift to the west end. Seems to be enjoying the job, also parcel on its way."

"Well, that's good news, let's hope it continues."

The phone rang, and Kathy answered on the extension line in the kitchen. The call was rather a lengthy one. She clonked the phone back on to the cradle. "There's been a change of plan as regards your schooling, Henry, will you go and call Jason to the house?"

Jason stomped across the yard with Henry in tow. "What's this all about?"

"Don't know, she didn't say" Henry followed Jason into the kitchen.

"Well?" said Jason.

"I've just received a phone call from Gertrude. A new influx of evacuees arrived from west London last week, Beaudesert is full. Bedfordshire education authority have sequestrated the small annex at the village primary school here in Eggington. A teacher, a Mr Stearson from London, will be in charge for the evacuees, and some older village boys and girls for the unforeseeable future."

"That's a turn up for the book," Jason said," it's a bit cramped in there,

We used that room to dry our wet clothes in when I attended the school. Still anything's better than nothing, what do you say, Henry?"

"Well at least I shall be with my pals."

"Do you know of him, Henry? Mr Stearson?"

"No can't say I do, perhaps from the West End."

The day to start school was given as the second Monday in October. Henry had a problem, though, an old ambition surfaced to occupy his mind. Before the evacuation, Aunt Lillian had high expectations for Henry and his artwork, now she wasn't around to guide him.

Henry was quiet at the breakfast table next morning.

"Is anything troubling you?" Kathy asked.

"I only hope the new teacher has art lessons for the class," he replied.

"Well, if not, I'm sure Tom Gunn wouldn't mind stepping in to be some sort of tutor for you."

Jason and Alec joined Kathy and Henry at the table, Gyp remained outside whimpering, the Widdup Grandfather clock struck a quarter past nine, while the kettle whistled on the hob.

"Just in time for your break." Kathy had made a fresh brew for the men.

"Are you ready for apple picking Henry?" Jason frowned at Kathy." You've got a good pair of sturdy legs, Henry, just the job to pick the lower branches. Alec and myself, we'll pick the high ones, there's three Bramley, three

30

Pearmains, and three Newton Wonders to gather. You can help Kathy push the handcart when the boxes are full. Alex and I have laid straw in the loft above the mixing shed. Kathy will show yur what to do."

Henry didn't know the names of the apple trees. "I won't shirk anything you ask of me, mum taught me to stand on my own two feet. So this will be my first job on the farm; where do we begin?"

"Whoa, not so fast, we have other jobs to finish before we begin picking, In the meantime we'll show you where the empty boxes are stacked. You can cart them all through to the orchard; Dotty Oddbin's calling round later this afternoon to pick blackberries in Longbrier Meadow and Sweetacre field. If you like, later on you can have a go with the tall briers; call it your first learning curve." Jason winked at Alec.

Every so often, a wet spell of weather would pass, followed by a dry spell; this was the dry spell, calm and mild, just right for gathering apples. As they made their way to the orchard, Dotty Oddbin cycled into the yard,"Coo-oo!" she called.

Gyp ran to meet her. Henry gazed at this strange being that rode up to them. She was plump, she was wearing a red, white, and blue woollen beret, yellow breeches and wellington boots; her greying hair was combed into a tight bun held with a tortoiseshell slide. She was a jolly person, full of nonsensical clichés. "Have you sent the lad for some skyhooks yet, Jason; we shall need some for blackberry picking."

Dotty rode the cycle round and round. Henry frowned at this.

"She's only joking, take no notice." Jason grinned, everybody laughed as she rode off with her wicker basket swinging on the handlebars. "See you later!" she called.

The afternoon, to Henry, couldn't get any better. While Jason and Alec set their twenty-six round ladders high into the first Bramley tree, Henry and Kathy used stepladders to pick the lower branches on the second tree.

Jason spotted them first; flying from the direction over Sweetacre field three R.A.F fighter planes zoomed past at treetop height. What a noise. Henry ran into the clearing to get a better view. Jason and Alec waved to them, threw up their hats in to the air. "Do you think they saw us?" Henry shouted. "That was something, I'll keep this moment in memory for drawing" he was so excited at seeing real imagery of war machines.

"Oi, back to work you two!" Jason shouted.

By the time the afternoon had passed, two Bramley trees had been picked. It was time for milking; the cows were standing at Longbrier gate, waiting to be let in. Jason and Alec stowed the ladders under the hovel, as Kathy and Henry pushed the handcart to the doorway of the loft ready for the winter storage. Kathy made her way to the kitchen to make ready the evening meal, while Henry ran off to Longbrier to join Dotty Oddbin's crusade in the picking of blackberries. His thoughts turned to the guardian's remarks on the train; they were indeed to enjoy true blackberry and apple pie.

Henry's race to reach Dotty Oddbin's crusade of gathering blackberries failed; her wicker basket overflowed with juicy ripe berries. "Yer too late, me boy, but ere hold the basket, you can do the onner's and carry them to the kitchen. That's where we divide the spoils alf for Kathy, a punnet for Alec, and the rest fer me.

"What part of London do you come from then?"

"Well. The East End, Shoreditch" Henry replied.

"What's it like there now?"

"Heap of rubble, we lost our shop, direct hit, we were

down the tube when it happened."

"I'll bet you feel lucky to be alive, then, is your family still surviving?"

"Mum and Aunt Lillian are, but dad died near here, I think."

"Aw, sorry to hear that son, near here you say?"

They arrived at the kitchen swelled with pride and set the basket proudly on the table. Jason and Alec came through the doorway in time for a cupper before milking commenced.

"Did you know the bull was in Longbrier, Dotty?" Jason asked

"If I'd a known, I'd a painted me lipstick on. Will Henry come to the harvest festival supper end of month, Kathy? "She asked. She rolled her big brown eyes. We have a right old do, and everybody loves me baked potatoes after the sale.

Dotty surprised Henry by pulling out a packet of Willy woodbines, and stuffing one in her lips, lit up, inhaled, and exhaled. "Ah that's better, does the lungs a world of good."

"You ought to know better, Dotty," Kathy said with a profound sadness for her friend. The Widdup Grandfather clock struck a quarter by five. Jason was in a hurry.

"C'mon, you lot, share the blackberries out."

Soon the party dispersed across the yard. Henry's last job was to collect the remaining eggs, if any were laid, in the nest boxes, and not to forget to search in the stinging-nettle beds, maybe the hovel, and climb to the hayloft, eggs nests could be discovered everywhere, this was the fun about the farmyard, the satisfaction it gave. Kathy set the table for dinner.

***

Monday, October the twelfth, dawned a grey and overcast sky.

"It may rain before you get home, Henry, you can borrow an old cape of Jason's" said Kathy, ever thoughtful. Henry said goodbye to the Smiths, and Gyp became inquisitive, her head cocked to one side, Henry strode off for his first day's encounter with Mr Stearson at Eggington School. The school, a mile from the farm, had taken Henry just over a quarter of an hour to reach. He ran some of the way, hoping to exchange views with his pals, how were they coping, what were they up to?

He hadn't set eyes on them since their arrival in the village. Their meeting was a bit muted, to say the least, owing to the circumstances that prevailed. Everyone was apprehensive as to what would happen in class.

The acting arbiter called from the front doorway of the village primary. A Mrs Dangerfield clapped her hands for the pupils to file into the main classroom. Henry remembered the last time he was in there, amid a feeling of loneliness, but now he felt safe with a feeling of togetherness.

Mrs Dangerfield called for them all to stand in line. At the front were the infants, in the next line, behind the second row of desks, were the six-to-ten year olds, and behind them were eleven-to-thirteen year olds. These older boys should have been at Beaudesert s.m. and the four older girls at Mary Basset s.m or the Cedars school, whichever one that would have been appropriate. The register that Mrs Dangerfield opened on her desk contained all of the children's names who attended the primary school that morning. She called each name in turn, looking up and acknowledging the child's response, after which she duly introduced Mr Stearson, who on the morrow would arrange his own register for the class. His pupils were made up of five evacuees, four village girls, and five village boys. Fourteen in total crammed into the small anti- room.

The large window that looked out over an orchard to the side of the school playground, and road, had brown sticky tape stuck in the form of an x across each pane of glass. The two rear windows, ditto. It was here for the next eight months Mr Stearson would teach Henry his colleagues. He never broached the subject of where he had come from, only he'd taught at the William-Ellis school, Putney. So he was from West London, Henry thought, I was right.

The lessons, which were on a wall chart, were hastily draw pinned to the back of the lobby door adjoining the small anti-room. (Monday) geography, reading, maths, history, English, p.t. - weather permitting. However, no art class, which left Henry disappointed.

***

Henry replied to his mother's letter, having stored the envelopes and writing paper in the small locker by his bed. He wrote the letter on the table in the alcove provided by Kathy for his artwork, when finished; he tiptoed along the corridor, as Kathy would take a nap Sunday afternoon. Jason snoozed awhile in the easy armchair by the range, and would soon wake up and go for a bath. It was Alec's turn to do the milking today. A week had gone by since he started school.

Henry popped his head around the kitchen door and saw Gyp lying on the doormat. She raised her head, knowing Henry was ready for the walk to round up the cows in Longbrier meadow. "Just a minute," he whispered to Gyp. He stuffed the letter into his pocket ready to post on his way to school Monday morning. They walked across the yard, out through the orchard where the hens were still scratching under the hovel and along Thedeway Lane and walked the long way to Longbrier meadow.

Henry snapped a short thin spur off the willow tree, which grew beside the babbling brook, he thrashed at the hedgerow, pretending to sword fight, while Gyp sulked, and thought, "what's he up to, this is not the way to behave on the farm,"

She did not like his behaviour at all and stood and barked at him; the cows saw them coming, it was time to give up chewing the cud, they all knew what to do. The bottom hedge of longbrier grew to a few feet of the Leighton Road, which branched off the main highway to the midlands and the north of England, that passed through the village Hockliffe a couple of miles to the east.

Henry had heard and seen the traffic from a distance, but never ventured this close before. He found a partial opening and a stile, which had not been used for quite a while, and clambered through the bars, and at that precise moment, an army dispatch rider on a motorcycle came chugging along, leading a convoy of army vehicles. Henry stood with Gyp and waved to the soldiers in the vehicles that passed. A cap was thrown by one of the soldiers from the rear of one of the vehicles, a black peaked cap. The soldier who threw it leaned out and shouted something, which Henry didn't understand. The convoy passed and Henry returned with Gyp through the gap. As they walked back, the cows were far to the furthest end of longbrier.

Henry fingered the cap and metal badge on the front of the peak, where inscribed the words Carter Paterson. The soldier had come from his part of London. The company were great hauliers to all parts of London and northern England. Henry knew of them, and decided he would keep the cap to show his mum if ever she came to Claridge Farm.

Henry's three weeks at the village school would soon bring the month of October to a close. The days were getting shorter, British summertime ended on the twenty- first day, two days to go..... What would he do with himself in the long winter evenings? He asked himself.

Mr Stearson might be a reasonable sort of teacher; if I approach him in the right manner, perhaps he could slot in half an hour of art somewhere in the lessons on the wall chart. A free time, say last period on Friday. At playtime Henry knocked on the annex door.

"C'mon in!" Mr Stearson called, "Yes what is it?"

Henry explained. "Sir, is there any time in the week when you could arrange an art class of painting and drawing?"

Mr Stearson gazed hard at Henry above his horn-rimmed spectacles. His bushy brows merged with furrowed lines on his forehead.

"I don't think I am qualified to teach art, Kneally. However, if you know of anybody who fits what you are after, there's no reason why we shouldn't look at your proposal. I assume you draw yourself?"

"I'll bring my sketches with me tomorrow, sir, if you like"

"We will go from there, then."

"Sir"

"Yes?"

"I did not mention it before you agreed, there's a gentleman in the village who I met briefly who's an artist in his own right. If my guardian has a word with him maybe he could oblige."

"What's his name?"

"Tom Gunn, he lives in the manor house adjoining the farm where I live."

"Right, Kneally, I will leave it to your discretion to get things moving."

"Thank you, sir"
When Henry left, he was quite pleased with himself.

CHAPTER FIVE

THE GUNNS

Tom Gunn stood, legs wide apart, wearing a collarless shirt with sleeves rolled up to his elbows. He stroked his waxed moustache, his flat cap almost touching the top of the doorframe of the kitchen, and greeted Kathy and Henry with a wide friendly smile.

"Hullo, what brings you to my humble dwelling?"

Henry could smell the earthy pungent odour of lichen and mosses along the stony pathway. Ivy grew the length of the manor, giving the manor that dark atmosphere.

"Can you spare some time teaching an art class at the village school?" Kathy asked," it seems that no lesson is scheduled to art and Mr Stearson, who teaches Henry and his classmates, agreed after being told about you, as he has no knowledge of art. If you could fit in the last half an hour on Friday afternoons for his pupils.

"Humm." He rolled his waxed moustache and thought a while. "Well. Let me dwell on it, and I'll give you my answer tomorrow morning when I pop over for some eggs."

As Kathy thanked him, Henry was confronted by Fred, Tom's elder brother.

"You've come over to view my brother's new portrait," he said, pointing to the French windows with his black sword cane. "Come son; feast your eye on a masterpiece." He opened the doors and pulled back the green velvet curtains.

Standing at least seven feet high was a full-length portrait of a Zulu warrior in full ceremonial dress. To Henry, it was inspirational; he stood transfixed and in awe of the picture.

"Well, what do you think? I have been told you are a budding artist, would you care to comment?"

"Err' not really." It was far too much above his aspirations to dare speak about another's work.

He just stood spellbound, but glad he'd been shown what Tom had achieved. Tom had visited Africa when, as a student at London College of art in 1920 he was offered the opportunity to visit the Dark Continent, where cultures were vastly different from England. Henry could not wait, hoping that his answer would be a resounding yes.

***

Tom Gunn strode purposefully along the footpath that lead from the Manor in-between the pigsty's and the dung heap to the farmyard, lighting his calabash pipe as he went to neutralize any pong the heap was hiding. Gyp bounded to meet him.

Henry meanwhile sat at the kitchen table finishing off a marmalade sandwich. Kathy spotted Tom Gunn striding towards the kitchen, having himself passed the time of day with Jason.

"Henry" Kathy said, "Get ready, I think we've got a decision on the art class."

Henry stood with Kathy and waited for Tom to knock the door.

"Good morning, Tom, I have your eggs ready in the outhouse." Tom smiled and sat down at the kitchen table, knowing a cup of tea would be placed before him.

"Well, now," he announced, "you're wondering what sort of answer I will give you after yesterday's meeting."

Turning to Henry, he added, "I don't suppose you know how many classmates are interested in the art class, at a guess?"

"Hmm, I don't know, but I will find out today, and let you know tonight." Said Henry.

"Why I ask, is that I know perfectly well that none of the village children have the slightest inclination, or remotely any interest what so ever in art. As for your mates, are they into the art world? If it's only you, then the only sensible solution is, for you to come along yourself, say, one day of the week to my studio, and see how we get along."

"Which day?" Kathy asked.

"Say every Saturday afternoon, till five p.m. better to draw and paint in daylight."

"That's settled, then, Henry." Said Kathy.

This was more than he really expected; at least he was being taught by the Master.

"Any time you cannot make the studio, just let me know."

The first question Henry asked Tom Gunn was "Where do you get your inspiration?"

"From the very depths of your soul, son. Look around yourself, what gives you the most satisfaction to draw; portraits, landscapes, classical architecture, miniatures? Then ask yourself what do I choose to work with? Charcoal, brush, oil, the list goes on, so show me what you've achieved up to now."

Henry opened his file, which Aunt Lillian had given him for his eleventh birthday. He would be twelve in two months' time, he thought. December twenty second. He became a little nervous as one by one he passed then to Tom. Tom scrutinised each one, observing the boy at the same time.

"Well what's your verdict, Mr Gunn?"

"Tom, please, and I call you Henry."

"That's ok by me."

"Right, my first thoughts are, I notice you have used a soft pencil, and drawings of buildings, so architecture springs to mind. Buildings that were once buildings, and now destroyed by bombs. I notice not so many people, but red London buses, so its movement, architecture, movement, which of these are your strongest point, or putting it another way, which is most pleasing for you to draw?"

Henry, with his quizzical mind, answered, "Could you point me in the direction I should go?"

"Well that's for you to decide. To me, though, building is your strongest point; I would follow this line of art." Henry thought so too.

For the next few Saturdays Tom Gunn inspired Henry to be weaned off the pencil to painting pastel shades in watercolour. Henry never paid a penny, Tom was very glad to be the tutor for a very gifted boy. In the middle of November the first, sharp frost covered the roofs of the farm; the light of day was perfectly good. Tom Gunn, as usual, collected the eggs from the farm. The third week, the last day of school being Friday, Henry was already on his way to school.

"Does Henry hear from his family?" Tom asked

"Yesterday, he received a letter from his mother; Kathy called from the adjoining outhouse, as she returned with eggs." I'm not supposed to say anything. Jason and I are planning a surprise party on the twenty second, being his birthday. His mum will travel the day before, and Jason will meet her at Standbridge station, hopefully by mid-day."

Henry kicked at some gravel as he walked to school. Mr Stearson walked a few paces in front and, as his digs were I Dunstable, sometimes Henry met him passing the farmyard entrance. Both saw the dispatch rider in the distance leading a convoy of army vehicles. The rider raised his arm and the line of trucks came to a halt. He beckoned to Mr Stearson to read something, and a puzzled Mr Stearson was shaking his head. By the time, Henry had joined them, and seeing Henry had caught up, Mr Stearson turned to him and asked, "Do you know Furrow Field?" he pointed to the dispatch rider's map.

"No, but if you move on a little further, on the right on the bend, you'll come to Claridge Farm. Ask for Jason, he'll surely know."

The rider thanked them both, drew down his goggles, and waved the convoy on. As the wagons passed, they saw everything was sheeted; At least, they both knew from the shape of one of the trailers being towed, maybe an anti-aircraft gun. The others they weren't quite sure. As they strode together, Mr Stearson enquired if he, Henry, was still pursuing his dream of becoming an artist.

"I know which direction to take now, thanks to Tom Gunn, it seems my artistic talent leans towards architecture," Henry said.

"Well that interesting," Mr Stearson said.

"Why?"

"Because, after this war is over, son, London will need your talents. There will be so much work you won't know what to do first."

The day passed without any further excitement, until Henry, walking home, heard lots of noise, and people shouting, and now Henry could see thick billowing clouds of white and black smoke, and flames reaching above the trees. Henry ran as fast as he could, he raced to the bend and saw the manor was on fire. A cacophony of sounds greeted him. Henry could not believe his eyes.

Jason, Kathy, and Alec stood there helplessly; the fire

tender from Leighton had not arrived. Jason murmured, "It's old, it's dry." The heat unbearable, Tom and Fred Gunn were nowhere to be seen. Soldiers came running into the farmyard. Henry stopped in amazement at the sight of so many people, but there was nothing they or anybody could do.

At last, the fire tender sped into the yard. Henry captured the scene in his mind.

Jason took command of the situation, first by moving the pigs to safety, soldiers rushing about, and now the fire chief shouting instructions.

"Where's the nearest hydrant?" he shouted to Jason. Jason pointing and running to the lane outside the gate. "You should know all this," he said, panting to the chief.

"I'm new here, arrived yesterday, and haven't had time to acclimatise as yet."

At last, the hose filled with water, and the fight to save the manor was on. The fire chief had two hoses to work with, one from a hydrant, the other from Thedeway brook. He took command and played the hoses onto the end elevation of the old manor where the kitchen and dining area were, and where the fire had taken hold most. The bedrooms were above.

Henry couldn't stand by any longer. He ran into the orchard and jumped over the wooden fence, which had a strand of barbed wire strung across stapled to posts. Henry vaulted over and jagged his right knee, and with blood pouring from the wound, he ran through the Gunn's privot hedge maze garden and across the rising lawn. To his astonishment, the studio was still intact, but embers from the beams were falling all around. It wouldn't be long before the fire reached this part of the building. He had to act fast. Smashing the French windows with a piece of old timber and once inside, he carried the Zulu portrait out on to the lawn. He made several journeys into the studio, carrying as many pictures as he could hold. At last, Jason and Alec caught up with him.

"Well done, Henry, can you see any sign of the Gunns?

The smell of charred timber became overwhelming, choking and spluttering they covered their faces with handkerchiefs but to no avail. The fire beat them back and they retreated with sadness.

Taking stock of what they had salvaged, most if not all of the canvases were untouched by the fire, but where were the Gunn brothers? The fire had spread to the roof timbers above the studio, the fire chief wanted this fire out, he did not want this fire burning all night. Suddenly, out of the fading light, three fire tenders from Dunstable arrived. Pumping water straight from the brook, the extra fire crews soon had control of the fire. Jason and Alec quit earlier, as milking and feeding of the livestock needed their attention, and now extra fire crews were on scene, there was little else that would be of any benefit.

Henry returned to the kitchen. The blood on the wound was caked dry to his skin; his face was blackened by the fire.

"I've done all I could" he said to Kathy.

"I'm sure you have, I've heard of your heroics from Jason and Alec. Get yourself up to the bathroom, waters hot, and get you a bath."

Meanwhile, Kathy made ready the supper. The Widdup grandfather clock struck nine o'clock.

A very late supper that Kathy pre-pared was laid invitingly on the kitchen table. Henry respected the Smiths, and waited until they were both seated. Drawing up his chair underneath himself, he, waited for somebody to begin a conversation, but none came. They ate in silence.

Jason pushed his plate away and shook his head. "I just cannot think how and why it happened." The shock of the fire had hit him hard.

"What have you" Kathy was about to ask after the paintings that were saved. Gyp growled. A loud knock pounded on the door. Jason opened it and found the new fire chief standing there. He donned his helmet and introduced himself as Roy Binfield. "Have you a moment?"

"Sure c'mon in, cup of tea?"

"Lovely, thank you. He stepped inside. "We've found the bodies of two people."

There was a short silence.

"Where exactly?" Jason asked

"One body in a small bedroom, and another in an attic type room. Unrecognisable I'm afraid. Foul play hasn't been ruled out. The police have informed the coroner. We are leaving one crew on standby."

Henry was curious about the soldiers in the farmyard.

"I can explain," said Jason "somebody in the village told the army that I would know of a certain field they wanted to pitch camp in."

Henry beamed "That was me, sorry."

"Well, Furrow Field belongs to Inwards farm, so that's where I sent 'em, as for what they plan to do there; perhaps we shall find out tomorrow, we shall see. I know something; the paintings we saved must be sorted and stored somewhere."

"We just can't bring them over to the farm; they are not ours to keep." Kathy said.

"Don't forget I have mine amongst them." Henry chimed in.

"Of course." Jason said, "I know. We'll store them in the small loft above the outhouse; we'll cover them with tarpaulin from the hovel. Henry and I can hump it on the sack-barrow and tomorrow I'll ring the police and see how the law operates on the subject."

"Another thing, "Kathy said, "They own a she cat, a fluffy Persian, answering to the name of Lolly" Jason bit his lip.

"Well, if she is alive, we'll take her on. I've seen her about the farm, she almost lives here anyway"

Another knock came at the door, a demanding knock above Gyp's warning bark.

"Who is it now?" Jason said, his voice a bit jaded. An army corporal stood at the door.

"Yea, what do you want?"

"The O.I.C. detailed me if tomorrow morning you could supply milk to the men."

"Awe, c'mon on in quickly, shut the door, we musn't show ant light," Jason said, irritated by the intrusion. "How many pints do you require?" there's a dozen men in the battery, we need at least twenty pints. That's enough for the cook."

"Okay and who pays?"

"That's the O.I.C's job, he'll settle with you ASAP."

"Well, tell him the army calls for the milk with their own container, and pays me here."

The corporal thanked Jason for his co-operation. "What are you supposed to be guarding." Jason asked.

"I cannot disclose any details. Top secret."

"I know there's only mangel-wurzel in Furrow Field, but I've enough on my plate to worry about the army. See you tomorrow morning" Jason closed the door on the corporal, who hurried away to the campsite.

Kathy, Jason, and Henry sat at the kitchen table. The Widdup Grandfather clock struck another quarter. Bless my soul, look at the time," said Kathy. "Ten thirty."

"The chickens Henry!" Jason blurted out.

They had forgotten the most important thing of the night, to lock up the chickens. With all the distractions going on, they had failed the hens.

Henry grabbed the torch. "Hurry. Else, you know who will beat us. I told you about old Reynard, so hurry."

They ran through the farmyard and out into the night. The orchard dark, where the chicken arks silhouetted against the night sky.

"Mind that torch, Henry, keep its beam on the floor." As each ark was inspected, the hens cackled a bit for being disturbed. Finally, at the last ark, two staring eyes confronted them.

"Blast, Henry that wily old fox has got here before us."

Jason hurled a broken piece of apple branch at the two eyes, "he ran off scared, the pest." Jason grunted, and looked inside the open door to find all hens perched. "Just in time, Henry, in the nick of time. Keep the beam low on the ground, Henry"

As they returned to the farmhouse, Gyp followed them, curious as to what both were up to. They could hear the standby fire crew still raking about, but Gyp had sensed something else, and began to growl. Because they were at the rear of the manor, the dog had sensed something or someone moving about in the Gunns rear garden, where earlier Jason and Alec had cut the wire fence to help Henry through. Whoever it was, moved quickly, not wanting to be seen or even caught. Jason shouted loudly at the figure and Gyp gave chase, but the figure simply disappeared through the evergreen covered pathway at the end of the manor.

"Perhaps the person was trying to loot the place," Henry quipped.

Kathy was waiting patiently for them. "Where have you been? It's eleven o'clock past."

Jason explained in detail. "But before we go to bed, I'll ring the desk sergeant at Leighton and report the mysterious figure we encountered on the Gunn property. He or she were up to no good."

Henry climbed the stairway wearily. Kathy ruffled his hair." You must be all in, have your wash; I'll run Jason a bath. Throw out your dirty clothes. Dotty will come tomorrow and do the tub for us."

"Good night," Henry said, and soon snuggled down under the soft eiderdown and drifted off to sleep.

The next morning he was woken by the Widdup clock striking five, or was it six? He did not know. He listened, not a sound, he lay for a moment wondering what day it was, or what month. His mind became aware, it was Saturday, and Alec's turn to work the weekend.

Sunday tomorrow, he thought, I'll write to Mum and Aunt Lillian about the fire, and how we managed to save all the Gunn's and my paintings. I'll drop a hint about my birthday and, of course Christmas. He checked the calendar. "H'mm, only six weeks to go. I will send a card, of course, but that's all I can afford." He heard movement on the landing, a tap on his door alerted him. "I'm awake!"

"It's Kathy, we are just getting up, breakfast in one hour."

"Okay." He replied, and gave a final stretched and left his bed.

Now that late autumn days were here the cattle housed in the spacious Dutch barn for shelter from the winter storms. Alec's only job was to let them in for milking from the barn, via a short walk to the milking parlour, and let them out via a walk-way behind the barn, and return through an open gate at the bottom end of the yard, where Gyp gives one or two yelps to hurry them on ready to chew another heap of hay and some cereal mix, which Jason and Alec had concentrated on during the week.

Henry assisted Alec to spread the feed along the troughs. The winter days also ensured Alec a job after scraping down the muck off the walls of the milking parlour to make for a fresh coat of whitewash to be sprayed on as soon as spring arrived.

CHAPTER SIX

FIRST CHRISTMAS

Sunday lunch consisted of rabbit pie and for sweet, blackberry and apple pie, that Kathy had preserved in Kilned jars, the fruits were picked after Dotty Oddbin's crusade into Sweetacre field. There was a lot to be said for Kathy's cooking. Henry hadn't tasted anything better; not that he would with this meal. Earlier in the morning, Jason and Henry counted and documented fifty-one paintings and drawings, were there any missing? They couldn't be sure. Scrutinising each one, Henry felt they were all there, but could not be one hundred percent.

Jason would love to have known who it was that was snooping around on Friday night.

"It's gone now," he said, "maybe one day we'll find out and maybe not."

The Gunn's charred bodies were transferred to the mortuary in Luton, where a pathologist would present the cause and nature of death, or would foul play be suspected? It could be weeks to find the answer. There was a certain amount of gossip amongst the pupils, especially with the village lads and girls who knew the Gunns considerably more than they let on, particularly one girl. She gave Henry some information that her mother regularly received a brown paper parcel every week. Tom Gunn delivered the parcel, which contained the washing, and he would let slip a snippet or two about themselves.

"Did you know," she said, "that they own two free public houses, and acres of land? Not here, not in Eggington. I think somewhere in Bucks"

"Where's Bucks?"

"The next county, silly," Henry felt somewhat belittled. Still, it will stimulate conversation round the kitchen table tonight.

Henry accompanied Mr Stearson most days on the way home due to the bus stop being on the corner of Furrow Field where the army had pitched their campsite. Mr Stearson lodged in Dunstable.

"How will you cope with your artwork now the Gunns have passed on, have you thought about it yet, or is it too early to ask the question?"

Henry replied that he did not know what the situation held for him, he just did not know.

Since Henry's arrival at the farm, time had passed by unnoticed; so much had happened in the three months he'd been at Claridge farm.

Sunday morning found the Smiths and Henry in conversation about the manor.

"I've known the Gunns since I was a boy." Jason said, "It must be all of thirty five years when they brought that property. Just after world war one, they moved in. I remember now, all their belongings were lashed onto a four-wheeled flatbed cart. Dad and I helped to unload and move them in. their furniture was a bit frugal to say the least."

"Where did they originate from?" Kathy asked

"Do you know, to this day I don't know, never asked, and they never told."

"One of the village girls told me her mother took in their laundry. She said that they owned two free public house and acres of land somewhere in Bucks, if that makes any sense to you." Said Henry.

Kathy pushed herself from the table. "That'll be Mrs Merrill; I'll have a word with her, see if she knows anything else about the Gunns when I'm passing."

Henry excused himself from the table, a drawing needed to be completed.

Jason helped Kathy wash and wipe the breakfast plates before plunging into the fireside chair to leaf through the Farmers Weekly.

"The old Fordson is getting a bit rough, I'm just wondering if I ought to get onto the war-ag for a possible new lease-lend tractor from America. Jim Fletcher's got one over Billington way, says they're a mighty fine bit of machinery."

"Can we afford one?" Kathy asked.

"I think you pay a nominal fee, the government pays the balance off later." The phone rang on the kitchen sideboard. Jason lifted the receiver. "Hullo, Claridge Farm, Jason Smith speaking." He raised his eyebrows at Kathy and mimed "Mary" with silent lips. He handed the phone to Kathy.

As Henry was out of earshot, they could speak freely. "How is he?" Mary asked.

At this moment in time, he is in his bedroom finishing off a drawing. We have the most hectic time here, the manor next door to the farm was destroyed by fire on Friday afternoon Henry was a hero, saving all the canvases which Tom Gunn and Henry had painted, but sadly both Gunn brothers died in the blaze.

Mary was shocked by this news. With the letters she received from Henry, she'd felt herself being drawn closer to the Smiths and Claridge Farm, had felt as though a bond of trust was beginning to evolve between the two families and now part of that had been taken away.

"About Christmas." She said, "are you sure you are comfortable I should visit?"

"Of course, everything here is being made ready. Your bed is aired. We will try our very best to see you have an enjoyable time. Keep yourself safe, and see you catch the train and give him the surprise he needs most.

"I don't like leaving Aunt Lillian on her own, with the blitz and everything."

"Well, you must not worry, Jason and I have thought about your situation, and we came to the conclusion that Aunt Lillian must accompany you. The double bed in the big room is more than adequate for both of you. Besides, it would be safer with each other for company, and traveling together."

"Are you sure, Kathy?" Mightn't we put too much strain on yourselves and resources? I have been buying a few things for a hamper such as I could afford, and I know Lillian will chip in to help things along."

"As I said, don't worry too much about food, you'll find we have stocks to last over the Christmas period, I'm sure Henry will be doubly surprised with both of you being here, and I know he can't wait for the holiday to start. We promised him we'll visit the cattle market in Leighton, and walk around the street stalls to see what sort of bargains we can pick up."

"I'll write a letter to you nearer the time." Mary concluded.

Two weeks before Christmas the holly berries were showing bright red out on the tree in the middle of a laurel hedge that surrounded the garden. Henry noticed that after two nights and days of early winter storms, most of the leaves were blown from the remaining elms and the apple trees were stripped bare. Heaps of leaves piled themselves against the walls, doors, nooks, and crannies around the farmyard.

Jason pointed this out to Henry. "If you want to make yourself useful, get a brush and handcart, and work round and clean the yard, make it tidy for Christmas, it's an extra half-crown for your pocket. It'll do you good."

The air was bright and crisp that first winter, Henry was away from London. Out there, he took a deep breath, and filled his lungs with good clean air. It made him feel giddy for a second or two, his cheeks turned to a rosy hue; gone was the paler city look, he felt good.

***

Gyp yapped as a black Wolsey car swung into the farmyard.

"Who have we now?" Jason said to himself.

Two detectives from Leighton police station stepped out of the car, and Jason strode out of the milking parlour to greet them in the middle of the yard. The taller of the two shook Jason's hand.

Henry carried on with his chore the other side of the yard, while Gyp gnawed and growled at the end of the broom as Henry swept. She would tug and growl with every sweep he made, and he teased her, it made him laugh. When did he last laugh so much? He couldn't remember.

He would like to know though! Being inquisitive, the conversation being held in the middle of the yard. Hopefully, all will be revealed at the kitchen table that night. As he swept the leaves, his thoughts were on today being Saturday; another week at school, and he and his classmates would be on holiday.

It was Jason's turn to work the weekend, then Alec's and for Christmas, both would work to ease the workload to complete the feeding in good time for the two festive days. First and foremost, Kathy and Dotty Oddbin would decorate the church ready for evensong, which the Smiths never missed. Henry was invited to accompany them. He'd never been to a church service, let alone a festival. It didn't mean that he didn't believe his mum and dad had never made time, though Aunt Lillian attended St Leonards Anglican Church in the high street from time-to-time.

Henry was apprehensive at first, but the Smiths would never browbeat anybody into something that a person would not want to participate in doing.

The dinner table laid, and Kathy busy over the range stove, Jason appeared at the kitchen door and drew off his wellington boots. "Where's the boy Henry?"

Kathy turned, saucepan in one hand, tea cloth in the other. I've sent him to the apple store, he'll be back soon, I thought we would have apple and blackberry crumble tomorrow, with the piece of beef I managed to secure from the butcher.

"Aw, that'll be grand, what have we to-night, though?"

"Well, I've boiled us a Bedfordshire clanger see what Henry makes of it." A wry smile from Jason pleased Kathy, She served each plate with a portion of clanger, mincemeat in one end, jam the other. Henry pondered, not knowing wheather to eat it with a knife or fork or spoon first.

The Smiths smiled at Henry; he chose what they chose.

"Firstly, about the two detectives on their visit to the farm." Jason said.

A date has been fixed for the inquest of the brothers Gunn. Guess what, the eighteenth has been pencilled in just at Christmas time.

This perplexed Kathy. "What was their findings on what happened to the brothers?" She asked.

"They wouldn't comment. Whatever the outcome, the bodies will be released for burial the very next day. Should we want to attend the inquest, it will be held at the second courthouse, Upper Wellington Street Luton, or we can wait for the report in the local Observer paper.

Jason mused. "I think we'll wait for the paper."

Henry became absorbed in their conversation, and on reflection, he asked, "Will they be able to say whether they were murdered, or just an accident?"

Jason eyeballed Henry, "Well if the bodies they found were charred so much that they were unrecognisable, as the fire chief said, I can only assume the verdict will be accidental death."

"What happens in the meantime? I mean there must be somebody in the legal profession who represents them, surely to god." Kathy said

"Well, if my memory serves me right, I believe when they moved in, I can remember a solicitor chappie from Northampton, meeting with them, and they both signed documents he had with him. Mind you, it's a long time ago."

On Sunday morning the dawn rose with a hard frost, the Widdup clock in the hall chimed six times. Jason, already downstairs, was clinking cups. "There'll be one for Kathy in bed before she gets up to make the breakfast," he said to himself, Jason stepped out in his boots, crunching the shingle. His turn to milk today, next weekend would be Henry's first Christmas. After dressing, Kathy reminded Henry that the decorations for the house were packed away in the attic; would he kindly climb the upper floor stairs where he would find a box with a slogan Swan Vesta printed on the side.

"Just check," she said, "and bring them down to the lounge."

Jason had completed the milking, and Henry's only other job was to feed the hens, collect the eggs, and return them to the outhouse for washing and sorting into small, medium, and large trays.

They had just sat down to egg on toast when Gyp signalled a stranger approaching. A heavy knock pounded the door.

The army corporal had come to inform Jason they were on the move; No more milk was required. The O.I.C. gives his regards and thanks, but could return at any time.

"Right, so what was it all about then?" Jason asked.

"Oh, a reconnaissance party for future engagements, that's all." The corporal waved, and the detachment waited; then passed on.

"Well, I think there was more to this little recce then he lets on. I wonder." Jason said, "I wonder."

Henry packed his drawings into a manila folder, which he had borrowed from Jason. School had broken for the holidays. Henry would find himself running errands for Kathy, and the usual chores for Jason, and yes a Christmas card to send to his mum, must remember to post first thing in the morning. You could feel Christmas coming, you could smell Christmas coming. Kathy had two large saucepans boiling with plum puddings in each one, which she had mixed as best she could manage, improvising as she went. Some of the ingredients came from overseas, but most of the mixture was mostly home grown, but Kathy had somehow kept and stored a few sultanas and currents a cherry mix, suet bread, stout, rum and peeled apples.

Twenty light Sussex cockerels were fattened up over the last six months. These were killed and plucked by Alec and sold to whoever wanted one. Henry had a sudden qualm of misgiving, but this was a living farm, this was life and death rolled into one.

The Christmas card he would draw and send to his mum was one of the farm. He went outside across the yard to look back at the farmhouse with Gyp sitting guarding the kitchen door. Henry chose to sit on an old sawn off tree stump and began sketching the scene.

Jason came by carrying a couple of buckets of swill for the sows housed in the sties.

"Do you mind?" he said leaning over and studying what Henry had drawn. Henry only became aware of Jason standing next to him when Kathy called to him. "Henry, can you help me for a little while?"

Henry nearly chose to ignore her, but thought otherwise, his train of observation gone.

"I want you to dig some parsnips for me," she said, I know I'm interrupting your drawing, but the weather being dry, I thought perhaps we could utilise and benefit, should the weather turn nasty. Dig about six roots; do you remember which vegetables are which? Also, pick some Brussel sprouts and a savoy cabbage. The carrots are stored in a box of sand in the mixing shed, select plenty for Christmas."

He grabbed the fork that lay on top of the wall and waltzed through the little gate and into the orchard where the garden had been lovingly cultivated by Alec and Jason, and sometimes Kathy when she had the time, which was not often.

I know what brussels are, he thought, as for the others, well, these are curly kale, and this row are parsnips.

Pointing, Kathy said, "These are savoys." She had quietly walked up behind Henry. "I thought you would have trouble, so I came to guide you for the future, you would then know what we are talking about."

Henry was relieved to find Kathy's knowledge of the

garden content much better than his, in fact he knew very little about the difference between a savoy and a january king cabbage until Kathy pointed to each in turn. Another lesson learned about country life. Such was the intensity of the work involved on the farm that he might not have the energy or backbone to attain what was asked of him. His enthusiasm remained second to none; it was all about understanding the difference names and their identities. For instance, a pitchfork, an Alfa-Laval milking machine, a seed drill, a bouting implement, a grinding machine, a tumbril-cart, harness for the welsh cob, the list was endless.

Henry retired to his bedroom to brush in the finishing touches to the card and realised that not once had he become homesick.

Kathy and Jason sat in anticipation at the kitchen table, wondering what sort of drawing Henry would surprise them both with. Before taking his place at the table he proudly showed them the card.

"What do you think?" he said, trying both to look too smug about it.

They both admired what he had sketched, an exact copy of the farmhouse, with Gyp in the foreground guarding the kitchen entrance.

"Perfect," Jason said" and this is your mums Christmas card present?"

"Well, I hope to send it first post tomorrow morning." He replied.

"I'll tell you what," Kathy said "I'm going to the shop; I'll post it for you." Knowing what they both knew of the surprise that awaited him, Kathy would not post the card but keep it safe in their old chest of draws until Christmas day.

"We are bush burning tomorrow, Henry, do you think you could manage enough strength to pitch some on to the fire?" Alec at some time, had trimmed and laid the hedge along Thedeway Bottom, as Henry otherwise attended his schooling. Now was the time to burn all of the discarded dead wood on to the fire. With Christmas just five days away, bush burning to Henry's delight was a total distraction from the chores and running errands. Firstly, Alec pulled some dry hay from the bottom of the hayrick, which had stood since July after cutting the Thedeway Meadow.

"Gather as many small dry twigs as you can, I'll show you how to form a good base to the fire once she takes hold. We'll have a hell of a job to keep up whatever."

He was dead right. Henry found himself running in all directions, trying his utmost. The more he threw on, the more the fire raged, through the red and white hot ash glowing and dying in its fierce attempt to beat them all, until Jason heaved one great big bundle into the middle, which quietened its race. "We must finish today, no fires burn after dark. How about staying on, Henry just that she might flare up?"

"You are joking. Can't we dowse the embers from the brook?"

Jason thought, smart lad.

CHAPTER SEVEN

THE THANKSGIVING

Mary and Aunt Lillian pre-pared themselves for the journey to Eggington, ever eager to be on their way, and excitement gripped their imagination as to what sort of day it would turn out to be. First came the taxi ride to St Pancras, where they caught the eleven o'clock slow train to Luton. Here they crossed over a walkway and changed to the two carriage Buzzard flyer via Dunstable. They had slight reservations here about the steep incline, which Henry mentioned in his letter, hopefully to stop at Standbridge station where Mr Bott, the local taxi-man, supposedly should be waiting.

The day before Christmas amounted to a somewhat crowed scene. Service personnel were everywhere. Sailors, Soldiers, Airman. Mostly Polish, New Zealanders and Canadians. The chattering of different nationalities washed over them and it was the most rewarding day they could ever imagine. To mix with such company opened their eyes as to how the war progressed; shunning the posters-, "Walls have ears!" The comradeship and banter lifted their hearts. Their spirits rose even further, the land army girls entered their carriage at Luton, for they had caught an overnight sleeper from the north, and were expected to arrive at a hostel near Leighton. They would be traveling companion's part of the way until their stop at standbridge. The accent of the girls bemused Mary and Aunt Lillian, sometimes they understood and sometimes they had to pardon them, which was very frequent, scouse's they maybe, but their sense of humour made the journey worthwhile.

Mr Bott was anxious to fulfil the fare he promised to honour at Standbridge station, but Mrs Peck the owner of Ashoo, the parrot, was intent he should be driving her and the parrot to the vet, the opposite direction to where he wanted to go.

"Very well, Mrs Peck, but first let me make a phone call to Standbridge station to remind Tom I will be a little late for the fare from London. " Does he talk the parrot I mean?"

The drive to the vets was interesting, as one would have hoped for, every time Mr Bott spoke, the parrot would reply, "Bloody Germans, bloody war, bloody hell."

"Have you taught the bird to swear like that?"

"Not really, he was given to me by my cousin who resides in Northampton, he got called up for the army, and the parrot became unwanted, so ended up in my care. My cousin asked me to consider leaving Eggington and live with him in Northampton. I said I would think about it."

"Has the bird a name?"

"Why yes, he responds to Ashoo."

***

The carriage rang with laughter, especially once they had boarded the Buzzard flyer. Doors were slammed shut, cigarette and pipe tobacco impregnated every carriage. The seats were well worn, the windows were filthy with dust and dries raindrops, they could barely see out.

The banter shifted from one topic to another. The girls were travelling to Leighton. Mary explained how she and Aunt Lillian were on their way to visit son Henry who had been evacuated four months ago and was staying at Claridge farm not far from Leighton.

"Perhaps we might get a chance to meet him," one of the girls said, if we are detailed to work on the farm, you never know"

The little train puffed into Standbridge station as Tom Goodright waited patiently on the platform, flag in hand. The train came to a shuddering halt, surrounded itself with steam and smoke. Tom shuffled along to open the door for two women to step out on to the platform. He knew they were coming, having been told by Jason two days earlier, and Mr Bott would be there to collect them, but Mr Bott hadn't arrived.

Tom greeted the women as they stepped of the train. "Just a minute," he said, and closed the door shut and raised his flag to send the train on its way. The two women waved to the girls, wondering if they might ever meet them some time in the near future. "Now, I believe you two ladies are here on a surprise visit to Jason Smith's Claridge farm, am I right to be collected by Mr Bott and his taxi?"

"Yes," they both answered.

"Well, he hasn't arrived as yet, I dare say." But no sooner had he spoken, the phone rang.

"Well, I'll be blowed. Hullo, Standbridge station, a'rrgh, hullo, Mr Bott –right,-right, yes, I've got that. Well they are both here waiting for you." He set the phone back on the cradle.

"I'm afraid you'll have a quarter of an hours wait, would you both like a cuppa tea while you wait?" Mary and Aunt Lillian accepted the offer gratefully.

Mr Bott drove the taxi into the station yard, tooted for Tom to send the ladies out. What was waiting for them, was a clapped out old Ford twelve HP car, a near- sighted taxi driver and an elderly woman carrying a cage with a parrot that could swear repeatedly as an old trooper could.

"You don't mind sharing, missus?" he said, "Been one of them days."

***

The day had passed quite quickly for Henry, until his soul mates had borrowed two ladies cycles from Gertrude Wilson's garage, and took it in turns to ride them to Claridge Farm. Here they rode round and round the farmyard, having lots of fun, but Jason thought he could make better use of their time.

"Hi there lads!" he shouted, "Do you want to earn some pocket money while you're here?"

They didn't need asking twice. The four of them, with Henry looking on, stopped what they were doing.

"Depends on what you had in mind," one of them said cheekily

The Burnett brothers, with their mates the Spillmans, were curious as to what Jason might ask them to do, and remembered Gertrude's warning. If you are calling on Henry at Claridges, don't get your clothes in a mess; also, be mindful, I know what can happen on farms. The lads gathered in front of Jason.

"Henry, I want you and your pals round the back of the mixing shed, as Alec has left a tumbril cart fully loaded of mangel-wurzel to unload. You'll find pitchforks in there. Henry will supervise, and mind you don't stab your feet. Be careful, and watch what you are doing."

The lads' enthusiasm knew no boundaries. The Burnett's climbed on to the Tumbril, while the Spillmans raced inside to receive the wurzels which through a small aperture they would make a heap aside of the grinder. They made short shrift of the load, working as a team. Henry switched on the grinder, which sliced the wurzels to make a ready mix with Chaff, Oats, Black treacle, and Linseed cake. They mixed enough food for Christmas day and Boxing Day. Jason was very pleased with what the lads had achieved. All grinning, their shirtsleeves rolled up, as the weather was dry and mild, and still pleasant for the time of year.

"Here's two bob, I'm well pleased and no accidents," he said; and thought, I'll bet the lads will spend the money on sherbet dabs at the sweet shop on their way home, there would be no parents for the brothers at Christmas, but I'm sure Gertrude will create a splendid spread.

***

As Mary and Aunt Lillian climbed aboard the rear seats of the taxi, they weren't to know they would be sharing seats with another lady carrying a parrot cage.

"Sorry you had to wait," she said, "How do you do, I'm Mrs Peck, meet Ashoo, I had Mr Bott transport us to the vets, I think he's caught a cold." Ashoo joined in the conversation; "Bloody Germans, Bloody war, Bloody Hell."

Mary and Aunt Lillian couldn't contain their laughter any longer, at the parrot swearing and flapping in the cage, and Mr Bott trying to negotiate the car out of the station yard; anybody looking on would have thought they were all a bit drunk. As the taxi tootled along the country lane to Eggington, the parrot went quiet.

"Has he nodded off?" Mary asked, and "he's a cock bird?"

"Yes, I think if we stay quiet then he is quiet, but if we all talk together he likes to join in."

"What if we sing?" Aunt Lillian asked between her

spluttering's.

"I don't know, never tried him in front of a choir."

"Well shall we sing a Christmas carol?" Mary chortled, "What shall we sing?"

"I know" Mr Bott said, "Ark the herald angels sing. C'mon then."

The strains of the carol could be heard all the way to Eggington. Now they were drunk, drunk with happiness. "Bloody Germans, Bloody War Bloody Hell." All forgotten; no bombs, buildings, rubble, deaths. A taxi of wonderful people who were enjoying the moment in time. Tears rolled down Marys face, she knew Henry was in for a real surprise.

They were but a few minutes away from the farm, but a slight detour first down a gravel lane that led to a little whitewashed stone and slate cottage, standing all alone.

"This is where you live?" Mary asked. Above the door was a wooden plaque inscribed, "Rose Cottage."

"I certainly do." Mrs Peck more or less rolled out the taxi, being plump and very friendly woman. Mary handed Ashoo out to her, and wished her a very good Christmas. She paid Mr Bott her fare, and presented a key to the oak panelled door and stepped inside with Ashoo safely on his perch.

Aunt Lillian wiped away a tear, "It's been a strange day Mary, but a quite exciting one, one I shell never forget."

Mr Bott turned the car round and drove out of the lane.

The warmth of the fire made Henry a bit drowsy.

"Wake up, Henry!" Kathy shouted across the kitchen void. She was in the middle of cooking very large stew. Henry decided it must be for two days, and noticed two extra places set on the table. Strange, he thought to himself, no one mentioned anything. Henry completed his routine task of collecting and washing and grading the eggs long before

Jason and Alec had finalised their work about the farm. His only remaining job of securing the arks for the night was to see himself out into the fading light.

"Hurry up. Henry, you'll be the last in for the stew tonight," Jason said, as he passed him in the yard, Henry went about his task, dutifully checking each lock was firmly fixed, and Gyp ran about chasing will-o-the- wisp spider webs, snapping and missing by a mile." C'mon Gyp."

They both ran as fast as their legs would allow, and reached the farmyard just as the dimmed lights of a car swept into the yard. Gyp barked, and ran beside the car until it screeched to a halt. Henry stood back, and called Gyp to heel. He could hear muffled female voices. Mr Bott stepped out to open the rear door for his passengers to alight, and Henry instantly recognised his mum's voice, and Aunt Lillian. He ran to her embrace. "Happy Birthday son."

Kathy, hearing the commotion, came to the door with Jason towering behind.

Mary paid Mr Bott the fare and bade him goodnight and a merry Christmas, but not without a request for the return journey after the holiday.

"Jason has my number, give us a tinkle, anytime." he said. The taxi pulled away, leaving the families to file into the kitchen once preliminary introductions were over. Henry couldn't help feeling the happiness inside and yet with a certain irritation that he'd been kept in the dark about the whole affair.

"Sorry Henry," Kathy explained," I wrote to your mother, and under the circumstances that prevailed, I said we would leave everything to her and Aunt Lillian whether of not they would be able to make the journey. Your mother telephoned me while you were at school, we confirmed the date, and said we would surprise you."

Two nights before Christmas Eve, Claridge farm kitchen resounded with laughter and tears, only tears of happiness, and inner self-belief that all of them and friends near and far, were still alive. The German Luftwaffe bombed Luton. The area around Eggington too was becoming a little uncomfortable at times, more and more army patrols and convoys were passing through the village. The conversation turned towards Mary and Aunt Lillian about their ability to cope with the blitz on London.

"How do you manage to work and live with life such as it is, don't you feel you've had enough? You know, get out of it altogether." Said Jason.

"To where?" Mary replied, "Where on earth could we possibly go? I have no relatives anywhere other than Aunty here."

Kathy served another round of Irish stew; the first was devoured with such relish that she wasn't sure she had estimated the needs of her guests. Conversation flowed freely between the Smiths and the Kneally family. Aunt Lillian turned her attention to the Christmas tree standing in the long room. "That's a fine tree. Did you purchase it?"

"They don't," Henry, said, Alec lifts the tree every year from their garden, and I helped to decorate."

"Well, our presents we bought will sit nicely underneath till Christmas day."

Henry couldn't wait to see what sort of gift mum and Aunt Lillian had brought with them.

Mary and Aunt Lillian offered their services for washing up duties for the next day or so, and a co-ordinated plan to assist Kathy around the house was devised. Kathy would cook meals, so Mary and Aunt Lillian cleaned and dusted, made beds, and made sure that any linen and odd bits of clothes were washed and ironed after they acquainted themselves with the Burco electric copper boiler. Henry gave his mother a detailed historic content of the boilers usage, the boiler became the central function; washing of clothes, hot water when the pig was killed and cured, hot water for sterilising all dairy implements, hot water for the vet, hot water for almost anything, the boiler's status on the farm and its importance was equal to that of a Fordson tractor and the Welsh Cob anytime.

To the astonishment of Mary and Aunt Lillian, Henry had become a member of the village choir of St Michael and all Angels. First service on Christmas morning opened with the singing of the carol, "O come all ye faithful," Mary and Aunt Lillian joined the congregation with Kathy and Jason, who had never missed a Christmas morning service, ever.

Dotty Oddbin, who was part atheist, always came to the farm on Christmas day, and Alec deputised ever since Jason's parents had passed on, .Alec would make an early start for the afternoon milking. the readiness of their feed, and the bedding down, would finish early, all the animals, the Welsh cob, and the pigs, cows, chickens, were all locked and secured for the night.

Dotty Oddbin, meanwhile would oversee the Christmas dinner, and the oak table set in the long room, which was only used for special occasions such as today. The table could easily sit ten people, and Gyp was allowed to lie by the roaring open log fire. Every time Dotty came to set some more places with cutlery, Gyp's doleful eyes would follow her, and this year was special; strange people were joining the celebration.

The service over, Kathy, Jason, Mary, and Aunt Lillian exchanged pleasantries with the vicar reverend Stefans, whilst waiting for Henry to join them outside the vestry. The walk back to the farm was brisk, enthused by the now dry cold but sunny day, which gave Mary and Aunt Lillian a chance to survey the village surroundings.

"I think I could settle here." Mary said. "So quiet." The only sounds they heard were the cattle lowing in the confined of their deep litter barns. You would not think there was a war going on.

Gyp came bounding to greet them as all five walked into the yard. Dotty Oddbin stood in the kitchen doorway waving a wooden ladle. She called to Jason, "The fire in the long room needs log replacements, and quickly."

"C'mon Henry, grab the hand cart, we'll soon fix her moaning" he said.

Alec slouched into the farmyard to start the afternoons milking, as Christmas dinner would commence as soon as he finished. Henry and Jason would see to the feed of the other animals, wash and sterilise the dairy implements, and make ready the churns for the milk wagon to collect the next morning. The journey for the Milk Marketing Board wagon was never ending; milk was a vital commodity for the nation.

The time had arrived for everybody to take their seat at the table. Dotty carried in the cockerel for Jason to carve. Plates were passed along from one to the other, along with brussel sprouts, roast potatoes, and parsnips. Homemade stuffing, which Kathy had prepared the day before, was placed in the middle of the table. Jason said a prayer of thanks giving, and to remember what other people might be suffering. Then they all tucked into Christmas fayre.

Two candles mounted in brass holders provided the light. Jason intoned with a toast. "To absent friends."

"To absent friends, may this war soon be over." Aunt Lillian choked a little on the Elderberry wine, which was rather potent, but went down the throat with an intoxicating tingle. Henry, however, contented himself with a glass of dandelion and burdock. The chatter around the table was endless. Kathy was consumed in conversation with Henrys mum about his schooling.

Aunt Lillian continued chatting with Dotty about the produce of elderberry wine, which Jason and Alec consumed more of, while Henry was running out of patience. The gifts under the Christmas tree should be unwrapped! Gyp nuzzled up to Henry, her tail wagging and desperate to lick somebody's empty plate.

CHAPTER EIGHT

THE BEREAVEMENT

Christmas and Henry's birthday passed all too soon. Mr Bott drove the taxi into the yard, and Henry, with Jason and Kathy and Gyp, bade farewell to Henry's mum and Aunt Lillian. The Standbridge flyer would meet the main line train at Luton, leave for London at five past twelve. A few more days and another term of school would begin. Henry had thanked all and sundry for the presents they gave, and would not have realised that the gifts were bought on the black market. He was still none the wiser until his mum remarked, "This is what happens when war gets in the way. But try not to worry and be strong."

Henry stood for a while, the smell of petrol fumes still invading his nostrils. Gyp squatted by his side. The farm was quiet, not unusual for this time of day because the cattle were being fed with hay, which Jason and Alec were on the point of delivering. A call from the farmhouse kitchen snapped Henry to his senses. Kathy needed him to run an errand to the village shop; she was short on milk-of-magnesium. Henry had noticed in the past few weeks that Kathy would purchase a bottle every time they visited the market in Leighton, or he had to run this special errand or call in to the shop on his way home from school. The thought didn't occur to him that something was wrong, he just imagined it was a grown up sort of thing, that grown up people suffered some ailment, and the solution would cure whatever she was using it for.

Christmas had been misty and cold, but dry, the air felt as though snow could be on its way. As he walked past the lane where Mrs Peck lived, something was definitely afoot; a large pantechnicon was parked in front of Rose Cottage. To Henry's annoyance, he could not tell if it was a removal van, he couldn't be sure. He would, on his return, try not to be nosey, but try to find out if the van, that was parked outside had any name on the side. How could he find out? There was a way, he thought, he would detour around the allotments, skirt round the back and down the other side of the cottage where he could peep through the hedge. That way, if the van advertised a name, he would know for sure she was moving.

Henry made sure he wasn't found snooping. By the time he reached the spot to get a better view, the van had been moved to the end of the lane, which made it easier to identify, but sadly there was no name on the side of the van. What he did discover was a board on a post, which had been hammered into the verge at the end of the lane advertising Rose Cottage to Let. This was good news. Henry hurried to the style as the van roared off in the direction of Leighton, or could have been Hockliffe; he raced along the road into the farmyard, through the outer gate to the rear of the farm, just in time to see the van turn right towards Hockliffe. On returning to the farmhouse, he met a village lad delivering the local Observer newspaper. He exchanged a few words with the younger boy who scooted off on his bicycle to finish his round. Henry would scan the property columns to let later. He opened the kitchen door, and placed the items on the table.

"Thank you, Henry," Kathy said, "don't take your clothes off just yet. Do one more chore for me. Go pick some brussel sprouts; you know the little cabbages that grow up the stalks."

"I think I know which ones to pick," he called, forcing a wry smile.

He returned to find two mugs of steaming tea on the table. The milk of magnesium had disappeared from the table.

Kathy called to Henry, "can you summon Jason for me, please, and he'll find me in the lounge!" Henry sensed something was wrong by the tone of her voice. He would not intrude on any private matter, only that everything he knew about the running of the farm and the routine practises that occurred daily would be affected if Kathy were ill. Alec picked at his nails. Between sips of tea, he asked, "Is there anything untoward?"

Henry thought, must be careful what I say. "Well, she's consuming teaspoons of Milk of magnesium of late; I've run errands this morning for her."

"Hmm, perhaps a bout of indigestion, yeh, indigestion." Alec seemed to have diagnosed the trouble even without a second thought.

"I just hope you are right," said Henry.

Jason called Henry from the lounge, to pass the local newspaper to him. As he reached the door, Jason met him with a very serious face.

"Everything alright?" Henry asked.

"Well, we are going to have a bit of patients, Kathy recons a couple of hours rest, and then we'll see how she feels."

Henry retreated to the kitchen, while Alec disappeared to the barns. Meanwhile, Jason sat down on the otterman and scanned the local news. Kathy closed her eyes, she really was tired.

"Ah, here it is inquest on the Gunn brothers." Jason read

each line, scrutinising every word as he read, it became obvious that no one knew what happened that fateful afternoon. The coroner summed it up as accidental death. The bodies were unrecognisable for anyone to determine what happened, and the post-mortem revealed nothing other than an accident. The bodies would be released for burial in a few days' time.

Jason dropped the paper to the floor and knelt beside Kathy, gently caressing her hands. There were perhaps times in his life when he felt hopelessly out of touch with reality and this was one of them. "If only! I should have realised you needed more rest time, I've pushed you too much ol' gal, the situation on the farm, the visitors, Christmas, perhaps was a week too much, he muttered to himself.

Kathy stirred a little, and turned onto her right side, sensing Jason was still in the room. She clutched at her chest and sighed a deep sigh.

"Alright Kathy?" she didn't answer. Jason knew what had to be done. If the worst came to the worst, the farm would survive.

An atmosphere of gloom descended on Claridge farm, the doctor was called for. Henry retreated slowly to his bedroom, unable to come to terms with the absence of Kathy, if anything untoward happened; Henry envisaged his stay at the farm would be cut short, or, he might even be sent back to London. It was unthinkable, just as he was getting used to the country way of life. Maybe land army girls would be hired.

A thought struck Henry. Mum said if I recall, she could get used to this sort of life, and then another thought struck, maybe, just maybe, Mrs Peck's cottage. Yes, I'll put the question to Jason. What if mum and Aunt Lillian could move into Rose Cottage, they could help Jason out on the farm, it's a brilliant idea, Henry thought.

Kathy was confined to her bed pending a short stay in the district hospital at Luton and Dunstable where a consultant would monitor and diagnose the cause of Kathy's illness. In the meantime, Henry ran to Dotty Oddbin's for her to stand in for Kathy's incapacity.

The Rover saloon, with Jason at the wheel, drove slowly out of the yard. Dotty Oddbin waved and brushed a tear from her eye, Gyp lay down, her doleful eyes followed all the movements; she knew the difference between happiness and being sad. Alec, meanwhile, felt his presence and ability to up his workrate would impress, and preserve the farms' survival.

Henry fulfilled his second week back at school, he would write a letter to his mum, give her all the facts, and tell her the situation and the dilemma they all faced with the farm. It might just prompt her and Aunt Lillian into some sort of action, he would ask Jason first, though and put the question of Rose Cottage to him, see what his reaction and line of thought would be on the subject.

For the trio at the farm it was an agonising wait, until the Rover Saloon returned. Jason drove the saloon quietly into the hovel; the shaded headlights dimmed and switched off. He walked over to the kitchen, with Gyp at his heels, while the three devotees waited patiently round the solid oak table. Jason slumped into a chair and clasped his hands about his head. "It's in the lap of the gods now," his voice trembling.

Dotty boiled the kettle. She had no relative as such, there was talk of a cousin, but best be forgotten. Her neighbour would pop into her house every now and again to see that the place was kept warm for her return.

Dotty would sleep in the large bedroom and would carry on her duties as if nothing had happened. Jason accepted this as the norm. Dotty had helped out on numerous occasions, it came as second nature. The kitchen would function as normal as possible; no doubt there would be a few hiccups from time-to-time.

Dotty dreaded the phone ringing. It was the doctor calling for Jason. In the past if Dotty wanted anybody she stood in the kitchen doorway and squeezed an old car horn, which Jason's dad had left, to summon anyone who was within earshot. Gyp joined in to add to the cacophony. Dotty then carried on with her chores at the drainer-sink.

Jason replaced the phone on its cradle. "I gotta go."

"What now?" dotty said.

"Yea, to the hospital, gotta hurry." He horned on his shoes, raced across the yard, slammed the door of the Rover Saloon, and was gone.

They waited most of the day. Alec had completed his work; Henry had collected the eggs and locked up the hens, and retired to his room. They waited in utter anticipation; the Widdup Grandfather Clock struck five-thirty when the Rover Saloon drove into the hovel. Dotty had an early tea waiting for Jason, he came in, and burst into tears and Dotty comforted him, put her arms around his shoulders.

"It's her heart, he mumbled, they say it could be tonight or maybe a couple of days, who knows, where's Henry?" he asked.

Dotty called him from his bedroom.

"Sit yerself down son," Jason explained the facts to the three of them; it hurt him to say this, "If she survives only until tomorrow, I'm afraid there'll have to be changes here at Claridge's."

Everyone was mortified at the news. The kitchen fell silent. Would this be a good time to let him know about Mrs Peck's one bedroom Rose Cottage to let? Henry thought, and asking Aunt Lillian and mum to move to Eggington.

There was a moral obligation to both families, first and foremost, Mum and Aunt Lillian had, more than enough of the blitz, and more importantly, Jason needed everyone's help, he mused to himself.

Dotty moved away from the table. Her fat pink arms showing from her rolled up sleeves. She grabbed the tea cloth, opened the black range oven door, and the aroma of toad-in-the-hole wafted throughout the kitchen, she poured Jason another cup of tea.

"So what about these changes you're on about?" she said.

"Well, I'm thinking of employing a couple of land army girls, I've got to do something." They all sighed with relief.

"What?" he said.

Henry seized his chance and blurted out, "I'm writing a letter to mum and Aunt Lillian because there's a cottage in the village to let. I would ask you if you could ring the letting agency to find out the rent, and would it be alright for them to move here and help out on the farm, because we are in such trouble?"

"Whoa, Henry, Whoa. I did not know about the cottage, and besides, if I do decide on the land army girls, we should be fine."

Henry's heart missed a beat. Land army girls, the more the merrier, he thought.

"But wait a minute; didn't I hear your mother say she would like to move here?"

Henry cut him short. "Will you find out? I know the name of the agency, its Connaught's of Leighton."

"First thing tomorrow, I'll ring and find out. What's today?"

Dotty shouted from across the kitchen and shook her

head in disbelief. "It's Thursday!"

"Very well, that's settled. You write your letter, Henry, inform you mum of the facts, and when we know for certain that they can move, we will ring immediately,"

Dotty served toad-in-the-hole and gave Alec a sausage sandwich to eat on his way home.

"Let's hope tomorrow brings better news, boss." With that, he closed the kitchen door, only to let Gyp in to sit by Henry and nuzzle round his legs. Henry and Jason tucked into their meal with relish and both thanked Dotty for being so good a stand-in, after which Jason retired to the fireside chair.

"Just a minute you two, I want some more coke here for the range."

Henry volunteered to do the chore, and he and Gyp went out with a zinc scuttle. Jason gave a little cough, and chose a make believe sleep pose.

"You know, that boy is a good'un, he deserves to have his mum and Aunt with him here. If we pull together there's no reason for the farm to suffer any failing." Jason stirred and shifted the cushion. Dotty almost believed she was talking to herself.

Henry returned with the coke, and Gyp remained on guard. The night was pitch black. Just as he sat down at the kitchen table to write his letter, the phone rang. Jason. Who had taken a little nap, awoke with a start "Who's that?"

"You better answer," dotty said, her arms deep in the washing bowl.

Jason rose wearily from his fireside chair." Ullo, Claridge Farm," he listened, never speaking. The call lasted no more than a couple of minutes. He put the phone softly on to its cradle.

"She's gone."

Dotty stopped washing up, Henry stopped his writing. "They done all they could for her, in the end she died peacefully. I've to call the hospital tomorrow, nine o'clock, they will issue the death certificate for me to collect, and then I have to report the death at the registrar's in Luton."

"Do you need me to go with you?" Dotty asked, Jason shook his head "That's a no then." She said feeling a little peeved.

"I'll go run a bath, and then sort my crumpled suit out, you know, the wedding suit, and now the funeral suit. He looked a broken man as he climbed the stairs. The Widdup Grandfather clock struck seven.

"She really loved life." Dotty cleared her throat and wiped a tear with her flower- covered apron. "They were made for each other."

***

The wheels of Mr Bott's taxi crunched to a halt on the thick bed of ash discarded by Tom Goodright's two slow burners. The station yard was covered with all sorts of soft core. In the distance white smoke from the flyer puffed out in small regular revolutions as it made its way from Dunstable. Mr Bott waited patiently for Mary and Aunt Lillian, and a sad reunion between both parties ensued as they entered the taxi.

As Mr Bott revved the taxi out of the station yard, the two women sat in silence. "To think it was only three weeks ago we were singing happily on our way to the farm for Christmas, and how are you two coping with the air raids on Lunnon?" he said breaking the silence.

"Well' we've survived so far but for how long, god only knows," Mary replied.

Mr Bott glanced at the two occupants in the taxi through

his rear view mirror, keeping one eye on the road, and the other on his fare.

"Jason asked me to do a slight detour, he thought you both could make your minds up about moving into Mrs Peck's cottage which is to let." Would you mind?" not at all, I says, if it means you coming to live here and to be nearer your boy, then yes. It's the best thing that could happen in the village, cos I for one'll be glad."

The little stoned-walled cottage came into view; last time they saw the property they remembered only a dim outline of Mrs Peck entering with Ashoo in the cage swearing about Germans.

"Well. Here we are, what do you think?"

"Can we get out and have a peek around?" Mary contemplated a sort of sojourn.

"Of course, of course." He said. "I can tell you it has a scullery, a small garden at the back, it has one medium sized bedroom, and a small living room, not much space, but you two could make it cosy, I know."

"Where's the lav."

"Ah, that'll be down the end of the garden, gets a bit scary these nights, I know, got one myself, earth closet, they call them, I bet you haven't got any in Lunnon?"

Gyp's bark alerted Jason and Alec who were working and cleaning out muck from the milking stalls, as the herd was kept in through the winter months. The cows were turned out to the Dutch barn, knee deep in straw for the day, let in again for milking, and remained in overnight.

The afternoon began to fade as Mr Bott's taxi drove into the yard. Dotty Oddbin was ready to squeeze the car horn.

"No need," Jason shouted, "we are coming in, make tea all-round Dotty!"

Mary and Lillian stepped out of the taxi. Jason looked

all in, Mary thought.

"Nice to see you again," he said. Mary noticed his sad eyes.

"Too soon," she replied.

Jason thanked Mr Bott. "I'll settle up later."

Mary and Lillian would not hear of it and paid the fare.

"Come in, come in." Jason said. Alec kicked off his wellies and hauled their suitcases up to the landing. The Widdup clock struck three thirty.

"Ah, Henry will be home soon, 'ere take yer things off and grab a seat." Dotty served tea all round. "I dare say you want to know what's going to happen at the farm," Jason explained, how he thought of employing a couple of land army girls, and Kathy not cold, Mary thought.

"True, I may have panicked, but miss her so much I thought that setting on some young people would lessen the hurt."

Mary slid her hand over Jason's. "I'm sure there'll be some good to come out of this in the end."

Gyp ran across the yard to greet Henry. "Hullo Gyp." He rubbed her ears, "Are they here?" Gyp yapped twice.

***

Thursday, the nineteenth of January; St Michael's was fairly full, if not almost. A dusting of snow settled around the parish church, and the service began with Kathy's favourite hymn.

"The day thou gavest, lord, has ended."

Tears welled in Jason's eyes. He could just make out vicar Stefans and the hymn board. The light through each window paled into blackness. He closed his eyes he wiped away the tears and pulled himself together. Soon be over, how I loved her. He clenched his teeth, bit his lip, and clenched his fist. The funeral arrangements had been first class, he thought.

The reading was taken from the Ecclesiastes, chapter two, verse four. Vicar Stefans began the reading.

Vicar Stefans took a firm hold of the lectern as he delivered the reading.

I made me great works
I builded me houses
I planted me vineyards
I made me gardens and orchards
I planted trees in them of all kinds of fruit
I got me servants and maidens and had servants born in my house
I had great possessions of great and small cattle
Above all that were in Jerusalem before me.

Everything else that day after the service was just a blur. Soon they all walked back to the farm. Only Dotty had stayed, at least someone was prepared to guard the farm, she had festooned the table with sausage rolls, cheese- cake, and spam sandwiches, and of course, a good strong cup of tea, which Jason laced with Napoleon brandy for whoever accepted the offer.

Mary and Lillian had met many local people this day because of Henry's presence. In the Smith family they were accepted as one of them, no doubt in Mary's mind, Eggington is where she wanted to be.

CHAPTER NINE

AN EFFORT OF WILL

The kitchen stove, which Dotty had managed to keep going with what little coke she has left in the zinc scuttle, needed to be replenished and banked down for the night, and Dotty reminded whoever was interested in that chore.

"I'll go," Henry said. He trudged out to the coal and coke bunker while the others took of their coats and settled round the table. More village people turned up to support Jason in his hour of mourning, his grief would subside in the company of friends, but Mary's astonishment there were no relatives for either Jason or Kathy.

Mary and Lillian were introduced to the vicar Stefans and his wife, Mr Bott and his spouse, and a few others, then Gertrude Wilson Green. Mary had been longing to meet her as Henry's letters contained some interesting snippets of information on how she had treated the other lads in her care. She was firm but very fair. They were living more or less in a mansion, and enjoyed rides in the Rolls Royce. Most of the village people moved into the study-come-lounge, leaving Jason, Mary, and Lillian together in the kitchen.

"I'm glad you made it today, did Mr Bott show you Mrs Peck's old cottage, and what do you think about moving to Eggington, have you thought about moving to these parts? I rang Connaught's letting agency and the rent is quite reasonable," Jason said.

"How much?"

"Ten shillings a week or two pounds a month, depending on how you want to pay." He'd cajoled Connaught's into a reduced rent.

Mary raised her brows. "We could manage that, couldn't we?"

Jason responded, "Of course, Henry would remain here at the farm."

"We wouldn't have it any other way." Mary agreed.

"Have a think about it" Jason gulped down the remaining dregs of his Napoleon brandy tea, and called Alec. "Sorry" he said,"gotta go, cows to milk, you know, farm work carries on. See you in a little while, say cheerio to the rest; Henry will see you to your rooms."

"Such care from the man," Aunt Lillian remarked, "I like him"

Mary reminded Aunt Lillian, "he's still wearing his best suit,"

Only one person remained as the others departed in dribs and drabs, saying their goodbyes and adding their condolences. After Henry oversaw his mum and Aunt Lillian in to the large bedroom, they came down stairs to find Gertrude Wilson-Green talking to Dotty Oddbin. Henry left in a hurry as eggs had to be collected, and by the time he'd washed and graded them, it was time to lock the poultry in the Arks.

"Ah there you are," Gertrude said, she had evidently made it her business to stay that little bit longer, and wanted to know what London was really like at first hand. " The papers sometimes exaggerate about the blitz, that the bombs not being very accurate, propaganda I believe."

Aunt Lillian responded first, "I can assure you that the papers are one hundred percent right in what they print, there's no denying London is like hell, no words can describe what it's like. It's like Dane's Inferno."

"Well, if you paint a picture as you say, why don't you come and live here, I'm sure Jason wouldn't mind under the circumstances. In fact, I should think he would be very glad, you see, he has no relatives, neither did Kathy, they were the last in the line of respected families, isn't that so Dotty?" Dotty nodded in agreement.

"So you know of Jason's history and lineage?" Aunt Lillian found the words to match whatever Gertrude knew about Jason's family.

"I do know we shouldn't be talking like this, but yes, Jason's family dates back at least a hundred and twenty odd years, that his forebears have farmed Claridges, and Kathy's family were village people too. Her father and mother owned the business of making coffins and anything in the carpentry world. She was the only daughter when her parents passed away; the business finished under the hammer and was auctioned off just before the war began.

"So there is nobody to carry on?" Mary said

"That's right, nobody, I'm sure Jason will tell you more as time goes by."

"Well we are thinking about renting Rose Cottage now Mrs Peck's vacated." Gertrude's eyes lit up on hearing this piece of news. The grandfather clock in the hall struck four.

"Good lord, is that the time." She said.

Dotty Oddbin had maintained an energy-sapping day, no wonder she looked worn out. Gertrude Wilson-Green offered her help, but was politely turned down. Dotty didn't want her in the kitchen, if she could help it. Gertrude bade her farewells and turned on her heel. As she left she called out, "if there's anything you need Dotty, just ring."

The kitchen door was gently latched by Henry who said

his goodbye to Gertrude as she passed him on the way out.

Dotty resumed her duties, leaving Mary and Aunt Lillian and Henry to support her. She hummed a tune as she washed the plates and cutlery, Mary and Aunt Lillian took to the wipes.

Meanwhile Henry returned with the Zinc scuttle to fill the fireside box with logs and coke. The night was drawing in fast. Jason and Alec bedded down the animals, now Jason could retire for the night.

Dotty would be going home tonight, leaving the four of them to cope. How would they cope? She thought. She was leaving them a saucepan full of stew to serve later. I dare say they will manage, they have survived the blitz, this must be a honey run to them. Just as Dotty dried her hands, Jason and Alec appeared at the doorway. Gyp as usual ran in between everyone's legs to sit in front of the range. Alec said his goodnight, and Dotty followed.

"See you tomorrow, you'll be fine," she called, her voice trailing into the night.

Henry had managed to show his mum and Aunt Lillian where everything was kept. They rolled up their sleeves and the table was soon cleared, then laid again for a late tea. The night was misty, cold, and dark and Jason blew into his cupped hands as Mary ladled out the stew into each of the bowls. Jason asked if they had reached a decision.

"We have," replied Mary, "the answer is yes."

Henry could not hide his happiness.

"We think it is a sensible solution to move to Rose Cottage."

Henry's face turned into a big grin; to have his mum and Aunt Lillian living just along the road were beyond his wildest dreams. He was very, very happy.

"I know it's a bit premature at be presumptuous and on

this day of all days," Jason said, "But time is the fundamental factor here. Grief, I know will hit me later, but what I'm about to propose may be odd to you. I think it's in the best interest of all of us if the farm is to stay productive, tomorrow, I'll drive you both to Leighton, and get the legal side settled at Connaught's then you both stay another night before returning to Lunnon."

Jason continued his narrative. "You can set a date on moving here, I'll keep the key safe, Alec and I and Henry will make ready Rose Cottage for you, don't bother your heads too much about the farm, Dotty will be expected to keep things running as she always does. I have many things on my mind, but this episode in my life I'm sure is one hundred per cent right," Jason could see no obstacles.

***

The Standbridge flyer puffed its way to the steep incline. It would take an hour before reaching Luton, and then a quick dash over the footbridge to catch the express from Derby to London. When they boarded the train, every carriage was packed with servicemen. The carriage, which they boarded, exploded with plenty of banter, and the jokes made the journey home that much more enlightening. On approaching St Pancras, their thoughts were of many friends they had made. It was so heart-warming to hear voices, smell the cigarette, and pipe smoke; some were eating homemade pies their mums and sweethearts had baked, but the comradeship above all provided Mary and Lillian with a sense of pride among all these boys.

Mary thought of Bert again, but the memory of that day seemed so far away, it no longer mattered.

They must pursue their own lives to whatever end may engage them.

Aunt Lillian paid the fare to the clippie, and then offered her a humbug, which she gracefully accepted.

"Oh, hullo, Mary, where have you been hiding these past few days?" the clippie and Mary knew one another as they operated out of the same bus depot.

"We've been to the country to see my son Henry, and we've made a decision too. We think a move there would benefit us, to get away from this hell hole, and to be near him."

"I don't blame you one iota for wanting to move out of this mad place."

"Why, has it been bad again?"

"We've had a couple of rotten nights."

"How's Old Street?"

"You'll find out a few more houses and tenements have been destroyed, it doesn't get any better, but we live in hope."

As they turned into the side street once again, Aunt Lillian's little terraced house was still intact.

"Thank the lord for that, I thought we would be turning round and heading straight back to the village." Lillian forced a wry smile as she unlocked the door and stepped into a very cold hallway. Aunt Lillian and Mary knew in their hearts that to survive was to organize and pack as soon as possible; the next few nights and days would be very scary.

They soon had a fire going in the small open grate. The electricity was still on, which was a blessing. The kettle was hastily set to boil, as water was still flowing from the sink tap. Overall, it seemed a miracle.

Aunt Lillian was a rock, without her Mary would be lost and it was with much trepidation that the night to come wouldn't be as bad as they both feared; as her clippie mate said, we live in hope! With their hands round their hot mugs of tea, Mary reminded Lillian that tomorrow she must go to the depot and offer her resignation straight away, they would understand that there was not much future here. The night passed with spasmodic air raids more to the south and east of them, and they were eternally grateful to come through the night. As usual, they bedded down underneath the large dining table, which offered little protection other than a psychological effect.

The morning sky offered little comfort for them; it was a misty, cold morning with a few snowflakes falling, just a few every now and again. With the kettle boiling, Aunt Lillian prepared breakfast while Mary made ready to report to the bus depot. Breakfast consisted of a bowl of Quaker oats and two slices of toast and marmalade, followed by a hot mug of tea.

Mary wrapped her top coat around herself and hurried off to give in her notice. Aunt Lillian busied herself with washing up and then resigning herself to pack and sort out what items were traveling with them to Eggington.

She pondered for a minute, thinking about last night's discussion on how they would transport themselves, would it be worth booking a taxi for them both. There will be quite a load, too much for them to carry on the train. She need not have worried, as the front door burst open, and Mary stood in the hall with an elderly man following behind. "Aunt Lillian" she said," I think I have solved the problem of moving. This is Bill, he drives the breakdown lorry for the depot, says he could move us this weekend. He can borrow a van off his son, and move us to Eggington."

"Phew, I was getting rather worried about how much we should take, and what to leave."

"How big is the van?"

"It's an old Carter-Paterson cast off. He bought it second hand at their sales up east, uses it for anything, he was in the scrap business."

"How much are you charging?"

"Shush Aunt Lillian, we only buy the fuel, a nod, and a wink job, Bill say's it's an honour for him to move us, wouldn't dream of charging. Besides, it'll be nice for him to drive out into the country, see what it's all about."

"Where is your son then, Bill?" Mary asked

"He's in the army, somewhere in Norfolk at the moment, he worked for Carter-Paterson, gave notice to leave, wanted to be his own boss. You know, always' on the go, then he joined the army ordinance. I hire the van out for him until all of this is finished, the war, that is."

Bill scoured round the little terraced cottage. In his meaningful voice, he said, "I can transport all of this if you want me to," with an air of authority, he added, "no sweat, can you manage to pack and stack ready, I can load the van. Have you arranged the day to move?"

"No" Aunt Lillian said," but now we know Mary," she said, "You must phone Jason straightaway."

***

Henry was leaving the farm for school when Jason called him from across the farmyard.

"Don't forget, before you come home this afternoon, call at the shop and collect dusters and cleaning fluid and tell Ma Leech I'll settle with her when I'm next by to feed the pigs."

Jason and Alec had been hedge trimming along Thedeway part of the morning. It was time for a mid-morning break and they were ready for the cup of tea, which Dotty had brewed for them. She tooted the horn as they entered the yard. "Coming!" they both shouted.

The Widdup grandfather clock struck a quarter to twelve

when the phone rang, Dotty answered "Ullo, Claridge farm" she said. "Jason it's for you" she handed the phone over.

"Yea, Jason ere." He listened intently to what Mary had to say.

"So you'll be arriving late tomorrow afternoon all being well, without any breakdown. Well, that's good news, this fits in with our cleaning of the cottage for you tonight, so everything should be ready. We'll leave a fire burning for you and don't forget to call in the farm for the key. Alec and Henry will help you unload, I'll be along later. Cheerio, be seeing you."

"Everything alright boss?" Alec asked.

"Yea, things couldn't have worked out better." Jason felt the warmth of the cup around his hands as he gulped the last dregs down. "C'mon, Alec, we'd better get that hedging done." He strode out of the kitchen whistling Rule Britannia. Dotty, her big brown eyes following him, realising she'd never heard Jason whistle before; his life was rejuvenated and he was feeling full again. Things were happening, she thought.

***

They left Ashford Street at precisely ten thirty on Saturday morning, the van loaded with most of Aunt Lillian's furniture and utensils.

"Are you sure this van is capable of making the journey?" Mary asked.

Bill was about to give a convincing and reassuring answer.

"Now don't worry, this van has travelled all over England, to my knowledge, and has never let my son down."

He surprised them both. "Eggington, it's a short trip, just

down the lane, joke, ha ha!"

"I hope you're right, and you know the way?" Mary was bemused with Bill's sense of humour.

"Trust me; I could drive there with my eyes shut, so long as you've packed the biscuits and a flask of tea. We will be in the village after twelve o'clock." He turned the ignition and the engine roared into life. Aunt Lillian took one last look and wondered if she would ever come back to Ashford Street and still find her terraced house intact. Bill had assured her earlier while loading the van that he would keep an eye on the place and phone the farm straight away if anything untoward happened to the house.

After a short drive the van turned on to the Edgeware Road, "There you are, the A5 , all we do now is follow this road all the way to Hockliffe, turn left and we are almost there; easy peasy."

Bill's confidence instilled them with faith, and gratitude.

They passed numerous buildings still intact; in fact, this part of London had escaped the damage so far, and was with much trepidation that the van sped out into the countryside, it wasn't until they reached St Albans they were surprised to be following a Carter Paterson van, a much larger one than theirs. Whoever the driver was, he kept his speed to the permitted limit, strict and to the book. The A5 was a good Roman Road. When they reached Redbourne they followed the larger van into a lorry park and café.

"Here we stop for a stretch and a cup of tea." Bill checked his watch. He glanced at his passengers, "Just an hour, we have made good time." He pulled up alongside the larger van and turned off the engine.

Bill made his way to the café to use the toilets and in doing so passed the time of day with the driver of the larger van. The conversation led from one thing to another. It turned out that Bill's son in his earlier days, at the beginning of his employment with Carter Paterson, had been this fellow's cabin mate on journey's to Scotland.

Aunt Lillian and Mary also made the comfort stop. Relieved, and with a stretch, they climbed aboard their van but not before being introduced to the driver of the other van, a few words and pleasantries were exchanged, and Bill and his companions , would follow the other van to Hockliffe.

As they passed through Dunstable, Bill saw that the trunk road lay between a huge chalk cutting. No doubt, whoever knew that the hill in decades past had to be hewn out for the road to continue north; the work must have been a monumental operation for them.

Just as the two vans were entering, the high chalk cutting all hell was let loose.

Explosions burst all around the vehicles. A tremendous sound enveloped them as a German Junkers 88 roared overhead, spitting fire from its twin guns, strafing the larger van in front. Out of control, the van skidded over the pathway and over a small embankment to land on its side. Bill, in an instant, stopped his van and ran to try to rescue the trapped driver.

"Oh, my god!" Mary shouted. She and Aunt Lillian jumped out and hurried as fast as they could to help .Bill tugged at the door as other drivers came to his aid; he was frightened of the van being set alight, as petrol vapour hit his nostrils.

"Careful!" he shouted. He could see the driver had been knocked unconscious. He must have hit his head on the roof of the cab as the van went over the small embankment. In no time, a fire engine arrived on the scene and began dousing the large van. An ambulance arrived; then a police car came, and Bill, with the aid of others managed to rescue the driver.

As for the van, the police would inform Carter-Paterson whereupon it would be up righted and towed to a garage back at Redbourne. This episode cost them over two hours delay.

***

Henry, Dotty, and Jason were getting concerned as the hours ticked by.

"I wonder if anything has happened." Jason stood in the hall glancing up at the Widdup clock, which always kept good time, the hands showed three fifteen. He was about to say he would call London just to make sure, when Gyp barked loudly, and the grey green van made its entrance into the yard.

The three of them stood in the doorway intrigued by their lateness. Mary was first to jump down from the cab followed by a rather flustered Aunt Lillian. Bill allowed them to get clear before he manoeuvred the van round ready for the off to the cottage.

"Why are you late, mum?" Henry asked cheekily.

"Well, we were attacked by a German plane."

"Pull the other one, mum"

"No it's true." Aunt Lillian explained how and what happened on the main road just outside Dunstable, and after they listened to her story, all were astounded.

Mary interjected. "Well, I think Bill deserved a medal for how he rescued the van driver.

Dotty clasped Mary by the hand. "You must come in and sit for a while, I'll boil the kettle, and we'll have a cup of tea. Where's your friend, go and call him in Henry." Dotty made haste to get them all some light refreshment.

"They fight dirty, them Germans, that's all I have to say." Jason was angered as it sunk in what happened. "I'll phone the observer paper first thing Monday morning, and tell them I have a story to give. You don't mind do you,.....You two?" nodding at Mary and Lillian. Many in this country ought to know how the Germans are fighting this war, firing on innocent civilians. I suppose the Gazette'll run the story as well."

After they rested, Bill reckoned they ought to get moving as he had a long journey back to the metropolis.

"I think you should stay over, there's a bed here for you." Said Jason apologetically.

"Are you sure? It would help me inasmuch as I wouldn't be rushed."

"I should phone the missus, tell her what the score is, she'll understand, though I don't like leaving her on her own for too long. Maybe I could get an early start tomorrow morning." Bill sought an answer from Jason.

"I'm up at five thirty or thereabouts, so it's no bother to me; Jason said," I'll make breakfast for the two of us and see you on your way."

Dotty fidgeted, more in protest at being overlooked. "So that's settled , I'll go and air the sheets for you, it's no trouble, it will be the best. Besides, you'll need the rest after what you've been through today.

They moved off in the van, with Henry and Alec squeezed into the back to help unload and move into Rose Cottage, Jason was to trot along later to see how they were coping, as he had milking to see to. Dotty would collect the eggs and see to closing of the Arks.

The van backed up to the front door. Mary climbed down and inserted the key. "Make a wish." Alec called, "as you cross the threshold;" Mary's mind raced. All she wanted now for all of them to be safe until the end of the war. She also thanked Jason in her mind for being so kind to the, and so soon after Kath's death. It must be hurtful for him; at least she and Lillian would be together again, and Henry would call in every so often. She would take on most of the chores from now on. She and Lillian were prepared to help out on the farm as and when time allowed.

The move was near complete when Jason arrived, the fire was roaring in the hearth, beds were made and there was little more anybody could do except for Lillian to make a cup of tea for the very first time. They made a toast. "Here's to a successful life in the country and to Rose Cottage and all who live here."

"I'll drink to that." Jason said.

Mary's eyes met Jason's as they clinked cups. "To the future."

CHAPTER TEN

LEGALITY

Stanley Hogg drove his decrepit Austin twelve through the leafy country lanes of Northamptonshire to arrive in the town centre just before nine o'clock at his office of Royal Ancient of Liverpool Insurer's family law and general litigation. This morning he was earlier than usual, as last night his attention had been than stretched over the last will and testament of the brothers Gunn. After reading the will at least three times and just to make sure everything was in order, he would read it one more time before he made the phone call to Claridge farm. It was customary in this case to dig around to see what caused the blaze. As the police Inspector said three days after the fire that one of his detective came across a tin box in the central hallway, under the stairs, while searching for clues as to what caused the fateful fire, he came across the information, which led them to this office in Northampton.

Stanley Hogg pulled at his frayed tweed coat sleeves. I must get my wife to repair these with a bit of leather, he felt his elbows; these as well if there is time. Austerity, Austerity, he mused to himself, still to the will. Something bothered him. He read through again, opened the casefile on the Gunn's death; verdict Accidental death was recorded; also there was the insurance file to deal with. He rang an internal number and asked his secretary to bring the Gunn's file into the office.

He duly thanked her and proceeded to read through, as in all insurance schedules there are articles, which are insured, and articles that are not. It wasn't until he came to a brief summary that a sentence made him sit up.

On no account would the insurance will not be paid out until the number of the fire insurance, which could be found on a plaque bolted to the outside wall had been registered with the said company. He fingered through the document. "Hmm, they must have forgotten to register," he murmured to himself, as he could find no number listed. This caused him some sort of dilemma, should he say something now, or wait until he visited Claridge farm?

Stanley pondered for a moment as the secretary entered with a cup of tea." Ah thanks, very kind of you, Muriel." He was about to ask her in a polite way if she knew of this short coming in the file of the Gunn's when he remembered she'd only been with the R.A.L.I. for a couple of months, not enough time to be aware of the situation regarding the file. Although he'd never met the people who lived at Claridge farm, Fred and Thomas Gunn apparently stipulated in a letter to the company that they were good honest beings. English through and through, and if anything happened to themselves, these were the people he would contact and deal with whatever the circumstances. Stanley would meet these people sooner rather than later.

He glanced at the clock on the office outer wall. "God, is that the time?" he said to himself. Quarter past eleven. He dialled a number to Hockliffe exchange. It rang for some time. Either the incumbent wasn't about, or not in. at last, a rather subdued female voice spoke.

"Ullo, Claridge farm who do you want?"

"May I speak to Mr Smith please?"

"Who's calling?"

"Is Mr Smith there, please?"

"Just a moment, I'll toot the horn.

Stanley gave a quizzical smile, and waited a couple of minutes before an out of breath voice answered, "Yea, who's calling? Jason Smith here."

"Ah, Mr Smith, it's Stanley Hogg of Royal Ancient and Liverpool, I wonder if I could have a few minutes of your tome?"

"Of course."

"I have some important documents that need to be read to you, but not over the phone. May I fix a date to come and visit you?"

"Sure"

"In two days' time, say Friday the sixth of April, and can I ask, is there a Henry Kneally living with you?"

"There is." Over the phone, Jason heard papers being shifted.

"The purpose of my phone call is our office has reason to believe from the police, and the fire officers at Leighton that we can proceed with the evaluation for insurance claims, but a problem has arisen in regards to a fire number which to all intents and purpose may have been accidently left off the policy. I wonder, would it be too much trouble for you to find this number, it's generally located above either the front door or the rear door lintel?"

"How do I identify the number?"

"It should be inscribed onto an oval or oblong plaque; the number will be indented in the name plate and bolted to the outer wall. I also understand that most of the building is still intact?"

"Well, yea, you'll find the building, except for the scullery and stairs and landing, and two bedrooms, in a blackened state. As for the rest of the manor it's in a pretty fair condition."

"Our mission on Friday, with the aid of an assessor who will accompany me, shouldn't take no more than a couple of hours. Expect us, say, about ten o'clock."

"That'll be fine, Mr Hogg, that'll be just fine, you have my word."

The Widdup clock struck twelve noon.

"Did you hear that, Mr Hogg? It's twelve noon."

"I heard. Right see you Friday the sixth at ten." With that he rang off.

Jason placed the phone in its cradle. "Well Dotty, we've got our work cut out if I'm not mistaken. We shall need a good pair of shears, and Henry and Alec will assist in discovery of a very important number."

The ivy that surrounded the manor had grown incredibly thick, inasmuch as the fire had not touched or even singed it. Jason lifted his cap and scratched his forelock. "We'll make a start after tea with what little light we've got left of the day." He remarked.

***

Henry arrived home from school breathless. "Where's Jason?" he panted.

"Lor, you're out of breath, lad here sit yerself down, now what's with all this hurrying?" said Dotty.

"They are back"

"Who's back?"

"The soldiers, I've run alongside their waggons, they drove in to Furrow Field on the corner. You never heard them?"

"No. I'm busy getting your tea. If you want Jason, you'll find him and Alec preparing themselves for a bit of ivy cutting."

"Ivy cutting, what do you mean?"

"Go to the Old Manor, you'll find them there." Henry stared at the hot bread and butter pudding Dotty had just retrieved from the oven.

"Oh go on then, just one slice. Mind you eat it before you join them both."

By the pigsties, and along the narrow path that led to the now defunct and charred shell of the manor. Jason was snipping away at the evergreen above the front door of the manor. Henry was curious as to why they were both trying to grapple with the climbing plant.

He joined them as he swallowed the last piece of bread pudding and, licking his fingers and lips, said" Can I help in any way?"

"Yes" Jason answered and glanced over his shoulder, "Stand back a little on the lawn and keep your eyes peeled for underneath the ivy, a number should reveal itself. I just hope I'm cutting at the right door, so yell if you spot anything."

Henry stood motionless still licking his lips and Alec gave him an inquisitive sideways glance. Two minutes of snipping went on until the last of the ivy was cut away. No number appeared.

"Perhaps you're cutting too high," Alec, reminded him.

Jason fumed, "Well, you come and have a blinking go!" They swapped places. Alec cut lower, above the lintel height, within two or three snips, and there it showed; a number appeared on an oval cast iron plaque.

Gyp sat by Henry's side, slapping her tail on the grass, impatient, as Alec cut a small section away and passed his hand back and forth across the plaque to wipe away any leaves and remaining dust. The numbers indented into the iron plaque were small in comparison to the size of the thing.

"What does it read, Alec?" Jason was full of curiosity.

"Let me read it," Henry said

"No, it's my duty to do the honours, c'mon down, Alec, I'll read it out to you."

So again they swapped places. Jason climbed the ladder and stared at the numbers on the plaque. He lifted his cap and scratched his forelock.

"Well, if I'm not mistaken, these are roman numerals, I don't understand 'em"

"Neither would I," said Alec.

Jason called to Henry to run to the study and return with pencil and paper. Jason would copy the figurers and translate them back at the house that night. As they walked, back to the kitchen the aroma of cooking reached their senses. "Aw, Henry, smells like stew and bread pudding." Jason rubbed his hands with pleasure.

Later, after all the chores on the farm had been seen to, Jason and Henry tried to relate the numbers into English. Gyp barked a welcome as Mary and Aunt Lillian strode in to the farmyard, which was fortunate for Jason as he reminded himself that Aunt Lillian had taught at school. Well, two heads are better than one, he thought. Mary and Aunt Lillian had by this time acquired a routine of helping Dotty to manage the farmhouse; they would do the night shift, ie, wash the dinner plates and cutlery, any sewing and ironing, general tidying up and making ready for the next day. Meanwhile, Jason moved himself into the study. Henry had permitted himself to bath and change his clothes.

CHAPTER ELEVEN

NEW ARRIVALS

The evening proceeded with Jason wrestling with a decision whether or not to apply to the War-Ag for help. He needed two more hands on the farm. With spring arriving in the weeks ahead, work schedules would be stretched to the limit. Six sows would be shedding litters all over the place at the smallholding he rented off a near neighbour. Jason's farm was a mixture of arable and dairy. He grew swedes, mangel-wurzel, potatoes, carrots, all to be sown. Jason rubbed the stubble on his chin.

"Trouble?" asked Mary

"Not really, just thinking about how to use a couple of land army girls, it would release Alec and me to concentrate on other work that needs to be done, and 'sides, I've decided to invest in a new tractor, one of them American G.M. lease-lend jobs. That would really set the pace."

"So you're upping the workload all round?" Mary quizzed.

"I've got to, no ifs or buts, if the farm is to survive at all."

Henry butted in. "What about these Roman numerals?"

"All in good time, son." Jason said.

Son, he called him. Mary considered what Jason had just said, she looked at Aunt Lillian, whose eyes told her everything she needed to know; her place now would be there at Claridge Farm.

Jason retrieved the piece of paper from the study. "Here you are then, put your Lunnon heads together, and tell me in plain English what these figurers mean."

Aunt Lillian was the first to react. "Well, at first glance the first two figurers are two-two, then one-two, then one-nine and three- nought."

"Are you sure?" Jason said

"As sure as night is from day."

"So that makes a number 22121930?"

"It certainly does." Nobody spoke for a second or two, until Mary and Henry chuckled in unison. They pointed at each other and declared simultaneously, "Henry's birth date."

"Well I'll be dang'nd, that's a hell of a coincidence, if I may say so," Jason beamed, his face a picture of total bliss. "Right, thank you Lillian I'll leave the number locked in my study desk until Mr Hogg calls next week."

***

There were rumours and counter rumours that a change of school was imminent, the pupils were excited as to which one they would be attending. It would happen quickly, even as early as the following week. The evacuees and older village boys and girls would be bussed to Beaudesert and Mary Bassett schools respectively.

On Monday, 2nd of April, 1943, as the boys and girls waited eagerly and nervous as to what lay ahead on this first day at their new schools, the coach driven by Sidney Roper, an elderly jovial character spoke of himself as he drove. Being a twenty seater coach the one where the driver sits with his passengers, he chatted to the kids who sat nearest to him about the time he was Mr Churchill's driver after he returned from Africa and fighting the Boers. He told them of

Churchill's exploits fighting Zulus. Henry thought for a while, funny, Tom Gunn never mentioned Churchill at art class, perhaps it was a different time and place.

The coach pulled to a stop outside Beaudesert. To their surprise all the windows had been bricked up, the school was dark until the caretaker switched on the lights for the whole of the day.

Doors were left ajar and small apertures with vent were cut into walls, the only air to circulate the classrooms, but the size of the rooms at least gave them freedom to breath and learn. Henry and his pals were surprised to see some school friends who had been billeted in Leighton; they were amongst at least thirty pupils, which made a classroom full of London children, and being taught by none other than Mr Shaunessy from his old school in Shoreditch. Mr Stearson would act as deputy head. This indeed made Henry and his pals a lot happier.

The following morning at precisely seven thirty, a khaki canvassed covered wagon braked to a halt amidst dust and grit. From underneath its canopy two pretty girls jumped down dressed in corduroy trousers, green sweaters, and pork pie hats, each chattering between Gyp's nerve shattering barks. The girls, frightened for a second or two walked on with self-belief that no one, not even the farm dog, would stand in their way for their first morning at Claridge farm.

Henry, hearing the commotion, finished off his ablutions and, running along the landing, peered out the side window overlooking the yard, only to see two strange hats disappear under the eaves to the kitchen door.

Hmm. Land army girls, he thought and quickly descended the stairs, breathing in the aroma of spam and dried egg being fried by Dotty. Plates were laid out ready for this, and Jason and Alec's breakfast. Two of the prettiest girls he'd ever seen in his whole life greeted him with a cheery, "Hullo, who are you then?"

Henry gave them a wry smile, and said, "I'm Henry, the evacuee from London. Who are you?"

"I'm Laura," said one, "I'm Jenny." Said the other "Where's the governor?" they chorused.

Dotty thought, being a bit too chirpy for their own good, and she served Henry his breakfast.

"Can we have some?" they chimed in.

"No you can't, I'll sound the horn for Jason to come and sort you two out." Dotty thought, I'll have to keep an eye on these two, I know.

It was up to the farmer to provide for the personnel who worked for any length of time, Jason reminded himself to speak to Dotty that in the future she would be responsible for the meals however many worked on the farm, so there would be more trips to town for shopping.

Jason slipped his wellington boots off, and called Alec to hurry. He did not know what sort of reaction he would receive on greeting his new employee's; he did know they would be starting this morning. Since Kathy had gone, time was he could face anything; this was a new challenge. He turned to face the Land Army girls.

"Ullo, I see you've made yourself comfortable?" the two girls squirmed on their chairs, and introduced themselves. Alec came in, followed by Gyp. Jason lifted off his cap and scratched his forehead.

"This is Alec; he'll tell you everything you need to know about the farm. Me, I'll walk you round the farm so you can familiarize yourselves, then we'll get started." The two girls were dying to know about their first job.

Gyp growled, as she heard somebody approaching the kitchen door. It was the corporal from the detachment; he wanted to order milk from tomorrow morning onwards.

"You back again?" Jason said in an agitated sort of manner.

"Yes gov, and there's more of us this time. The O.I.C recons on thirty pints, if that's alright with you."

"Okay same as before, bring your own container and pay on the dot, no I.O.U'S."

The two girls nudged each other as the corporal eyed them through Jason's outstretched arm what was holding the door ajar,

"See I told you we'd be alright for company," Jenny whispered into Laura's ear," Laura nudged her in the ribs.

Jason drained his last dregs of tea. "Right, c'mon you two, let's be having you. Alec start the Fordson up, we'll meet you in the Dutch barn, then make for the Little Dinge Field."

As all of them were preparing to leave, the postman cycled in to the yard delivering a few letters. Jason hurriedly fingered through them, cast aside the bills, and opened one from the War-Ag. He scanned through the letter as the others looked on. A big smile crept across his face. "Ooray!" he cried, "the new tractor arrives next week."

For their first job on the farm, the girls would get ready the potato sets. Alec, meanwhile, would drive the old Fordson tractor to cultivate a furrow to receive the potato seed. After six rows, he would unhitch the one sheared plough, and hook on to the tractor a contraption consisting of a small platform and a trailer. The girls would sit on the plank of wood and he would slowly pull the contraption along, covering two rows, while from their seats the girls would drop seed potatoes into the furrows, guessing two feet as the tractor chugged its way to the other end of Little Dinge, five acres in all, by the end of the day. Over half would have been set and earthed up. The girls were very tired when they returned to the farm after their first day's toil; they washed their arms and hands at the outside tap by the dairy.

"Well, girls, how did your first day go then?" Jason was changing the churns from underneath the cooling apparatus.

"When do we get a chance to milk the cows?" they chorused.

"It'll come all in good time. Now can either of you drive?" Laura raised her arm and Jason saw the lilywhite skin, her dark curls hung beneath her pork pie hat. If I were twenty-one again, he thought.

"Where?" he asked

"A year ago my dad taught me to drive his Morris 8 through the city streets of Liverpool, so I know how to change gear, that's about all I know."

"So, you're from the north?"

"We both are."

"I can't expect Alec to continue much longer, you can see he's in retirement age. You'll be expected to drive the new tractor as soon as it arrives."

The girls were hungry to break for a cup of tea and a cheese sandwich. Aunt Lillian was just about to buzz the horn from across the yard. She could just make out the features of the first girl as they walked closer and it was obvious to her that she recognised the dark hair girl.

"It's you!" Aunt Lillian called with a surprised voice," come on in" The two girls were happy to see her.

"Where's your other friend?" they asked.

"She's in here, come in."

The girls were tired after their first day on the farm and glad to sit down on a comfy chair. Mary greeted them as she poured the tea into two mugs; it didn't take too long for the girls to register their delight of meeting the two Londoners again.

Jason entered and the gregarious chatter that greeted him took him by surprise, in fact he learned later of the train meeting between the women and of their banter that had passed back and forth. Jason was outnumbered four to one. He'd never been in this situation before; he was overwhelmed with female company.

Henry came in at just the right moment from school and gave Jason that bit of support he needed to counterbalance the difference, as they sat round the solid oak table. Jason knew he'd made the right decision in taking on the girls. Just what the place needed, some life. `

Jason sipped the remains of his tea; he still had plenty of work to finish. The girls would be there tomorrow to complete the sowing of potatoes and small seeds of swede and mangel-wurzel. Henry had settled in at Beaudesrent School, and the rotation of Dotty for early morning, Mary, and Lillian in the afternoon was working like clockwork.

CHAPTER TWELVE

PROPOSALS

As with his father, Jason was brought up to be prudent, so it was no surprise to any of the villagers to see him cycling to the shop for a few sundries. The new Hudson cycle had proved a godsend for Jason inasmuch as it saved on fuel and time, and money. It so happened that Mary needed to buy a few items herself. The timing was coincidental; Jason pulled up just as Mary reached the shop doorway. A chance meeting had brought the couple together for a few minutes on their own. Jason was fifty-two years old, time was slipping by and a widower; Mary was forty-six and a widow, yet their lives had somehow inexplicitly been thrown together through no fault of their own. For a second their eyes met, and for a second both felt a little embarrassed, but why should they be, they were free birds.

"Oh hello, I didn't know you could ride a cycle." She said.

Jason rested the cycle against the shop window ledge. Seeing Mary in her print coloured dress and small grey crochet waistcoat, and black half-heeled shoes, her mousey curls with just a hint of grey hanging down on her shoulders, she looked positively demure. Why hadn't he taken any notice before? Perhaps because of Henry being part of the family beforehand. Jason had been reluctant to make any advance on Mary so close to his bereavement, and now here, she portrayed a figure that he knew from his youth he would have tried to court. they both laughed as the cycle fell away from the window ledge and knocked over a box tree being displayed, its contents spewed all over the path.

"Cor blimey." His face reddened.

"I think you better apologise to Mrs Leech, I bet she's wondering what's going on out here." Said Mary.

It was late April the sun had warmth as Jason stretched down to recover the cycle. Mary noticed his brown sinewy arms, having lost none of the sunburn from last summer through the winter months. He must be as strong as an ox, she thought; with his shirtsleeves rolled up, his blue overalls still had the crease line in from Mary's last ironing session.

"Oh, so you two have finally caught one another's eye?" Ma Leech could spot a chink in anybody's armour, be it bad or otherwise.

Mary continued with her browsing the shelves with what little the shop had to offer. Jason, meanwhile, stood the other side watching her every move.

"What can I serve you with Jason?" Ma Leech's voice snapped his senses back to the present.

"Ah, just a few…." He'd almost forgotten what he'd called in the shop for, he was thinking as fast as he could but he could not get Mary out of his mind. "Tell you what, Ma, I'll go to the pigs and call on my way home." With that, he stomped out of the shop. He even forgot to apologise for knocking the box tree over. Ma Leech and Mary laughed their heads off.

Mary had picked the items she needed and arranged them on the counter for Ma Leech to tot up the values, while she counted; she asked Mary how she was getting on at the farm. Everyone in the village knew the way the farm was being managed, this encounter at the shop re-enforced the tittle-tattle that would emerge from Ma Leech's counter.

"How's your Aunt getting on, is she well, I haven't seen her about?" the conversation went back and forth.

"I can't understand why you are both not living at the farm, surly there's enough room for you?" Ma Leech could be rather inquisitive at times.

More times than not she got under your skin, but that was village life. As Mary walked back to Rose Cottage, passing Little Dinge, the land army girls, Laura and Jenny, had almost finished the ten rows of sowing swedes. For his work, Alec had used the Welsh cob and a one-shear plough, after which he would hitch the cob to a lightweight roller to flatten the top furrow. The girls followed each with a dibber to indent a hole into which they would sow half a dozen seed, as later in the year they would thin the weaker plants out with a hand hoe. The same procedure would apply for the mangel-wurzel.

Mary clambered up the small embankment, her wicker basket over her arm. She called out to the girls, "hullo there, I've something for you!" the girls raised their heads to see Mary waving at them over the hawthorn trimmed hedge. Mary rummaged through her shopping and passed two hot cross buns over, that she had purchased in the village shop. Alec could be seen unhitching the cob at the far end of the field unaware of the treat the girls had been given, he would not be envious; he was too old in the tooth for any favouritism, whatever it was. In the distance, Jason, on returning from his trip to the pigs, could see Mary chatting to the girls.

"What's this, then? I don't pay you to idle," he joked, knowing that another opportunity had arisen for him to ride alongside Mary as she walked back to the cottage. Had she deliberately delayed her walk hoping Jason would catch her before she turned in to the lane to the cottage, or, had he shortened his visit to the pigs in order to be by her side? The girls giggled as Mary and Jason sidled along the road together.

Since the girls arrival at the farm, all manner of tales circulated in the village, to the dismay of Henry's ears; Claridge Farm was becoming a hotbed of females all seeking attention. A surprise awaited Henry who waved goodbye to his pals on the coach, which dropped him off at the gate. The Rover saloon, parked outside the kitchen door had been washed and polished. Henry stroked Gyp who greeted him every night, now that his time at Beaudesert meant he arrived home much later.

He threw his satchel over one of the oak chairs. "I've something to tell her."

"Oh yes, and I've something to tell you too Henry," Aunt Lillian said in rather an excited tone.

"You go first, Henry." She said.

"Well, I've learned today that through my exams I could earn myself a place at Luton Technical College, if I want it."

"That's excellent news, Henry, your mother will be thrilled to bits, and I'm pretty sure Jason will be too."

"Where is everybody, anyway?" Henry wasn't sure what to expect. He pulled the oak chair from under the table and slumped down. "Something is up, isn't it?"

"Well in a way, yes. Your mum and Jason are going out tonight."

"Is that why the car has been made ready?"

Aunt Lillian was about to reveal the venue when Jason appeared dressed in his crumpled wedding suit, cum-funeral suit, cum- on a date suit. A suit for all occasions, Henry thought.

Jason sat down beside Henry while Aunt Lillian poured them out a cup of tea. A plate of beans on toast was waiting for Henry.

"Something to be going on with," she said

Jason fidgeted with his tie. "Here let me fix you the knot," Lillian set down the teapot and with a dexterity of a true Aunt, her hands flicked over the tie and slipped the knot up to the collar. "There." She said you and Mary will make a handsome couple."

"Where are you going?" Henry felt he'd been hit with a sledgehammer.

"Now don't worry son, your mum and me have been, well, I had been invited, and the invitation said two, so I asked your mum if she would accompany me to the Grand Theatre over at Luton, a night of laughter and music all in aid of war orphans. It's being promoted by the Farmer's Co-operative, should be a good night providing Jerry doesn't come calling."

Tommy Handley's topping the bill, he'll make us laugh."

Henry thought, when was the last time mum had laughed? He couldn't remember, and yes why not? It's time they had a break from this humdrum mode of life.

Aunt Lillian, Henry and Gyp, grouped in the kitchen doorway waiting to see them off. Jason started the Rover Saloon and made ready for the journey, he glanced at the petrol gauge. Just enough, he though to get us to Luton and home. Can't do many of these jaunts, he said to himself; still, all in a good cause, and besides, I'll have Mary by my side. He felt good; she was a fair looking woman.

He felt proud as he and Mary walked up the steps of the Grand Theatre and into the foyer. Two or three groups of farmers with their wives were talking amongst themselves as Mary and Jason walked through into the auditorium. They touched their foreheads and Jason acknowledged likewise, the hairs on the back of his neck standing proud against his shirt collar.

He was beginning to feel like a nineteen year old. This was the first time in many a year since he'd had a night out. Mary slipped her arm into his; the first sign of intimacy had taken place without each other being aware, something each had done with their former partners unconsciously without another thought.

The couple settled down in their seats and Jason fumbled with the programme. When everyone had seated themselves a silence descended on the hall and as the gold and red curtains drifted apart, the orchestra struck up an introduction, to the BBC tune of. "In Town Tonight." A show, which the BBC broadcast every Saturday night, and tonight there was a surprise guest of an American thespian.

The hall resounded to roars of laughter as Tommy Handley acted out many sketches with other cast. Next, a young local girl came on and sang Vera Lynn's song" We'll meet again, don't know where, don't know when, but I know we'll meet again some sunny day." Jason's hand met Marys and clasped together tightly, and when Jason squeezed again Mary was receptive to the gesture and her eyes filled with tears if remembrance as well of tears of happiness. The confines of the hall, the warmth of the audience, engulfed them

"I never thought, I –I- forgot the toffees I bought to share with you," he stammered.

"Shh." Mary squeezed his hand but never said anything.

The show over, the cast assembled along the front of the stage while an official of the Farmer's Co-operative stepped forward and made an impromptu speech. He dwelt sometime on the plight of the war orphans in which tonight's proceeds would help in purchasing a new building down in the West Country as far away as possible from the war zone.

He raised his arms for the audience to stand as the orchestra played "god save the king."

As Jason and Mary made their way out into the foyer, someone touched Jason's arm. It was Fletcher from Billington. They exchanged pleasantries and a few words about their work. Pushing open the outer door, they found themselves completely in the dark, and surrounded by a thick fog. Fletcher reminded Jason that the reason for the fog every night, was that Luton was enveloped in a mist to confuse the enemy planes as to where they would release their bombs on the town; the whole area stank of paraffin.

"Now, where the heck did I park the car?" Jason could not remember. Fletcher by this time had disappeared with his wife on his arm. Jason stood scratching his head. "Christ Mary, I'm lost."

"What's the time?" he asked, Mary slid her cardigan sleeve back to reveal her wristwatch that Bert had given her for her twenty-fifth birthday. It was an ingersole-rand luminous. Cupping her right hand around the watch, she read ten twenty nine." Nearly half past ten "she said worried.

"Can't you remember at all where we parked?"

"I ought to know I mean, I know these streets through delivering milk to the co-operative sometimes." Jason guided her to the right.

"This should lead us towards the railway station, I'm pretty sure that's where I parked." As they reached the corner, an express train thundered through the station. Walking up to the footbridge, he found the car. "Thank the lord." He turned to Mary who stood by his side; they stood close, he could make out her face, and he held her for a second, then softly kissed her, the mist surrounding them in a quiet embrace.

***

Aunt Lillian glanced at the kitchen clock. Ten forty five. She carried on reading her book, and then raised her eyes at Henry who was busy with a sketch; some angles needed restructuring. The grandfather clock struck a quarter to eleven. "Eh, don't you think you ought to make tracks to bed, Henry it's getting late." "I'll just draw in some more infill to the building and that will be the final stroke to the drawing." He slipped the drawing into a sheath with others; a black manila held all of Henry's works.

"I just hope everything is alright on their journey home." Aunt Lillian became more agitated as clocks struck eleven.

***

Jason started the Rover Saloon, switched on the headlights, dimmed down through their shuttered grilles. He could barely see. "It's no good. Mary, you'll have to get out and walk in front until we are out of this blasted fog."

"But I don't know the way"

"Well you drive and I'll walk in front."

"But I can't drive."

Luck was on their side. A car came along very slowly and stopped behind them. The driver jumped out and asked if they were ok. It was Fletcher." I thought you had long gone home." Jason said, as the two came together in the middle of the road.

"No we changed our minds, had a quick half in the Midland pub along the street. What's the trouble?" Jason felt embarrassed.

"I can't seem to get my bearings in this blessed fog."

Fletcher was quite a few years younger than he was.

"I know the way, follow my tail lights." Jason felt relieved, but a bit humiliated in front of Mary. They followed Fletcher. "I recon he could drive blind and still find his way home." Jason whispered into Mary's ear.

"Good job he came along then."

The further they travelled the more the fog thinned, and when they finally could see, the geography told them they were passing the L&D hospital.

Jason gave Fletcher a quick toot on his horn, although the law stated no horns to be used in time of war. Fletcher acknowledged and raced away.

Jason drove at a more sedate speed, and nearing home, he slowed in Nursery Lane and turned the car into a low type of building, a landing stage, in fact for the sandpit quarry, disused now, but an ideal place to be on one's own. He switched off the ignition and lights, and pulled on the handbrake. A deathly silence followed. The pitch black underneath the rickety worn out stage completely concealed them from anyone passing by; it was a perfect hideaway.

"Don't be frightened, Mary, I just want a few words together on our own. I know I took advantage of you back there in Luton, I'm sorry, it shouldn't have happened. It's, just, well I've been thinking a lot of late."

Mary raised her finger to his lips. "Don't say no more, I'm old enough to know what's going on in your mind, and yes. I have feelings just like everyone else."

"So you didn't mind me kissing you?"

"Not one bit, but I'm not anyone's bit of old skirt, I do have my pride. Besides, I have to think of Henry and Aunt Lillian's emotions how will they react to us becoming an item?"

"Wouldn't it make sense if you moved into Claridges, we could be a proper family, or am I moving too fast for you?"

Mary sensed friction. "They will understand, besides, it would relieve Dotty from making the tedious journey every day, and I'm sure Aunt Lillian would revel in living on her own in Rose Cottage, it'll give everyone a bit of space. When will you announce our intentions?" Mary said, her heart missing a beat.

"Tomorrow."

"Do you think that's the right time?"

"I do."

"I think we should be on our way, she said. Aunt Lillian will be getting worried."

Jason reversed the car out of the shadows of the stage and drove slowly through the village. Turning into the yard, Gyp's eyes reflected in the subdued beam of the headlights as Jason swung the Rover car under the hovel.

Aunt Lillian made ready two hot steaming cups of coco as the latch lifted on the kitchen door. The couple entered and Gyp gave a little yelp.

"Be quiet Gyp." Jason removed his cap. "Sorry we're a bit late, got lost in the fog in Luton."

"Fog?" Lillian said with surprise.

"Yes, fog, Aunty, apparently the release this sort of mist from tin barrels along the streets, a deterrent to confuse the Germans."

"Well never mind that, you are home now."

The couple sat down at the long oak table and cupped their hands round the mugs of coco, and sipped the beverage in silence. Aunt Lillian sensed a mood at the table, and carried on with her chores.

"Goodness, just look at the time?" she said. The clock in the hall struck twelve midnight and broke the tension.

"C'mon, you too, I'll drive you home." Jason said as he pushed his chair in under the table.

"No, we can walk; do us good, besides you cannot leave a child on their own."

Good point, Jason thought, Aunt Lillian wanted to get to the bottom of this, and walking home was a good time to talk.

The night was fresh for late April; blustery showers had prevailed all day. As they sidestepped the puddles, Aunt Lillian pursued her line of thought.

"You can tell me, Mary, I know something's on your mind."

"Well. Jason has asked me to move in and be the woman of the house, he thinks the time is right for everyone to know tomorrow at breakfast that's how far we have progressed."

"I am pleased to hear that Mary."

"He thinks that by moving in it will release Dotty from her chores, which I think she would be well pleased, also he will ask you if you don't mind helping me out in the afternoons, and you would have more space for yourself at the cottage.

"What about Henry, what about his thoughts?

"I don't know, but one thing is certain, if Jason asked me to marry him I shall accept. That way we would all be family again, you know, proper like."

***

Dotty rose earlier than usual. Something was on the cards at the farm, she knew instinctively, and rubbing her eyes, she rolled out of bed. The alarm was set for five-thirty. Pushing the stop button, she waddled into the kitchen, ran some water to boil the kettle, and waited all through eating her breakfast and riding her cycle to the farm her mind was troubled as to what awaited her.

Jason was already up and herding the cows in for milking. Alec followed Dotty into the yard.

She opened the kitchen door and noticed straightaway a

letter propped up against the kitchen clock on the sideboard. Curious, she peered through her pince-nez spectacles to see who it was for. "TO HENRY KNEALLY ESQ." She murmured.

Now, she really was interested. She fingered the letter and placed it back against the clock, then she had second thoughts, she tiptoed up the wide staircase and gently slid the envelope underneath Henry's bedroom door. She quietly made her way downstairs as the clock in the hallway struck six forty five. He'll soon be getting up to make ready for school, she knew, or she would give him a call.

Henry awakened rubbed his eyes and peered out of the alcove window. From there he could see everything turning green, the blossom on the hedgerow, their small buds all raised against the warm sunshine. The air, though humid, was glorious. He turned over and noticed the envelope under the door. Slipping out from under the covers, he picked up the letter and wondered. A voice within said, you'll only find out if you open it. Sliding his thumb along the top flap, he did so. To his surprise, it contained two one-pound notes and a folded note; it read.

Henry, love from mum on your scholarship to Luton Tech we are all in admiration of your effort to succeed in life. Love mum and everyone on the farm.

The two land army girls Jenny and Laura arrived at the farm chatting to each other about last night's outing to the Peacock in Leighton. Henry could hear them; laughing and teasing Alec that he should be their companion for a night out. Three steaming hot cups of tea awaited them. Henry finished his ablutions and joined in the banter.

"Look what I've got?" he proudly waved the two notes in his hand.

"It's two pounds a gift from mum and Aunt Lillian

because of my gaining a place at Luton Tech.

Congratulations were in full swing when Jason entered the kitchen.

"What's this, then?" a bit early for a party."

Dotty was the first to speak. "We are celebrating Henry's academic achievement"

"Well, being's that you are all here, I've got an announcement to make."

The gathering went silent.

"Here's something for you to chew on." Jason wasn't one for making speeches, not this early, anyway. He cast Henry a sideways glance and blurted it out.

"Henry, how would you like me as your stepdad?"

Henry was taken aback at the announcement; he composed himself and, sitting alone at the far end of the oak table, replied, "You took care of me when I needed someone badly, and now I'm to become family again. I think I'm over the moon.

"Hold on a minute, I haven't asked your mother to marry me yet."

Jason knew in his silly way he'd been a little too impetuous. In unison the party shouted, "When will there be a proposal so we can all witness the event?" Jason kicked himself now forever mentioning it.

"No, I'll wait until she gets here whenever."

He turned on his heels and fled to safety of the dairy, fuming at himself for being too premature.

The girls and Alec departed across the yard as their work for the day was sowing onion and swede seeds at Little Dinge. Jason meanwhile was contemplating how he would approach the subject of proposing to Mary. Then he had an idea. Finishing off the washing down of the milking apparatus, he was about to run the churns to the loading stage outside the main gate, when Dotty began tooting the horn.

He called "Won't be a minute!"

She bellowed "phone!"

Jason rushed in and lifted the receiver "Ullo," he said panting.

"Sorry to trouble you, Stanley Hogg, Royal, and Ancient. How are you?"

"Wondered when you would call," replied Jason

"I'm just ringing to see if I could make a visit, if it's alright with you?"

"Tomorrow, say ten o'clock?"

"That'll be fine, we'll see you then."

He replaced the receiver and went on his way to complete the job of lifting the churns on to the stage. There were many jobs to sort out before Mary and Aunt Lillian would enter the farmyard. Jason wanted to time what he had in mind to perfection. He remembered how he proposed to Kathy a long time ago when he courted her along by the stream on the style in Thedeway, and his mind wandered back to those halcyon days, he had played a blinder at batting for the village cricket team, needing twenty-eight to win the match. He hit six fours, and ran five singles to beat Slapton in a thrilling game. That evening after a couple of pints of Benskins bitter, he and Kathy were walking out and he plucked up enough courage and proposed to her as they sat on the stile in Thedeway. The night and stars were made for love.

***

The day had been still and humid; Jason felt thunder in the air. He'd tapped the barometer as he passed in the hallway. He looked closer, it registered a drop in pressure that was five forty this morning; it was nearing mid-day and the air was heavy. He walked out to the main gate and gazed south. Sure enough, thunderheads appeared. Could be here in an hour or so, he thought. Gyp followed at heel and Jason stroked her head, "Things are going to be different, old gal.," he reminded himself. With her doleful eyes Gyp looked up at him, head tilted to one side, ears cocked, her sixth sense a perception even some human beings were not conscious of but Gyp knew Jason had a preconceived idea. Something or other was about to happen.

Jason sent Gyp to her kennel just as the sound of a heavy vehicle roared into the yard. Jason's eyes lit up, for there anchored and strapped to the flatbed chassis was a shiny red General Motor Tractor.

"Christ, I'd forgot all about the tractor." He beamed more than ever when the driver leaned out and asked. "Where do you want her Gov?"

"Right here where I'm standing, I'll propose here."

"Beg your pardon, Gov?"

"Nothing, just another idea, unload her first here."

Jason half ran into the hall, rummaged about in the study, and found the brownie camera. As he charged out, he shouted to Dotty to follow him.

"Oh bless my soul, now what?"

They stood and waited while the driver unloaded the tractor. I only hope the film is okay, Jason thought, as he reeled off a couple of shots. I don't remember when I last used the thing.

Mary and Aunt Lillian strode into the yard, surprised at the scene that confronted them.

"Here Dotty, take a shot of me and the tractor." She did as she was told, held her hand over the viewfinder, and clicked away. The tractor was shiny and new in the middle of the yard. Jason climbed aboard and asked Mary to join him.

"What, up there with you?" "Yes" he pointed to the tow bar behind him. She stepped up and held on to the seat.

"Will you marry me?" Jason said nervously.

A clap of thunder rebounded around the farmyard.

"I didn't hear you!" he shouted

"Yes! I said yes" and she wrapped her arms about him.

Dotty, Aunt Lillian, and the lorry driver, and Gyp all looked on in amazement at the couple on the tractor, wondering what was going on.

"It's alright," Mary, said, "I've just agreed to become Mrs Smith."

They stood and clapped, the rain now teeming down, and then they all bolted for the kitchen. Once inside Jason repeated, "well that's the best declaration I've ever heard. Dotty, boil the kettle, we'll celebrate, I'm sure the driver would like a cup of tea" the man nodded in accord, set his manifest on the oak table, and asked Jason to sign for the tractor. "Where have you come from?" Jason asked.

The driver informed him that three more tractors of the same type were unloaded at the sidings at Leighton that morning. "I'm due back to collect them and distribute them to farms all over the south of the county.

"Never mind his distributions" Dotty said "What about you two getting married? We all saw it coming, you know.

Jason felt a colouring in his cheeks and neck. "Well, it makes sense, don't you think".

"Of course it does," Aunt Lillian chimed in," and we are all happy for you both"

"What about Henry?" Dotty said

"What about Henry?" they chorused. Sheepishly, Dotty slid the teapot back onto its stand. She had become very fond of Henry, knowing when he first came to the village alone with just four other friends. Dotty knew only too well what loneliness was like, having lived on her own for many a year.

"Your quite right, Dotty," Jason said, "I shall ask Alec to be my best man, and Henry will be chief sidesman at our wedding." They all gave a resounding cheer.

The driver of the contract lorry waved goodbye and drove out the yard, while Gyp scampered about the shiny new tractor sniffing the new rubber tyres.

"We shall have no hesitation in getting on with plenty of jobs." Jason was thrilled as a schoolboy with a new toy.

Alec, Laura and Jenny stood admiring the new tractor, the storm cloud having passed, leaving rivulets of rain draining off the machine.

"Where are we going to house her, then?" Alec perspired now from the humid weather.

"I thought we'd move the Fordson's power take-off onto the new G.M and leave the Fordson belted up to the mixing shed's crushers permanently. We'll tarpaulin the Fordson over for the present."

Everybody dispersed to their allocated jobs, leaving Jason to enjoy the moment in time. He took Mary's arm, wanting so much for this city woman to know how much a tractor raised his enthusiasm for farming. He climbed aboard, and picked up the manual having been left in the steel sprung seat and flipped through the handbook acclimatising himself with each switch and control. He pulled the gear into neutral, pressed the starter button and the tractor roared into life.

"Cor, that was magic! No more cranking the old Fordson only when necessary." Jason slipped the gear into first, and gently turned the steering wheel round and round. He de-clutched, hoisted Mary aboard, and gently went round and round again before heading for the hovel to park up.

"This'll make life a lot easier for all of us." He proudly said.

"What's the first job you will be using her for?" Mary asked.

"Well ten acre's beyond Sweetbriar will be ploughed later in the year ready for spring wheat to be sowed, that will be its first major job. Other than that, there's some sawing of logs that's really needed."

The afternoon passed by only too quickly, as both turned to walk back they were met by Henry with Gyp at his heels.

"Hello, son, we have something to tell you." Mary said.

Henry followed his mother and Jason to the kitchen where Aunt Lillian prepared a snack for all of them. Jason pulled out the chair at the end of the solid oak table, the noise ear splitting on the flagstones.

He removed his cap and stuffed it inside the pocket of his boiler suit. Henry chewed on a digestive, with his tea in front of him, his mum standing between him and Jason. The Grandfather clock in the hall struck half past five. Aunt Lillian lounged with her arms folded, leaning against the upright of the old kitchen range that used to be. Gyp yelped at the kitchen door.

"Henry," his mother said. "Jason has asked me to marry him?"

A small ladybird fluttered down into Henry's outstretched hand that held the half-eaten biscuit. Sparrows chirruped outside on the guttering, a ringed Dove cooed gently high in a chestnut tree, and thunder rumbled in the distance. Henry thought, only here it could happen, only in this rural England. This setting was just perfect, he jumped up threw his arms around his mother and thanked her, it was the most rewarding time of his life to be told they were soon to be a family again.

"Will this mean we are staying at Claridge's?"

"It certainly does, Henry." Jason said, "And I've asked

Alec to be my best man, and you can be chief usher."

Henry frowned. "What does a chief usher do?"

"Well, it means you direct all the guests and congregation who attend; you will show them to their seats. It's a very important task; besides, now we know you'll be moving to Luton Tech you need to have a secure family support. If there's one thing I could wish for, is for you to pass out with flying colours with whatever you study."

"Have you made up your mind yet?" Mary asked.

"Hmm, yes, as a matter of fact I'm thinking of architecture."

This was by far the best news that Mary and Aunt Lillian could have hoped for since arriving in Eggington.

The phone rang, breaking the narrative. Lillian answered.

"It's for you Jason." Jason took the call. "Ullo, Claridge farm, Jason Smith speaking. Who's calling?"

"Mr Hogg of Royal and Ancient. Are we on for tomorrow?"

CHAPTER THIRTEEN

STRIPES & COLOURED PATCHES

As Mary and Aunt Lillian made their way home to Rose Cottage, chatting to one another about how things had worked out, Mary suddenly stopped. She caught hold of Aunt Lillian's arm.

"What's the matter, Mary?"

"Well, everything that preceded today's events I've completely forgot. You'll be on your own. I've been a fool, thinking only of myself. I'll have a word with Jason tomorrow; see if he will agree to you moving in with us. I mean, there's plenty of room, and it makes sense."

"Just a minute, Mary, don't forget that Mr Hogg is to visit tomorrow, perhaps Jason will be too busy. Best wait a while. Wait till you are married, let things settle, I shall be alright, besides, you two will want time on your own."

"Maybe you are right."

They carried on and reached Rose Cottage. Full of themselves and brimming with confidence, Mary closed the shutters, the blackout in force, and slept in a dream of enlightenment.

***

The rusty Austin Twelve turned in to Claridge Farm. Gyp greeted it with a series of yelps and barks. Stanley Hogg stepped out of the car with a brief under his arm, and patted

Gyp on the head. "I'm sure you are a good guard dog." Sweating a little, and passed on to the kitchen door. In the middle of June a heatwave developed, sending the farm into a frenzy of activity, so much work, so little time. Mr Hogg surveyed the scene and patted his brow with his handkerchief.

An eventful journey had exhausted Mr Hogg, having made several detours on-route, because of the army manoeuvers, ending up in Aylesbury, twenty miles out of his way, thus being an hour late. The grandfather clock struck eleven o'clock as he tapped on the kitchen door. Dotty came out and sounded the horn.

"Ah, so that's what you meant when I rang earlier, I was a little bemused." He said.

In the meantime, Jason and Alec using long handled brushes were busy creosoting the chicken arks, when they heard the sound of the horn.

"I'll leave you to finish off, Alec, that be Hogg, I'll be bound."

By the time, Jason reached the kitchen Dotty had Mr Hogg seated at the oak table with a steaming mug of Bovril, something Jason couldn't quite get his palate accustomed to.

"Good morning." Hogg said, rising from his chair, and declaring his pleasure with the beverage Dotty had offered. He sipped. "Ah, this is lovely; I mean the surroundings as well. Shall we get down to business?"

"I daresay. Where do you want me to start first?" Jason said.

"Well, the number that I asked you to secure I need to clarify."

"Certainly." Jason shoved his chair noisily and made for the study. From the kitchen, Mr Hogg heard him rustling some papers about and he returned with a brown envelope, waving it and proclaiming how he had filed the vital evidence.

"We had a surprise when we finally uncovered the plaque." He gave the piece of paper to Mr Hogg who in turn unfolded the note.

"Well I never, roman numerals, and you deciphered them as 22121930. Can I see the plaque for myself later, above the portal?"

"One other question, does a certain Henry Kneally reside here?"

"Yes, he most certainly does." Jason answered with confidence." Call it a coincidence or not, but these numbers represent his birthday.

"Never" Hogg uttered. "Unbelievable coincidence.

"As true as I sit here," Jason added.

"We will come to Mr Kneally later. Now, I understand there are some paintings that were rescued from the blaze?"

"Yeh, we stored them in the loft above the outhouse."

"Can I see them?"

"Of course, follow me," Mr Hogg followed Jason to the outhouse which, being attached to the parlour, had no electric light. Jason unlocked the door with a key he took from a hook inside the parlour. As they entered, the only light came from the door they just opened. The paintings were covered with a tarpaulin, but first they had to climb a small ladder.

"Drat it." Jason said, "I'll go fetch a torch, you won't see without."

Jason pulled back the tarpaulin cover, exposing them for the first time since the fire, and thumbed through the canvases, counting to fifty-one. "They look in pretty good condition considering their history." Mr Hogg proceeded to lift one out at random and inspect it with knowing intent. He made a note of each painting, its description, and when satisfied, he pulled the cover back over. "I think an evaluation will be our next duty, someone who can fix a price on what they're worth. I do have someone in mind; I will ring and let you know in due course.

Jason locked the door and both he and Hogg retreated back to the kitchen, as they entered, he asked Jason if he could talk in private for a while." Have you a study or another room we could use?" Jason gestured and guided him along the hall and into the small study, which was used for such matters.

Jason pointed to a leather chaise-longue, which had seen better days. Nonetheless, Mr Hogg made himself comfortable in the circumstances that prevailed.

Jason closed the door. Mr Hogg selected a folder from the brief he carried with him.

"The numbers you retrieved from above the portal I must insert on these papers." He shuffled them about and wrote in the numbers. "There, that's done. Now I can inform you that in two months' time I will need you to meet me somewhere; would you prefer here at the farm, or could you travel to Northampton to our offices?"

"What for?" Jason enquired.

"Well, the will of the deceased must be read."

"Ah, I've just asked Henry's mother to marry me." Jason spluttered out.

"Two surprises in one, then, congratulations, I hope people around here are not too narrow minded and read into the situation you are about to find yourself in."

"What are you saying?"

"Very well, you have been named as a beneficiary to the Gunn's estate, that's all I can say at the moment. On second thoughts. I think I should come back to the farm, it will be more appropriate, let's say won't need to scrimp and save as much as you are doing now."

"Phew. I didn't realise." Jason was really moved by the unexpected.

Mr Hogg shook hands at the kitchen door.

"I will ring you about the evaluation first." He drove off in a cloud of dust with Gyp running behind seeing him off.

The new tractor was earning its keep. Grass cutting had already started in Ten Acres beyond Sweetacre, the last days of June getting increasingly hotter. Henry's term at Leighton school was due to end at the beginning of summer holidays in July; his new term would begin at Luton Tech in September. Six weeks of uninterrupted farm life beckoned.

Henry was chatting to Dotty as he was about to leave and catch the coach for school, when an army vehicle with a canopy over the back pulled up outside the farm gate. He paused a few seconds outside the kitchen door and waited to see what the vehicle had stopped for Gyp by his side gave a muted yap.

A figure emerged from underneath the canopy. He stepped backwards, straightened his tunic, and walked across the yard. Henry, perplexed realised he was a German POW. He had round orange coloured patches sewn onto his brown uniform. Nobody on the farm had any idea that he was due to work on the farm. Dotty didn't know, Alec and the land army girls were on their way to Ten Acres. But, where was Jason? As Henry was about to greet the POW, Jason came swinging into the farmyard on his cycle.

The German hesitated, took off his cap, and just stood rubbing the stubble on his chin. He really looked lost.

"Ullo, old chap." Jason said, as he rode past him and propped his cycle up against the windowsill of the kitchen. "Shouldn't you be catching your coach, Henry?"

As Henry passed the German he greeted him. "Hello!"

"Guten morgen." He replied. Well that's what it sounds

like.

"You speak English?" Jason said, now confronting him.

"Yah" he nodded "Me understood, you Mr Smidt?"

Jason knew about the German being sent to Claridge Farm, but as usual did not tell anyone else, fearing they might express disapproval.

"Dotty?" Jason called, "See he has a drink and whatever's in the larder for later on!" Jason beckoned to the POW, to follow and sat him down on an old tree stump used as a stool, then gave him a short-handled axe and pointed to the hovel where all sorts if wood lay. "You chop firewood for fire in house and kitchen."

"Yah, Yah me understood," and so Lally as he became known, chopped wood until Jason found him another job.

Lally was still chopping wood when Henry came home from school. As Henry passed him, he pointed towards Henry with the axe. "You school? Com and talk, I understood."

"Understand." Henry corrected him, "Yah, un-der-stand."

"Yes, Yes," Henry said, "Very good, very good."

Henry smiled and ran to the house to get changed in to his old clothes.

Aunt Lillian and Mary were busy in the house. "Have you met the POW, the enemy?" he asked

"Don't be cheeky, he may have relatives just as we do, they might be suffering just as we are."

"Sorry mum I'll understand in future."

"You do, my boy." She said.

As Lally chopped wood, so Henry sketched the hovel with Lally at work. Being inquisitive, Lally rose from the tree stump and strode over to Henry, expecting to maybe find schoolwork. He was surprised to find a sketch being drawn of himself.

"You artist?" he asked, pointing to the drawing, Henry noticed Lally's hands they were large, the veins swelled out in a raised manner, his eyes were sunk deep under his highbrow. Lines furrowed his forehead. He must be at least forty, Henry thought, he was old to be a soldier in comparison with our soldiers camped in Furrow Field. "Yah I see." Lally nodded his head, "Yah I see," he repeated again, and walked away to his tree stump.

Misty light rain began to fall, cooling the hot weather from the southwest. Henry packed up his sketchpad and stool, and the army lorry collected Lally. The haymaking came to an abrupt halt, the girls came charging in to the kitchen expecting a cup of brew with which Mary and Aunt Lillian obliged, and Henry raced downstairs two at a time to greet the pair.

"Oh, where have you been?" Laura spoke first, "Thought you were coming to Ten Acre to help?" "Ah, got waylaid by the POW."

"POW," they chorused.

"He'll be working here from now on." Jason stood in the doorway "Sorry" he said "Slipped my mind, but you'll meet him tomorrow. We shall all get to know him better, I dare say"

The misty rain had cleared by six o'clock, the morning showed real promise. The last few wellington bombers were returning from their night raids somewhere over France or Germany.

Henry, his mum, Aunt Lillian, Jason and Alec the land army girls, Laura and Jenny, were all involved with the juggernaut that was the massive war machine that kept rolling on, and here they were, in their own little corner of rural England fighting to survive.

As usual. Henry got ready for school. Dotty could be heard clattering about in the kitchen; Alec tinkered with the tractor and trailer. The land girls harnessed the Welsh cob and would present her to the hay-turning machine. By midday, if lucky, they could well be building the hayrick inside the Dutch barn, if the weather held.

Alec raised his eyes to the sky, "It's going to be fine, with warm sunshine everything bodes well for the day." He said

Jason wheeled two churns out for the Milk Marketing vehicle, when the army lorry pulled up to let Lally off. Henry stood outside the kitchen door ready to be off, Gyp at heel. She gave a muted woof. "Shush Gyp."

Henry watched Lally climb down from the lorry, noticed he was clutching something close to his body, something resembling a figurine in his right hand. Jason joined Henry as Lally strode briskly to the kitchen.

Neither of them spoke, only Lally with an outstretched arm. He said, "If you draw me, then I carve this for you." Henry gave a quizzical look but accepted it with a degree of hesitation. He ran his hand over the smooth figurine, its texture was pleasing.

"I'm just off to school." He ran out of the yard to catch the coach, clasping the figurine close. Jason called "Don't lose it, Henry!"

"I won't, I will thank him properly before he leaves for camp!" Lally displayed an air of frustration, shook his head, and strode over to the hovel to his fixed abode to chop wood.

"Not today." Jason called to him, and pointed in the direction of the Dutch barn. "Here we make hayrick." Jason handed him a pitchfork "Make hayrick."

"Yah, 'ich verstehen." Lally said

Jason nodded and smiled.

138

CHAPTER FOURTEEN

TRAGEDY

Last day of spring, term and Henry fretted a bit; just as he was getting used to Beaudesert, it was time to move onto another curriculum in his young life. Everything bode well; he had made his mind up to become an architect.

The coach slowed to a halt, and a village girl with whom he had struck up a good relationship alighted from the coach with him. Goodbyes and cheerio's echoed in his ears, for the next journey to school would be on a National Bus traveling in the opposite direction, and his mother would have to pay out extra money for the fare. However, Henry noticed that mum and Aunt Lillian weren't unduly concerned; Still five weeks summer holiday beckoned after exchanging arrangements with his friends of the moment, Madge Willans, who incidentally was very good at sport. She played tennis quite frequently because her being a member of the Bell Close Club, she had made many friends and invited Henry to come along and join in.

Madge had completed her education at the Girls High School and would take a Pitman's course, hoping to secure a job at Barclays Bank in Leighton; that was her intention, or so she said.

Lally in the meantime, had received his first load of hay. He'd made ready its base with a thick layer of wheat straw left over from last year's crop. From the Dutch barn he could see Henry talking to Madge. She was shortish and plumpish, but had a good round athletic figure. In a while, Henry made off towards the kitchen, Gyp by his side. As he passed, Lally gave Henry a little whistle and a wave, then to Henry's surprise, Lally called "you jiggy jig."

Henry was angry with Lally forever mentioning the words, he knew what it meant, and his neck coloured beetroot red. Feeling embarrassed, he ran indoors straight to his room

Henry slammed the door, buried his head in the pillow, and lay prone face down on the bed, he mumbled to himself, "How could he, how could he?" His outstretched hand clasped the figurine Lally gave him, and instantly, the smoothness aroused the pleasure in himself. So this is what growing up really means; of course, he was not far off from adulthood. Slowly he raised his head and peered out the little window, still stroking the figurine. How had Lally made this so beautiful and smooth?

Activity in the kitchen embellished a different meaning; the pending wedding of his mother to Jason resulted in a furious abuse of cutlery being thrown around the sideboards and tables. Dotty was not a person to be around and interfered with, while being so busy, so trying to reason with her was useless. She was left alone. Henry and Gyp made their way through Sweetacre to Ten Acre where Alec and the land girls were in the last moments of loading the trailer to clear the hay to the Dutch barn. Henry rode back to the farm with Laura driving the new GM tractor. She was a very competent driver and one day he would be allowed to drive. The tractor's pneumatic tyres followed the previous indents of its tracks, not much steering was needed, Gyp trotted alongside, her tongue hanging out, and looking up at Henry occasionally. Laura drove the tractor and trailer into the yard and steered it exactly to rest in a juxtaposition by Lally's hayrick, which by now had almost filled the Dutch barn. This load completed the haymaking. Ten acre would be ready to plough and make ready for winter oats to be drilled and seeded. Farmers call it rotation farming. Mary and Aunt Lillian entered the kitchen, the aroma wafting out through the door, stimulating their taste buds.

"My, that's a savoury aroma around the kitchen, Dotty, what are you cooking?" Mary couldn't resist the temptation to walk over and lift the lid, dip her finger in and suck. "Oh, that's lovely. Is this for tonight's dinner?"

"Yes. I've made an Irish stew for all of us, a special surprise for you and Jason, a sort of engagement feast." She tried to describe it "Best end of mutton, onions, potatoes, stock, and rosemary, enough for six helpings."

"Good lord," Aunt Lillian said," I didn't know you could cook cordon bleu"

"Oh I don't understand that sort of lingo; I'm showing off, that's all."

"How did you purchase the mutton?" Mary asked

Dotty tapped the side of her nose. "Never you mind, you'll eat and enjoy."

***

The first week of Henry's holiday began the last week of July, five weeks in all, ending in the first week of September. All the hay work had been completed, Lally was back chopping wood. Alec with the cob in harness and hitched to a contraption with two angled flat hoes cutting weeds, the cob plodding wearily up and down the rows of mangel-wurzel with Jenny leading to keep the cob straight. Jason, meanwhile, was teaching Laura to reverse the new tractor and hitch the three-furrowed plough to the tow bar. Ten-acre field in effect was a triangular field, this made ploughing a bit difficult. The headland was fifteen feet wide, and to keep a straight furrow Jason had paced it out the day before and driven in steaks at intervals of twenty paces. The starting point being the longest to the point of the triangle. By turning left at that point and travelling twenty paces to start a new furrow, back to the straight hedge to the other end of the field, and so on. At each turn, Laura would twist-turn her body, lean back, and raise the plough by means of a screw handle. This was exacting and strenuous work.

By the end of four or five furrows, she had got the hang of it. Jason stood for a while confident that Laura would apply herself to the task in hand. Henry came racing through Sweetacre to Ten-acre calling out for Jason at the top of his voice and cajoling Gyp to join in.

"You are wanted on the phone," the calling message echoed through the air. Jason turned his head to be greeted with an out of breath boy, but not Gyp, she'd raced across these fields many times before.

"What's up? What's up, av the Germans invaded?"

Henry knew he was only kidding. "No. But Mr Hogg phoned, will you call him back this morning, if possible." Gyp sat on her haunches, tongue hanging out panting.

"Right," Jason said, "Run back to the farm, and tell your mother to phone Mr Hogg , his number is on the pad in the study, tell him" but Jason checked himself and his Hunter watch. "Tell him in three quarters of an hour, I'll ring. I can't leave Laura just yet; I want to know if she'll be alright on her own."

Henry and Gyp raced back to the farm with the message, wondering to himself what all this was about with Mr Hogg. I'll bet a pound to a penny it's the paintings, he thought, Henry walked through the farm gate and gazed at Lally who sat chopping wood, deep in thought. Gyp sidled to her kennel pretty dog-tired.

The kitchen table had been laid for the evening meal as Jason sauntered through the farm gate still worrying about Laura. If anything is wrong or she loses her confidence she should stop and wait for me, and with that in mind, he lightened his stride to the kitchen where Mary and Aunt Lillian were waiting. Gyp woke up from her daytime dream.

As he passed Lally, he called "I think that's enough wood, take a break, I've another job for you later on in the cowshed," Lally touched his forehead. I understood."

Jason strode into the kitchen and shut the door.

Mary and Aunt Lillian could not disguise the fact that whatever Mr Hogg had said it was none of their business, so they continued with their chores and preparing a brew for the staff of the farm, elevenses in other words. They could hear him talking loudly, a pause, and then the phone was replaced and Jason came along the hallway rubbing his hands.

"Have you lost a penny and found a pound?" Mary asked.

"You could say that, in fact, in a few days' time an assessor will be calling to evaluate the paintings."

Outside, mugs of tea were handed round to Alec Jenny, and Lally. Jason dispatched a flask to Laura later. He still worried about her. Mary knew in his voice and his actions that Laura was something special to him, he carried a torch for her; she had steel, she had what it takes. Perhaps, Mary thought, I came too soon for him.

Jason read Mary's thoughts, "She's young, Mary, very young, you and me were made for each other; a day, a year, another time, he kissed her on the cheek, smacked his lips. " Golly, this is a rotten cupp 'a tea."

"Go on with you." She pushed him away. "Not in front

of this lot," she said. The group outside chuckled a bit but knew when to be discreet. Alec and Jenny returned to their weeding and Lally headed for the cowshed.

"Now Henry, how about helping out to scrape the walls down of all the winter's muck. Then we'll whitewash the cowshed to make them spick and span; you know me, I'm ready when you are. "Gyp pricked her ears, but there was nothing much for her so she just lay down and dozed.

Henry was given a garden hoe and Lally was directed to lower cowshed to work on his own. He loved working alone, and hummed a tune to himself as he took to scraping and brushing the muck off the walls, while he and Jason scraped together in the large shed.

After half an hour's work Jason mumbled, "H'mm, it's no good, I keep thinking of Laura, Henry. I'll use the cycle to see how she's progressing; I've been far too long in leaving her on her own." He pushed himself off and peddled hard across Sweetacre as though rough riding. Henry thought, I'll do that one day, blow walking, give Gyp a run out.

Lally came to Henry's aid. "Have you finished?" Henry said, a bit taken aback that Lally had got through the work so quickly.

"Less talk, more work," he grunted.

The motor horn sounded at the kitchen door. Henry dropped his hoe and rushed to the kitchen. Aunt Lillian stood in the doorway holding a flask in her hand. "God, Jason took off so quickly before we realised where he was heading. We called, but too late, will you do the honours?"

"Right o, c'mon Gyp"

With the best will they set off once again through Sweetacre. Lally left on his own, a punishment for being the enemy. As Henry and Gyp approached Ten Acre, he could see the tractor, motionless, facing away from himself. As they passed through the gate neither Jason or Laura could be seen anywhere, Henry placed the flask in the well of the seat. Ten-Acre field bordered the main Hockliff to Leighton road and, peering through the hedge as he and Gyp neared, he could see stationary American army vehicles, he and Gyp made for the style in the hedge. It was apparent that something had happened; he could see Laura and Jason standing along the verge. Two American servicemen prevented Henry and Gyp going any further. Laura stood close to Jason, he with his arm around her shoulder. Henry could see why, one of the vehicles had veered off the road and smashed into an oak tree beside a deep ditch, the occupants being of Rangers Brigade, Jason and Laura turned away and beckoned Henry and Gyp back into Ten Acre.

"There's nothing we can do son, anyway, why are you here?"

"You forgot the flask."

"Oh heck, well on your way back, you can drive the herd in for milking. Laura I will wait until you've completed the furrow and then we can go home. Henry, be sure to inform your mum and tell her I'll explain what happened here."

*****

The day had been a weary one for Henry, what with double BST the evenings lasted forever. Sunset was due at eleven o'clock. Everybody, including Alec, sat at the long table in the kitchen.

It was right that Alec should sit one end, as he was to be best man and Jason at the other. Aunt Lillian and Mary opposite, and Henry with Dotty would fill the remaining chairs.

Jason explained; "Before Dotty serves this scrumptious

meal I think a few seconds of silent thought and sympathy for the American soldiers who were killed today. Dotty served the stew; she asked, "What happened?"

"Laura and I heard the impact. When we reached the scene, a serviceman said the driver must have dozed off at the wheel. The convoy had travelled all night from Heysham in Lancashire with only a couple of breaks, at least three in the cab died."

"No wonder," Dotty intervened," an accident waiting to happen, all the way from god knows where, only to smash into a solid oak tree, dearie me," Dotty carried on serving "God bless them," she said with tears streaming down her cheeks.

All savoured the stew, it was delicious "You know" Jason said, "What happened to-day and trying to plan this wedding, saddens my line of thought," Jason sprinkled more pepper on his stew and sneezed. "Bless you." Mary said her thoughts too, also, about arranging the wedding, "Can I suggest that Aunt Lillian be the overseer?"

"I second that," Dotty blabbered in between sniffles. Aunt Lillian accepted the position of importance. So with pen and paper she jotted her list of things to do, things to get and most of all, a date for the big day.

"So, your next move," she said "get yourselves to Rev Stefans and set a date and read the Bans." Aunt Lillian said.

"Are you booking the village school for the reception?"

"How many guests do you intend to invite?"

"How do we prepare food, and with what, may I ask?"

"Due to rationing, who is preparing to cook and make sandwiches?"

"Sandwiches?" Jason repeated, "We'll not have sandwiches, we're gonn'a sit down to a proper do, I'll see to the meat and veg."

Aunt Lillian frowned. Dotty sniffled in between her distress for the Americans.

"I'll do the cooking, if I can't then I shall very annoyed."

"Right, that's settled." Jason said quickly, knowing Dotty's sensitivity.

CHAPTER FIFTEEN
PLANS AND VERDICT

Jason made the call to Reverend Stefan's at Leighton All Saints Vicarage. That same evening after the meal, Dotty was sent home for a much-needed rest. Alec, once home, would check and sort out his best shirt, tie, and purchase a new suit, if rationing coupons stretched that far. Jason was prepared to foot the bill for everything, but Aunt Lillian insisted that the woman buy their own. Jason agreed this was the right and proper thing to do.

The appointment to meet the vicar at the village church of St Michael and All Angels would be Monday night after the weekend at precisely seven thirty. The Bans would be read, and called for four Sundays, and the wedding would take place on Saturday 7th September, at two pm.

Jason was a very pragmatic person. He was a hands on man, knew the very meaning of how one should behave in these circumstances, as everything was in short supply. He knew his contacts; he knew which person in Leighton to trust how to be discreet and dealt with. First, the butcher who he'd schooled with and became a good friend, and another good friend, the baker, whose wife had been Kathy's best pal at school. Their association had been a very special bond; she came to the farm as often as she could, a relief from their everyday existence, for their kneading of dough was long and hard work, so a visit to see Kathy, one could see the benefits she needed from the strain and stress in the early days before the war.

Henry would wear long trousers for the first time in his life. The Co-op in Leighton claimed to hold stock for young men as the best outfitters in town, so Henry would be duly dispatched, and measured for charcoal grey trousers with turn-ups. Mary's thoughts as she gazed at her son while he admired himself in the outfitters mirror were. If only Bert could see him now.

"Mum, what do you think?"

"I think you'll make a very good sides-man, you can wear your school blazer, and a red rose out of the garden for your button hole. That reminds me what shall I carry?"

"I don't know mum, you'd better confide in Aunt Lillian," Henry said. Still admiring himself in the vertical mirror. His mum pondered, "I dare say you are right."

***

Jason had thought long and hard about his mother's auriferous gold ring; one side of him said yes to slipping it on Mary's finger, another said no. The next morning after milking, Jenny and Laura had been assigned to Big and Little Dinge for a stint of digging out ditches, Lally was slapping a coat of creosote on the roof boards and sides of the chicken arks, and various other buildings, which would keep him occupied for a few weeks. Jason and Alec were crossing the yard for a quick, brew; the postman came riding on his cycle into the farmyard, whistling a patriotic tune. Gyp greeted him with a few sharp yelps, hens flapped and clucked and flew all ways, as he skidded to a halt in front of Jason.

"Morning," he said, "Three letters for you, two for Mr Smith and one for Master H Kneally, Good day to you both," he said as he pedalled away, amid more yelps from Gyp seeing him off the premises.

Jason shuffled the letters between his bid hands. H'mm, Master H Kneally, he mused, as for his own, blessed bills. Henry sat at the long table scoffing a toasted fried egg sandwich. "Taste good Henry?" Jason handed the letter to him. Henry used his knife to slit it open and the remains of the yoke on the knife smeared the letter. "Tut Tut" Jason said, go and fetch the proper letter opener from the study. "Sorry", he jumped up, reading his letter as he made his way to the study, on returning to the kitchen; Jason asked "Good news?" "In a way, yes it's from Luton Tech; my term starts the second week of September. Monday, nine thirty to four PM. I'm advised to supply my own sandwiches, although there is a canteen subsidised by the Education Authority, but a small fee."

"How much?" asked Jason.

"It doesn't say, I'll make a sandwich"

Jason slit open his letters, an invoice from the seed merchant, and a letter from Mr Hogg. He read it through and quietly slid it in to his side pocket. Henry, have you separated your paintings from Tom Gunn's yet?"

"Yes why?"

***

The intensity of war grew each day, rationing became a headache, but Aunt Lillian fully intended to give Mary another chance in her own sorrow-filled life. A certain or uncertain dispensation of her property in Ashford street which she guessed was still intact, as no message had come through from Bill Trantor to say otherwise. Hoping that he still lived, she had the property insured, but if the house had been destroyed by the blitz how did she stand to receive any monies? She would ring her insurer's first thing.

Mary was still dozing, when Aunt Lillian eased herself out of her small bed and crept quietly downstairs to fill the kettle to boil. Today she would right a list and instigate and compile an order of routine for the wedding. It needed careful planning, something she was good at.

Mary woke up from an awful dream, and found Aunt Lillian standing by the side of the bed. "Now get this down you, we have work to do." Mary rubbed her eyes "Where am I?" she said wearily. The dream still swimming in her head. "I dreamt that Henry and I were walking towards a huge blue mountain but the road was never ending. The nearer we trudged, the further the mountain kept receding its left me totally drained of all strength." Aunt Lillian sat beside her and stroked her hair. "You know, are you quite sure of yourself, about getting married?"

"That's a curious thing to say Aunty"

"I know, it's just that, is it what you really want?"

Mary nodded. "Yes, I'm sure as hell is...... " Before she could finish, a knock came on the cottage door. They both hurried downstairs. Henry waited with the letter in his hand. He kissed his mum. "What's the matter, has something happened?" she asked. Henry beamed.

"I start at Luton Tech second week of September, the week after you remarry!" he chortled.

"Oh Henry this is good news." They sat down to toast and marmalade." Aunt Lillian, do you think I'm doing the right thing?" he asked.

"Of course," her eyes raised to the ceiling, she replied, "Goodness gracious boy, how many times do I have to spell it out to you? You grab this opportunity with both hands; in later life you might just regret it." She stopped short, "here have another round of toast."

Henry stayed with his mum and aunt until the time for them to walk to the farm for their afternoon stint. "In a month's time, Mary, you'll be established at the farm, and this ambivalence will be a thing of the past. Wont' you be glad?" Aunt Lillian said with an air of optimism in her voice.

"Well under the circumstances, I think I have made the best possible choice available to us, and everybody in the village wants to be part of the celebrations. I hope I don't become too emotional or over confident."

"Just be yourself."

Together the marched into the farmyard, Gyp greeting them with huge loving eyes and a happy wagging tale, pleased to see them together. For Jason and Mary that evening they were to meet the vicar, as he had cycled from Leighton to address their needs and to call the bans over the next four weeks.

After the vestry meeting, Jason asked the vicar to partake in an evening soiree in the lounge. The hall clock struck nine o'clock when the vicar the bride to be and the groom made their entrance to the farmhouse. Dotty and Aunt Lillian had prepared light refreshments of cheese and tomato sandwiches, washed down with cider or in preference sloe wine. Alec also returned, as the vicar was to give him and Henry lordly advice on how they should proceed with their duties as best man and usher. Dear Aunt Lillian would give Mary away.

The vicar, not being the best of drinkers, set off to cycle the two miles home to Leighton. The next morning, a passing sand quarry worker found him asleep with his cycle on top of him in a gully, still snoring away the effects of the cider and sloe wine that Dotty had stored to maturity. The doctors prognosis of the vicar; he was drunk and in no fit state to continue with his duties, so, should retire to his bed and sleep it off.

***

As so many times before, Jason had overlooked the fact to notify anybody on the farm staff that the assessor would arrive to value the paintings, to the disgust of Dotty who would be asked once again to provide refreshments at short notice.

The following morning, Henry bemoaned Lally for slap dashing the creosote over all the locks and latches of the chicken arks. His hands dirty and smelly, he wiped them on what straw was left in the ark, after feeding the hens and collecting the eggs on his return to was and grade. After this chore, he climbed the ladder and pulled off the sheet that covered the canvases to admire once again the Zulu Warrior's portrait. It was magnificent; he thought and wondered what would happen to them all. For the last time he threw the sheet back over and resumed his chores in the outhouse.

At ten a.m. Mr White, the assessor drove into the yard in a baby Austin. With a squeal on the breaks, he pulled up in front of Gyp's kennel, to her profound disgust. She sniffed the smell of hot exhaust gases and slunk inside on to her fresh straw, which Henry had laid earlier.

Jason greeted Mr White and directed him into the domain of Dotty's parlour, where they seated themselves at the heavy oak table.

"Pour out tea for us, Dotty; I'm sure Mr White could sink one. Have you come far Mr White?" Jason asked.

"From Amptill. Hoggy and I used to work for an insurance company in Bedford before he moved to where he is now."

"Ah, I wondered how the connection. I'll show you the

way to the portraits."

Mr White followed Jason through to the loft above the outhouse where Jason slipped off the tarpaulin sheet for him to examine the paintings and presumably come to some sort of figure for Mr Hogg, but before Jason could leave, Mr White was adamant that the paintings be brought down into natural light. Jason cursed a little under his breath, as other important duties needed his attention.

Mr White worked diligently, first the Zulu Warrior, inspecting it with a microscope. He scanned every brush stroke, light shade, dark shade, etc. he admired this portrait very much. Next, he found the artist's signature in the bottom right hand corner and the date. His task was fifty-one canvases to record, write, and evaluate. Allowing himself ten minutes a canvas, it would be six in the evening before he called it a day. Emerging from the outhouse, he stretched his arms and aching back. It had been a long day, but well worth the visit. He had found a masterpiece in the Zulu Warrior, an oil. The rest were watercolours of which two were of local girls that Tom had painted and framed into small portraiture; very delicately applied, he thought.

Henry found Mr White a dedicated and profound man, and very astute, inasmuch as he felt confident to ask him a question or two about his own ability. As Mr White sipped the last dregs of a mug of tea that Aunt Lillian had provided, Henry confronted him with the drawing of the London Blitz, one that he had sketched before being evacuated. "Have you the time?" Henry asked.

Mr White cast his professional eye over the drawing, seemingly unaware of Mary, Jason, Alec, or Aunt Lillian all waiting with bated breath as to what his thoughts would be. He studied the drawing, which Henry held out to him, stroked his neatly trimmed goatee and said, "Well, now you know, I'm sure, no I'm positive you will be a great artist one day. In the meantime, carry on studying, and I'm sure you won't need me." he lifted his head, and looking over his tortoiseshell spec's," to give you that much reassurance. You have that ability and a rare gift in the first place."

With that, he bade them his farewells, slid into the baby Austin, and drove out the yard gate.

"Well, I suppose now we have to wait for the will to be read," Jason said.

CHAPTER SIXTEEN

NIGHT OF TERROR

The battle of Britain raged on, but there was talk of how soon the armed forces would invade Europe now America had thrown herself in to the affray after the devastating blow she received at the hand of the Japanese at Pearl Harbour. Every day the locals witnessed a vast amount of troop movements along the Hockliffe road. However, this route was blocked and cordoned off after a night of an unusual incident.

Henry had just concluded the rounds of closing the flaps to the chicken arks; the moon was peeping above a mighty cloudbank, the weather had threatened all day but kept well to the South most of the time, the air was humid. As the farm prepared for slumber, the cows that Henry could see through the five-barred gate grazed peacefully; nothing stirred much. Jason completed his rounds of checking and walked slowly across the yard, heeled his boots and entered the kitchen just as Mary and Aunt Lillian donned their coats to walk home.

Jason kissed Mary lightly as she passed. "Won't be long now, my love."

Henry slumped down into his favourite place and flipped open a Farmers Weekly magazine turning the pages and pretending not to notice. Jason had become a second father that he'd longed for, a guiding hand, a little word here and there. Jason never interfered, but his influence in some respect was having a good effect on the way Henry was behaving. Jason sat down heavily licked his lips and sipped the tea and biting into the cheese sandwich that Aunt Lillian had prepared before leaving for Rose Cottage.

Henry retired first, leaving Jason to lock up but not before giving an order to Gyp... "Your turn now old gal to guard the farm." Her eyes glowed in the twilight; the farm settled down for the night. Soon. Henry slipped between the sheets, but threw back the eiderdown owing to the warmth of the day's sun in the room.

As the lids of his eyes closed into a dreamy state, thoughts of the impending wedding crossed his mind. *Mum would be living with me in the same house, who would have thought when waving goodbye to them both on St Pancras station that Mum would come to the village and find another love in her life?* Henry sank into a deep sleep.

Jason stood over Henry shaking him, at the same time pulling on his trousers over his pyjamas.

"What's the matter?" Henry raised himself and rubbed his eyes. "I don't know, but somethings up Gyp's bark woke me. Didn't you hear her?"

"No what's wrong?"

"Someone's out in the yard." There came a tap on the bedroom window and Jason crossed the room and pushed it open. It was the corporal from the detachment on their site in Ridge and Furrow field.

"What do you want?" Jason's infuriated shout echoed around the buildings.

"Can you come down a minute?" the corporal shouted back.

"Why?"

"I'll explain!"

"You up Henry?" Henry had quickly dressed himself and followed Jason downstairs. On opening the kitchen door he found the corporal with a long pole he'd found under the hovel.

"Sorry about this," he said "But a lone German aircraft has penetrated the south coast defence and is circling around us."

"What for?" asked Jason

"We don't know, the OC thought it would be wise if you were up to be mindful for your cattle, we don't know whether it's just a reconnaissance plane or what, by the sound and the slowness, we recon he's loaded."

"Do you mean he'll bomb us?" Henry said with a faltering voice, half-afraid.

"Can you hear the throb of its engines?" the corporal turned and pointed in the direction of Leighton," this will be his third attempt." As he finished the sentence, the searchlight flickered on and off.

"Gor blimey" he said, "That's giving the position away." He ran like a scalded cat leaving Jason and Henry wondering what would happen next.

"A curious thing, though, usually the siren would sound at Leighton but I never heard a thing, it's unnerving, Henry." Jason said. The searchlight beam flashed on and straightaway they had Jerry in their beam. The bomb-bay-doors were open, its interior lights glowed inside the fuselage, and then the searchlight beam swung out of the night sky across the farm buildings and projected parallel to the main road.

"Christ almighty!" Jason bellowed. They both dropped to the ground; Henry himself spread-eagled with his head in Gyp's kennel. She backed away and sat licking his forehead. The bombs exploded to the left of Sweetacre, but in line with the Hockliffe road. Henry never thought that the war could reach as far as Eggington but it did, with almighty explosions.

Stillness prevailed. Only the drone of the plane flying on towards the east, its engines diminishing by every second, orders were shouted, and counter-ordered by the officer on their site in Ridge and Furrow filed. Jason ran to Sweetacre gate. The cows had panicked. He let them through into the yard and cowsheds and tried to calm them, but to no avail. It would be an hour or so before they settled. The bombs had set light to the middle hedge. The bowser was parked in the paddock where the cob grazed and in its panic, the cob had jumped the railings and mingled with the cows. All the time Jason uttered words of calm. He called Henry. "I'm going to start the GM tractor and hitch up the bowser. This always stood filled with water for emergencies. Henry leapt on to the back step if the tractor towing the bowser and heading towards the fire." What's that smell?" he shouted. Jason sniffed. "It's oil, its oil they were oil bombs, they dropped bloody oil, the swines!"

Jason positioned the GM tractor near the blaze, jumped off and uncoiled the hose and coupled it to the power take off. An adaptor fixed to the side of the PTO, allowed a two inch hose to squirt water on to the fire, but the blaze was too strong. The hose really wasn't adequate or sufficient to quell the blaze, but they stuck to the tack, taking it in turn to direct water until parts of the hedge were out and under control.

Aunt Lillian sat up in bed with a suddenness that she frightened herself into thinking she heard a vibration in the bedroom. She nudged Mary. "Wake up, wake up, Mary!" she turned from lying on her side.

"What's the matter?"

"I felt a big vibration, a bang," she said in a fearful voice.

"Heard what?"

"I'm sure I heard something exploding"

"You heard bombs then?"

"Well something like that, I'm sure."

Aunt Lillian got out of bed and peeped behind the blackouts. From the little window she could see the outline of Claridge farm, just the tops of the buildings and beyond, a glow in the sky." Mary, c'mon, Mary get up, we must get to the farm, it's on fire!"

"Good god!" they pulled on top coats over their night attire and half ran to the end of the lane, to be met by Alec.

"I was coming to knock you up. Christ I think the farm's alight, we'd better hurry."

As they approached the gated farm half running half walking, some of the cows were jostling about the gate.

"I don't like this," Alec said. "What on earth's going on?" he pushed the gate against the herd making them back away. They crossed to the kitchen, the door wide open. They went in shouting for Jason and Henry, but the house was empty. "I'll have a scout round to see where they are?" Alec trotted off out in to the night, now morning as the hall clock struck two o'clock.

"Well, wherever they are we'll have tea ready, I'm sure they will be thirsting for a cuppa." Aunt Lillian busied herself, and Mary meanwhile rushed upstairs to check the rooms. She pulled the blackout curtain in Henry's room to one side, and there in full view she could see figurers silhouetted against the blaze in Sweetacre.

In the wane of the moon Alec checked; he could see and hear the desperate call of people coming from the direction of Sweetacre. Soldiers and other people were trying to beat out the fire with whatever means available. Just as they thought the fire had beaten them, a fire tender from Dunstable arrived at the same time as an auxiliary unit from Leighton. They wasted no time in running their hoses to the moat behind the

Gunn's small estate, and within the next half hour, the fire was well and truly out. Just a few smouldering pockets of hot embers doused, and the trauma was over.

It would be daylight before anyone could reach any sort of explanation as to why this happened at this particular time, and at this particular spot. Alec managed to separate the herd into their own sheds and stalls, and give them bowls of cow cake to pacify them.

Jason was surprised to see Mary and Lillian, but was jolly glad they made the effort. He, Alec and Henry rested themselves in the oak chairs, while Aunt Lillian poured each a mug of tea. Jason's face was blackened, as was Henry's and Mary couldn't help laughing at the pair.

"What?" Jason asked, "Have you two not looked at yourselves lately?"

"You'd have thought they'd swept the chimney, wouldn't you?" Alec said, as he gulped his mug of tea.

The hall clock chimed five o'clock Jason and Alec looked at each other, each reading his own thoughts.

"It's not worth it," Jason said, meaning any sleep. I'll go and wash; we might as well start the milking. Get the parlour ready Alec and you Henry wash and get some sleep, and you two winking at Mary and Lillian, thanks for turning up like that. Go home, but leave Dotty a note to put her in the picture. It's a wonder she's not here, and Henry , when you get up for real, run the hose from the tap to the bowser and refill."

Salutations were given to Jason for his heroics. Henry retired to his room, his mind racing on the night's adventure, recalling the bits of shrapnel lying hot and silvery.

Daybreak revealed another injustice to the village. After their inspired effort through the night Dotty thought it only fit that a good breakfast was needed, Alec, Jason and Henry each tucked into a slice of bacon, an egg and fried bread, just what the doctor ordered.

"Thank you Dotty, for being so understanding," Jason said. She loved to see them eating heartily, and she loved cooking for them. After breakfast, the three of them with Laura and Jenny in accompaniment decided to investigate what damage had been inflicted on the countryside. It was hard to believe a solitary German aircraft could slip the defences of the country and drop bombs on nowhere in particular. As they approached the first crater, they saw thick lumps of shrapnel everywhere. The smell was pretty awful; as they stood on the mound, they counted five other craters in line about a field apart, a distance to the main road of at least half a mile. Further inspection revealed that the bombs had reached neighbouring farmland, the last two being one thousand pound bombs of which one was unexploded. This bomb had buried it's self in the soft blue gault clay underneath the main road, splitting the surface a foot wide. The stench of oil invaded their senses. Jason and his employ of four strode on across the fields following the line where the bombs had exploded, inspecting each crater until reaching the last vast crater; the thousand-pound bomb had created.

"Christ, this was a big one, and look. A convoy." Jason said.

"Who are they?" Henry cried out. Jason's party stood and watched as a line of army personnel had unhitched their camouflaged vehicles, which had evidently bivouacked on the wide verge overnight. Could they have been the target? He thought to himself.

A convoy of five lightweight army trucks drove past them. Not one of the occupants acknowledged the little party standing on top of the crater. The farmhands in turn started back to the farm, but Jason had noticed the military were wearing red caps. Could it be that somebody of importance was aboard? His thoughts were in fact dead right. But then again, it could all be supposition.

CHAPTER SEVENTEEN

PREPARATIONS

The damage to each dividing hedge had to be repaired with posts and barbed wire, which Jason thought why not in the middle of each field. Each bomb had dropped on each dividing hedgerow. It was uncanny, and the last bomb was meant to detonate or not. However, the authorities closed the road for a few months before the bomb disposal squad dug it out and exploded the dam thing right in the middle of a lesson at the primary school, much to the annoyance of the teacher who had not been informed about the explosion taking place. An army officer was sent to offer apologies for any inconvenience they caused, but was too late. She had fainted in front of the class, her heart weak. The doctor was sent for.

The weeks leading up to the wedding gathered momentum. Old dresses were given a new lease of life, the photographer from Leighton was ordered to capture the whole scene inside church as well as outside, and the church was decorated out as if for a harvest festival. A fortnight remained until the big day. Mary became a little irritable about the whole affair.

"It's no use worrying now," Aunt Lillian retorted," let's get on with it and run our own lives for a change. We'll start a new life here in Eggington." As if that wasn't the best news for Mary's ears, the postman called with an official looking document for Aunt Lillian.

"Who's that from?" Mary being a bit inquisitive.

"Well. I hope it's from who I think it is." Aunt Lillian opened the letter and unfolded the note. Sure enough, it was from the Co-Operative Insurance. Aunt Lillian read its contents.

"All's well?" Mary asked. "Yes" Aunt Lillian grew a big smile.

"There will be compensation if the property is damaged, and we should insure Rose Cottage here at the same time."

"Hold on, it says something about a grant from the war damage commission," aunt Lillian said. "So I could receive compensation for the shop?" Mary interrupted.

"You should look into it, "Aunt Lillian said obligingly.

They walked together arm in arm to the farm.

"Won't be long now Mary, this part of your life will be less daunting. Let Jason use his solicitor to help you with any information about your misfortune with the shop, they will fix it for you, I'm sure."

Gyp greeted them with a few tail wags of delight as they entered the yard. Everywhere was a mass of green. The tall elms wavered in the gentle summer breeze.

"Do you know, I've quite forgotten how good a British summer can be, the hedgerows out with Dog Rose blossom, the smell of life, Mary the smell of life is all around of it wasn't for this darned war,"

The Rover saloon was standing ready in the yard. Both became a little curious as to why the car was parked and waiting. Jason stood in the kitchen doorway dressed in grey trousers and open neck shirt, and looking like a man who owned ten thousand acres.

"Where are you going?" Mary thought she had better ask.

Jason looked up to the sky and said, "We are going to

Luton to purchase you a proper wedding outfit. Jump in."

"But I've no money on me to pay."

"Never mind the money, hop in, Dotty's holding the fort while we arrange the most important fitting for you and me."

"Is Henry coming, I must have his approval?"

"Of course, c'mon or we'll miss the bargains, you can get some good outfits in Cheapside."

"Cheapside! No thanks, it's got to be a decent shop or."

"Or what?" Jason said in a very tone.

Oh dear, Aunt Lillian thought, their first little tantrum. She butted in, "I'm sure there's a ladies shop somewhere, if not we'll make do with the Co-Op." good Aunt Lillian for diffusing the idea.

Off they went, Dotty waving, Gyp giving a few yaps.

The ride to Luton wasn't without its problems other than suffering a flat tyre. Jason pulled over on to the wide pavement outside the Jolly Tea Pot café in Dunstable Road. While Jason listened to Henry's none too expert advice on how to change a wheel on a busy main road, Aunt Lillian and Mary went inside to order four teas, and engaged in banter with the proprietor and proletariat alike. It was in this conversation that Mary learnt to her advantage of a certain ladies outfitters in Hightown. After the proprietor poured the tea into four mugs and was happy for Jason and Henry to use the privy and wash their hands, they smiled clinked mugs and drank heartily. As they continued on their journey, Mary told of their conversation with the café owner who obliged them with directions to Hightown.

"Do you know Hightown?"

Jason nodded "Yep, and I can park there somewhere, I suppose. We'll find the shop eventually."

The door creaked as they entered the domain of Ester's Lady Wear. The shop assistant taken aback as four people descended on her.

"What can I do for you?" she asked. A plump, small round figure with bouncy red hair and cheap perfume, fussed around them.

"I'm to be married in two weeks, and I've been assured by someone we met on the way here, I would find what I'm looking for," Mary said.

"Very well," the assistant fussed again. "Have you any colour in mind, and will it be a dress or two piece? Oh and by the way, most important, have you the coupons necessary?"

Nobody had thought of clothes coupons. "Never mind," she said," come through the back of the shop, mind prying eyes."

Aunt Lillian and Mary held each other's glances. Jason and Henry together remained dumb. He steadied Henry by holding his arm. "Not this time son." They eased themselves down into the two chairs provided for customers.

Blandishments from the shop assistant would neither alter nor persuade Mary's mind other than the pink two-piece she'd fitted on. This was a perfect fit for a queen, she thought. Aunt Lillian admired her sister-in-law; a bit of blarney didn't hurt anyone. Mary called Henry to come through to the back of the shop. "Well son, how do you think I look?"

Henry stood to one side and watched his mother moving around, the two-piece hugging her fortyish figure, yet still appropriating the lines of a younger woman. Henry rubbed his forehead seemingly a bit embarrassed at his mother's question.

"Well I don't know, what do you think, Aunt Lillian?"

"I think she carries it off ever so well, in fact yes," Aunt Lillian was very excited for her, "You'll make the perfect bride."

Henry traipsed back to the front of the shop, pursed lips,

and nodded to Jason in agreement with himself.

"Well?" asked Jason

"Very smart, she'll do." Henry felt a certain pride.

Aunt Lillian and Mary pushed through the slightly faded thick brocade curtains, smiling, the two piece already packed and held tightly by Mary. She beamed at Jason.

"The lady said go through and reckon with her." The three then went out and waited in the car, nobody daring to make conversation.

The single electric lightbulb enlightened the face of the plump assistant.

"You ready to settle?" she said approvingly.

"I've no coupons," he said quietly.

In a hushed voice, "don't worry," she replied.

"So what price to pay?"

"Ten pounds" she said, "Your bride to be said you are a farmer,"

"That's right, how about two dozen eggs, and five pounds. Does that sound ok?"

"Sounds good to me." She said. Jason paid the lady and by coincidence, two dozen eggs lay in the car boot.

It was jubilation all the way home. "I must get the tyre fixed before I start work, Jason said in a bemused sort of voice. His mind in overdrive there was milking, the hens to feed, all sorts of jobs whirred inside his head.

"Watch out!" Henry shouted, "You just missed that man on his cycle."

"Well he ought to have known we are in a hurry." Jason laughed at the sight of the cyclist picking himself up off the grass verge and shaking his fist in despair. The car swept on in a cloud of dust and pulled into the yard, Gyp mounting a growling session and running alongside the car before pulling up outside the kitchen door.

Aunt Lillian and Mary were glad to be home." Thank the lord we don't do this every day," said Aunt Lillian stepping out of the car. Dotty greeted them. "Just in time for a nice cuppa. C'mon in and rest yer'selves." When they settled, she said, "Now tell me all about your journey." Dotty couldn't wait, "And you'll show me your outfit?"

"Not until Jason departs for the garage to get the tyre repaired, then I'll show in the bedroom," Mary replied.

Dotty rubbed her hands, her impatience getting the better of her. Jason departed taking Henry and Gyp with him.

Aunt Lillian and Mary exchanged views on the ability of Jason's erratic driving. "That's not the first time he's been accused." Dotty said they adjourned, following one another up the wide staircase in to the bedroom, which was to be the couple's bridal suite.

Aunt Lillian and Dotty waited by the oak bedstead, Dotty pressing up and down on the mattress and grinning at Lillian. "Well the room has seen a lot of happenings in its time, I should know, some happy, some sad, his mum and dad, and before that grandma and grandad, have all shared this room. It's been a long journey, but I'm glad I'm still alive to be witness to this wedding."

Mary stepped out from behind the small screen, which provided cover for many generations for their first encounter between the betrothed.

"Oh you do look pretty" Dotty couldn't believe the transformation that stood in front of her. "I think you will make the perfect bride, Jason should feel proud of you, just look at you." Dotty couldn't take her eyes off Mary. "Come here, stand in front of the mirror."

"What about a hat?" Dotty asked.

"Oh my gord. I've completely forgotten about a hat."

"Never mind, I know just where to lay my hands on

one."

Dotty bounced out of the room along the corridor to a small box room. She opened many boxes that were stacked after Kathy died. "I know," she panted to herself "I know which one, yes, the purple coloured box." She opened the lid and there inside was Kathy's going away white pillbox hat complete with veil, still preserved intact. No moths had depreciated the contents. She lifted the hat and carried it very carefully to the bedroom. "Try it on," she said excitedly.

Mary fitted the hat over her soft brown hair; the pillbox fitted the crown perfectly.

"I think Jason wouldn't mind, in fact, I think he'd be pleased. Well there's nothing we can do now, just a fortnight to go, so maybe a blessing in disguise." Dotty waddled off downstairs to the kitchen.

CHAPTER EIGHTEEN

THE WEDDING

September, and almighty God had created a masterpiece of a late summer morning. Low mist straddled Sweetacre and surrounding field. Eventually this would burn off for a perfect day.

Dotty arrived long before Jason ever thought of rising to start milking. He should not have worried as Alec had already corralled the cows for milking, in fact, he was half way through the job when Jason entered the milking parlour and took over. While Alec interchanged to feed the pigs, calves and chickens. It was here where Henry met Alec who promptly handed over the feed mix and let Henry open up all the arks in the orchard. Alec revved up the GM tractor and wizzed off with the feed for the sows along to the overflow at the leased sites along the Standbridge road. Everything was going to plan; all jobs must be dealt with by ten o'clock, as the service at the village church was arranged for two o'clock.

Aunt Lillian and Mary would share Rose Cottage for the last time, after breakfast of toast and local honey. Next came Aunt Lillian's turn to prepare Mary in to a radiant bride. Mr Bott was to drive Jason and his best man and Henry to the church, then return to collect Aunt Lillian and Mary thereafter.

The school on Friday night had seen many helpers clear

the desks and make way for the borrowed trestle table's from the premises of the local carpenter who had stored them for the cricket club until better times. Everybody in the village had contributed a little something towards the food. However, Jason had somehow secured a joint of beef which Dotty had duly cooked, cooled, and sliced, that would sit nicely aside of mashed potatoes and main crop carrots.

Flowers decorated the church, and candles in brass holders adorned the tables for the reception afterwards. St Michaels and All Angels, although small, held as many as sixty or so souls, in fact, some remained outside, such was Jason's popularity. The photographer was already there with his tripod and camera in place before Lillian and Mary arrived, busy fussing about his lot, he was perfecting imaginary shots. At last, Mr Bott gently drove the taxi bedecked with ribbons, pulled up outside the church gate, and as they both alighted, a convoy of army vehicles swept noisily by. The troops spotting Mary rushed to the back of the canvassed lorries and waved their congratulations above the cacophony of engine noise and shouts. Both Mary and Lillian reciprocated as each vehicle passed. Mary thought of Bert for a brief moment. Aunt Lillian sensed something amiss.

"Now, come on, Mary, I know what you're thinking, you'll have to put whatever is bothering you to the back of your mind, let's get on with today." They adjusted themselves and quietly made their way toward the front porch of the small well-kept church, where well-wishers had gathered, as they posed for a few shots before entering to Handel's wedding march.

The organ was being played by an old repatriated friend from Canada who long ago lived in the village but came back before the war. Since then her husband from World War One had died of a gas attacks. They had settled in Winnipeg, but she came back to her roots, and had played the organ for any event for anyone for no remuneration. Henry greeted them both, he, feeling proud and very smart in his long trousers. He kissed his mum and gestured them in. Jason rubbed his knuckles anxiously. Alec fiddled with his buttonhole, and nudged Jason to be ready.

As Mary came along side, he too thought of Kathy, but smiled at his bride to be. The service, conducted by the Reverend Stefans, went according to the book, the congregation singing Jason's favourite hymn, All people on this earth do dwell, with gusto, their voices a distraction from the war, a vision of hope that they will hold in their hearts.

Dotty remained at the farm preparing for the homecoming. Somebody had to be there, and she reminded them she was that somebody, a dutiful soul one could depend upon one hundred percent. Humming a tune while she worked in the kitchen. The phone rang, "Oh the blessed thing." And she answered in a purposeful manner. "Hello. Dotty speaking."

"Hello Claridge Farm, this is Bill Trantor speaking, you know, the van driver from London, can I speak to Mary, please?"

"Oh, not just at the moment, you see, she's getting married today, in fact this very hour at the village church. What's it about can I take a message?"

"I'm afraid its bad news for her Aunty, the house has been destroyed by a landmine."

"Oh dear, oh dear," Dotty became very tearful.

He went on, "Last night's raid at least a couple of streets were completely blown apart."

Choking, Dotty said, "I'll pass the message on, it'll ruin her day, I know it will,"

"Well there's nothing here for her to come back to London for, tell her to phone me, Mary will know my number," he rang off.

As Mary and Jason came out of the service, six veterans of the village community made an arch with pitchforks as they passed arm in arm out of the porch and into a sunlit afternoon. The photographer took several frames at different angles, and the last being a shot of all who could smile into the lens.

More or less everyone in the village had something to eat; children and all joined in the happening. Alex stood and called for order. He read out a few messages of goodwill, and then asked Jason to give his sagacious speech to the assembled. He commanded their attention, a speech straight off the cuff as was expected of him. Halfway through, as everyone listened intently, a commotion appeared to be happening in the porch of the school.

"Let me through!" Dotty shouted, "Let me in," she burst in, all flustered and with rosy red cheeks, "Aunt Lillian, she called, she found her serving tea in the small annex to the school.

"Oh Lillian, there you are, oh Lillian!" she exclaimed.

"What on earth's the matter, Dotty? Sit yourself down, pray calm down."

"Calm down?" Dotty squatted on a seat provided by a member from the church choir.

"There now, what's all the fuss?" Jason ushered Mary to where Dotty sat, still trying to get her breath back. He asked, "Who's looking after the farm?"

"Don't worry, Laura and Jenny called in just as I took the call on the phone,"

"What call?" Jason enquired.

"For Lillian, a landmine has destroyed her house in

Lunnon; in fact the whole street was blown up!" Everyone murmured their sadness.

"Bill Trantor phoned, say's you've to contact him at the bus depot, he said Mary will know where to phone, says its nerve racking living in Lunnon.

"If ever there was a case for euphoria, then despair in a matter of minutes, this surely took the biscuit." Jason announced that they should return to the farmhouse as quickly as they could.

Mr Botts taxi could easily squeeze in six people. As Jason left the reception, he sportingly told everyone to eat up and clean up, and leave the school tidy. "I'll be back just to make sure, enjoy yourselves and thanks for turning up and making our day," the reverend Stefans stepped forward and assured Jason he would oversee, and call in on his way home to Leighton. Jason gave a nod and a wink and signalled Mr Bott to leave. He reversed the taxi and turned in the direction of Claridge farm. A ten-minute ride, and the taxi, Dotty who'd followed came peddling in on her trusty rusty bike; Laura and Jenny were there to greet them.

"You'll come in for a bevvy too, Mr Bott?" Jason asked

"I'll pop back and fetch the missus first."

"Ah, you can't do without a missus."

Mr Bott nodded in agreement.

They entered, but not before Jason swept Mary off her feet and carried her over the threshold; he kissed her in his arms, and set her down as she held on to her pillbox hat.

"Haven't I seen that hat somewhere before?" the kitchen fell silent. Dotty sidled forward. "It was my idea," she said, a little wary of what he might say." She forgot to buy herself a hat, so, I thought of Kath's hat in the box room, you don't mind?"

"Not at all, she looks just wonderful, suits you." He

kissed her again.

Jason stood at the end of the large oak table and admired what Dotty had provided, in fact he was amazed at the culinary delights she had acquired over the months leading up to the wedding day. Dotty fussed about with the teapot, pushing in between everybody as they settled down.

Gertrude and her four charges were invited to sit in on the private party at the farm. At least the boys could be counted on to eat any leftovers. In this case none would be available as there was just enough for everyone including Mr and Mrs Bott and the reverend Stefans who finally arrived just as Jason poured out a tot of four star napoleon brandy into the cups. "Just in time, vicar, you've timed it just right." The vicar sat down by the kitchen range and drank his cup of tea laced with the good stuff and promptly gave a toast to the happy couple.

"Cheers, everybody, blessed the day for you both."

Teacakes, lardy cake, swiss jam roll, bread and marge, blackberry jam to conclude the day, a surprise which Dotty had hidden from everyone the day before, when all were busy and doing their work. Dotty also, had arranged for Jason's friend, the baker at Leighton, to bake a special two tier wedding cake, the ingredients kept secret until cut, but before they took their places, the couple exchanged vows with each other, sealed with a kiss; the reverend Stefans blessed them again and the cake, it was a joyful event. The photographer called in for a group gathering outside, with Dotty, and Gyp taking pride of place between Jason and Mary, and then he happily called for one or two shots and confirmed the album would be ready in a fortnight's time.

As everybody had gathered in the yard, Jason thanked all and sundry for the time and effort everyone had achieved on the day, but there it had to end as milking and feeding had to be resumed. He held Marys hand and said. "Mrs Smith, now we start work, I'm sorry, but it ends here and starts here," Jason and his new wife Mary turned and entered the kitchen followed by the rest of the guests.

With Gyp fussing about Henry's legs and wanting attention, he bade them to sit around the long oak table pouring out copious amount of cider, or if anyone wanted brandy, just to shout.

"I can talk now that I'm in my own home with the people who have cared, and I've trusted over the year and a half. I know it's not been easy for any of us, but it's been a remarkable day for us all, I must say it went well." He raised his glass as they reciprocated. After which the guests drifted away leaving in an air of total bliss.

***

"First and foremost, Lillian, how can I help you?" Jason said.

"I don't really know, but since you ask, the solicitor, you know at Leighton, who is dealing with Mary's property, do you think I could use him too?"

"I can see no reason for him not to want to. I'll ring Roy Connaught first think Monday morning. Jason reminded them that milking needed to start. I've drawn up a plan, I hope you all agree that everyone here has a duty to perform, and if we keep a tight ship we'll come through these uncertain times." He leaned over and whispered to Alec, " Get changed and drive in the herd. " he tapped the table, " Monday morning Dotty, will you be here on hand to help Mary settle, and acclimatise herself about the house; Lillian, are you willing to help in the afternoons? Does the plan suit you all? I hope so." They all sipped the last dregs from their cups and glasses.

"Of course you will." he muttered. Each one at the table nodded in agreement none declined.

"Right then, that's settled, I can go to bed tonight with a clear conscience and a pure heart."

Dotty reminded them all that it was near to apple picking time, and blackberries need their attention in Sweetacre.

CHAPTER NINETEEN

IN A NUTSHELL

Mr and Mrs Smith aroused themselves from a good night's sleep as the hall clock struck six times. Mary stretched her lilywhite arms and placed them behind her home permed hair, which one of the village girls gave her prior to the wedding. Jason slid out of bed and pulled the curtains to one side. "You know, all the time I've lived here I've never been so settled and confident that we'll survive the war." He parted the curtains a little more, his eyes roving round the farmstead. Most of the machinery was from the Victorian age, apart from the new GM tractor. Something has got to happen, he thought, a new age will dawn after the war; with a little vision, more modern machines have to be invented if farming's to take its place in the world, I can see it coming, a revolution or mass production of all sorts of things.

"I can see it coming, Mary."

"What can you see coming?"

"A revolution," she clasped his shoulders, and he turned and kissed her lightly on her forehead. "It's time to make tracks." He said.

They readied themselves for the day ahead. For Mary, a strange day but not without its uncertainties, would probably raise its head before the day was through.

Dotty yoohooed in to the yard and leaned her cycle against the sill of the kitchen window. She waddled through the door. "Morning to you all, beautiful morning it is."

The air was clear and clean. Jason donned his cap and smock for milking.

"Oh later, he remarked, I'm taking stock of pigs at the lease sites, soon be able to sell some at Leighton market." He called; see you later, to Mary who at the time was calling Henry to get up. It would be his first day at Luton Tech College.

"You don't want to miss the bus!" she called.

Dotty smiled at Mary, "How are you coping? I know it might be a bit strange for you Lunnon people, you'll get used to it." She strung her apron round her tubby waist, humming a tune to herself, after they had cleared the table of breakfast things, and waved Henry goodbye to catch the bus to Luton, the next chore was to worry what would be for dinner that night. Mary could cope through the day with cheese sandwiches and cups of tea, but the thought of every day, and dinner to cook at night with all the shortages and ration coupons, frankly, it could drive her insane. Dotty assured her she would cope very well under trying conditions to say the least. To lessen the stress, Dotty said, "I will show you something, now come with me." Mary followed her along the hall. "This is my little secret." She opened the large pantry door, and stuck on the inner panel was a lined piece of paper, penned with instructions for each day of the week, and depending on how many food coupons were available. "So there, don't fret, today Monday, will be leftovers from the Sunday lunch, you'll serve cold, obviously, so Tuesday, we have suet pudding with bacon bits, Wednesday, sausage and mash, Thursday, a piece of fish if we are lucky, Friday, egg, spam, and potato, Saturday, rabbit pie, and Sunday, maybe a bit of beef with vegetables from the garden, which Alec grows for us. We'll take a walk to the garden and see what we can gather, usually at this time of year there's summer cabbage, carrots, onions, potato, and maybe some runner beans, we'll see."

"I don't know if I will remember the different varieties."

"You'll soon learn."

"What a difference, when in London you can walk to a café, sit down, order and eat, but here you have to be self-sufficient and do the best you can." The culture shock hit Mary hard, but she knew what she had let herself in for as early as when Aunt Lillian and she had moved to the country. She knew it wasn't going to be a picnic; her resolve during the days and nights in London would stand her in good stead. At least with Dotty and Aunt Lillian to give her a hand life wouldn't be as bad as first thought. She would come through this.

Mary peeled potatoes at the sink, while Dotty made the beds upstairs. She could see all that had happening on the farm. Laura and Jenny were in the mixing shed; Alec was wheeling the sac barrow with empty boxes to fill when apple picking begins. At that moment, Jason drove into the farmyard on the GM tractor, back from evaluating the pigs along the leased sties. The wind began to blow in the tall Elms at the gateway to Sweetacre, from the kitchen window Mary could see right through the orchard and way down to the far end of the large field. She shivered a draught cut through from the outhouse. "I'll get Jason to fix a door to stop the draught blowing in here." She said to herself. Autumn was just around the corner.

Dotty came shuffling along as the clock in the hall struck ten.

"Time for a cuppa, the staff, Mary mustn't keep em waiting. I'll get the mugs and boil the kettle, you squeeze the horn, they'll come running, you'll see."

They filed in and seated themselves at the long table. Lally had been moved to another camp and district, they missed him, but, nobody understood where his capture had taken place, he never once let on.

As they sipped their tea Mary beckoned Jason to the outhouse, the others looked on bemused. Surely not their first argument? As Mary made a lot of gesticulating movements, it was plain to see something was not quite right for the lady of the house.

"Okay, okay, you've made your point, I'll fix it tomorrow." Mary smiled at the three mates.

First points to Mary.

Mary sat down in the worn leather chair, she glanced about. Some of the furniture really needed replacing, but it was not the right time. She wrote a letter to Bill Trantor, of how they were coping and sorry for not informing him earlier about getting married to Jason in totally unexpected circumstances, though she allowed herself to make a quick and shrewd decision, which benefited her and Aunt Lillian and Henry. She also asked if he knew of anyone who had lost property due to the blitz to be compensated by the government or war damages commission. She signed herself Mary Smith of Claridge Farm Eggington. Mary gave Dotty the letter to post on her way home.

This afternoon she would assist Alec to gather the Bramley apple's and store for winter. Tomorrow Dotty and she would pick blackberries in Sweetacre. Jam making was Dotty's forte; Dotty, however, had saved every jam pot from last year's endeavour's, had washed them and sterilized the pots and left them to warm in the oven ready to fill when needed. However, Mary's thoughts were on rabbit pie.

How do you skin a rabbit?.... Oh heck.

Laura and Jenny were clearing the headland's over in

Big and Little Dinge making ready for the wheat harvest, which would be ready providing the weather held. The summer of forty-three was lasting into September.

Henry stepped of the bus and hurried along the lane. Madge Willans who had alighted earlier from the bus going in the opposite direction, waited for Henry to catch up.

"Your first day at the Tech, how did you get on?"

"Met some very good people. Yes I think I made an impression." They exchanged a few more words and Henry agreed to partner Madge at the weekend for a doubles tennis game. He couldn't wait.

Suspicions were mounting about the invasion of Europe; more, and more American military were coming to England, and war was gathering pace at an incredible rate. The battle of Britian had been won, the tide was turning in British favour, there was an air of expectancy and anticipation, something of significance was about to happen. Mary was finding life very busy. Gertrude Wilson-Green approached her to see if she would be interested in joining the W.V.S Mary knew that if she joined, something would have to be sacrificed at the farm, so she declined the offer for the time being. "Let me settle in for a while, and then maybe I could give a little time at a later date."

The wheat harvest at Big and Little Dinge started in earnest, with the new GM tractor hooked up, revised modification to the harvester, the power drive made life that bit easier, but the sheaves were still stooked and later carted to the Dutch barn to be stacked, then a wait of several months more before the Victorians still haunted the farmyard with a Black cumbersome magnificent beast hissing steam and spurting clouds of smoke. Mary and Dotty would have their work cut out to supply tea and sandwiches for the extra workers set on for the duration of their stay.

Two letters arrived by the morning post, a cheery "good morning" he called out, with Gyp yapping at the back of his cycle as he sped away. Mary collected and studied the postmark, one from Leighton addresses to Mr J Smith, and the other a Northampton postmark, likewise to Mr J Smith. She left them on the oak table for Jason to open and read at elevenses. The hall clock struck ten thirty, and she made ready with Dotty flasks of tea and some cheese rolls that were ordered earlier with their friend the baker from Leighton. Apparently, this was a standing Order each year for this occasion.

Jason appeared at the kitchen door. "Weather has stayed warm for September, always busy period. Mary" he smiled, threw his cap into the fireside chair and sat clumsily down.

"God I'm thirsty." Mary poured him out a long glass of Tizer. He belched, "Aagh, that's more like it." Mary handed the letters to him. "Came a while ago," she said.

Jason ripped both open and read them.

"This one," he held up to Mary," is from Roy Connaught, the solicitor" he fumbled with the first letter, "Say's you may get compensation provided you still have your house insurance policy as a bona-fide confidant."

"What's that mean?"

"Well simply, the country's broke. All depends on whether Mr Churchill will get all the gold he shipped to Canada for safe keeping and will still be there when the war is over."

The second letter from Mr Hogg read as follows. *"I will be obliged for you to contact me as soon as possible as the brothers Gunn's will is ready to read, and you are the sole beneficiary, it is in your interest to acknowledge this letter forthwith."*

"Anything interesting?" Mary asked, shooting a

calculating glance at the letter he was holding.

"You could say some of our debt may be rid of by this time next month."

"Why?"

"Well. I've to write a letter to Mr Hogg in recognition, and respond to a meeting. I suppose I am the inheritor of the Gunn's estate."

"Does this mean that Claridge Manor will belong to you?"

"I dare say, well, yes. I'll write the letter now and get Dotty to post it for the afternoon collection, where is she anyway?"

"Upstairs making the beds. By the way, when are you going to fix the outhouse door?"

"I'll do it straight after writing the letter." He gulped the last dregs of his Tizer and made his way to the study, and wrote the letter ready for Dotty to post on her way home. He called Alec from across the yard to call Harry the carpenter for two door sized four-ply. "I'll make it right with him when I see him next."

"Okay boss."

"By the way Alec, that'll be on your way back from collecting the girls at the Dinges."

"Okay boss."

"Later, we'll make ready the harvest, teach the girls how to oil and tighten all nuts and anything else that need attention to fix and renovate."

"Right you are boss." He said again.

Nobody suggested to Jason that he was about to commit a crime, all the time it was happening across the country; black market goods often found their way onto farms and into the country larders; to the village policeman a dozen eggs for turning a blind eye for lacing the milk with water, or how such a quantity of choice meat and offal suddenly appeared on a pantry shelf. Dotty would tap her nose and shake her head to Mary meaning, say now't, hear now't, you know what the papers say, walls have ears.

The hammering and sawing went on all afternoon, a few choice words for the occasional miss hit with the hammer, but eventually the door could be closed with some degree of application, in fact, an instant warmth was felt in the kitchen, to the delight of Mary. The draught had been eliminated, and she showered Jason with all kinds of complementary words and affection.

When Henry walked in, slinging his satchel and gasmask on to the floor, he slumped into the chair. "What's all the fuss, I could hear you two halfway across the the yard, even the girls were giggling."

"C'mon, look." Jason beckoned Henry through to the outhouse. "See, your mum wanted a door to sever the draught."

Henry scrutinised Jason's carpentry. "H'mm." he ran his fingers over the beading. "You've made a good job, in fact an excellent job, for something that only needed a curtain."

"Well, Henry, that's not nice, apologise at once."

"He knows what I mean, no offence to you Jason."

Jason frowned and lay the hammer on the table. "Are you up for some harvest work this weekend Henry? You have been here two years now, are you warming to the idea of farm work, or will your studies take you elsewhere?"

"I promised Madge I'd make up a foursome at Bell Close Tennis Club." However, he agreed not to be too cynical, and would help when help was needed.

Henry ran out of the yard and up to where Madge lived at Thedeway cottage. Her mum and dad managed to scrape a living from a small holding selling flowers and produce; her dad had no use in one arm, restricting him of ever holding down a decent job. Henry rapped on the door. Mr Willans answered. "What is it boy?" he was an abrupt sort of man small in stature but with powerful shoulders.

"Err; is Madge in, Mr Willans?"

He called Madge from upstairs. "Sorry, Madge, I can't make it for tennis, Jason needs me to help with the harvest at the Dinges," Henry said.

"Quite right, my boy." Mr Willans indicated plainly, "You'd do well, Madge if you offered your services as well. You know a little help goes a long way in these times."

"But dad I've made arrangements."

"Well undo them for a change, it won't hurt you."

Even Mrs Willans joined in. "I'm sure Jason would be pleased if you gave your time to help, you know harvest won't help itself."

"Alright then, I'll phone round and explain why, though it's a bit late. I'm sure somebody else will turn up."

Mr Willans was glad that Madge had thought fit to alter her plans and help. Over the years Willans and Jason had locked horns over certain rights that had dogged them at council meetings, such as sheep grazing on the green, a covenant that stipulated it was common rights for animals to browse, a thorny subject that one could not see an end to, but perhaps if Madge were to help it might possibly mend some bridges between the two families.

Madge and Henry worked side by side, both building long stoked sheaves, Henry soon pulled his shirt sleeves down when he realised the roughness of the stalks chaffer his wrists, which bled leaving little pinheads of blood. Madge on the other hand wore a long sleeved wool jumper; she had anticipated what was to come. The both worked tirelessly with no thought of resting for tea, they were happy in each other's company. Jason and Mary wondered about their relationship.

The weather held fair over the weekend and into the following week. With the land girls, Laura, Jenny, and a couple of rough necks from the village they managed to fill the Dutch barn with a rather large stack. The dry spell helped enormously to ripen the wheat in what appeared to be a good yield, so, in a couple of month the contractors for threshing which Jason had ordered would huff and puff in to the yard. The black and green painted steam traction engine would highlight the November days.

Jason whistled Rule Britannia as he entered the kitchen, milking concluded, four churns standing ready in the cool of the dairy would be collected with tomorrow mornings milk. Alec remained a while after the farm work had been completed. He then set about digging the main crop of King Edward potatoes he'd planted earlier in the year. He dug up six rows in the farm garden, covered them with haulms to protect them over night, then uncover them the next day to dry before bagging up and storing them in the loft with the Bramley apples. Jason was the unmitigated yeoman. Mary had put the finishing touches to the blackberry jam when he folded his arms around her, kissed her, and thanked her.

"What's that for?" she turned her body into his and kissed him back full on the lips and they embraced for a full few minutes.

"You know, I'm lucky I met you how could I have known my life would turn out the way it has?" she said.

"You could have been a gold digger, a-ne'r-do-well, a tramp, but you're not, you're my love, and I admire you, Mary Smith."

***

Henry came in from Luton Tech, and slouched into the chair. "Anything wrong lad?" Jason noticed Henrys unwillingness to greet them.

"I don't think I'm cut out to be an architect, I'm considering cartography as my subject."

"What's brought this on?" Mary could see Henry was in some sort of emotional state. "Perhaps you could have a word with your tutor about your change of mind, or would you rather have Jason to confide in?" Henry's attitude surprised her she thought he was happy with his life, and being taught about architecture was uppermost in his mind. "Anyway, what is this cartography all about, other than your hobby sketching and painting, I thought you would have enough to occupy yourself without compromising your main subject? Still it's your life, we won't stand in your way if you think it would be a more beneficial to your education." underneath Mary was saddened at this sudden turn of events. "Jason, try and talk some sense in to the lad."

"How about a cuppa, Mary?"

"Now Henry, in a nutshell, what's cartography, tell me?" Jason said.

"It's simply map making, I'm pretty good at geography and geometry, I thought that somewhere between these two subjects there'll be a need for new maps after the war, and interestingly geology and exploration of earths minerals for the future."

Jason studied Henry's train of thinking. This boy was no fool how far can a young mind look into the future such as this.

Mary served the tea, sat down, and listened to what Jason had to say.

"You know Henry, when I first met you at the local school, I selected you remember?" Henry nodded. "I thought this boy is right for the farm, because of our situation, then I thought that with a bit of persuasion he might consider a farm life, and then, I thought, no, he's from the city, different culture altogether. What I'm getting at, lad, is nobody is forcing you to do anything against your wishes, but if I were you, I would give serious thought about your later life. You only get one chance, and you grab it. Maybe, you could take this cartography as a second subject. If all else fails, there'd be no harm done."

Henry sipped his tea, pondered and fiddled with his cup.

"You are right, I'll carry on with the architecture and choose cartography as a second subject, I know I can achieve both. I must knuckle down and study, there's too many distraction going on around here."

Jason advised him. "Why not draw up a plan for each month, allowing yourself the time and space and that little bit of relaxation from stress. We do it on the farm. We have a planned rota system, and it works. Work on it and pin the schedule in your bedroom, and stick rigidly to the plan. If it gets too much, we are here to help in any way we can."

CHAPTER TWENTY

THE WILL

The phone rang. Jason answered and Mary and Henry listened to the conversation. Jason gave them the thumbs up sign, and rested the receiver back on to its cradle. "Well Mr Hogg will be visiting tomorrow at eleven o'clock to read the Gunn's will." After a year's wait, they will finally get to know what Tom and Fred were really worth, and who will benefit from their estate. Henry made his way upstairs to change. Jason called "Are you up to helping me clear out the pig sties along Standbridge road? This is the perfect relaxation Henry!"

Mary reminded them that dinner was at six o'clock, and not to be late. She watched them both as Jason drove the lease lend GM tractor out of the yard with Henry sitting in the trailer on the new straw litter for the pigs. They would load the trailer with manure, then transport the load back to the farms manure heap which when mature the girls would be shown how to use the muck spreader on the fallow field of Longfield for next year's grass crop to grow, after which they would chain harrow to spread it more evenly. In the meantime, the girls were given a light job, cutting boar thistle armed with sharp sickles.

***

Alec called Mary to come and inspect the potatoes he had just unearthed.

"Look at these, the best King Edwards you'll ever see and taste, especially with Christmas dinner not too far away." Mary rubbed some of the dried soil away. Alec could see she was becoming a dab hand at being a farmer's wife.

"I'll have these bagged up tomorrow and store them in the loft for you."

She left Alec musing over the crop. Gyp followed her into the kitchen. "No Gyp," she pointed to the kennel. "There's a good dog" Mary rested at the kitchen window; her life had changed forever.

***

Jason called Alec, Laura, and Jenny in to the study. He gave them strict instructions for the day. He wanted the farm to be devoid of all humans other than him and Mary. At eleven o'clock, the situation needed no interference while Mr Hogg's visitation passed without so much as a miasma on the farm.

The morning progressed slowly for Jason. The farm was eerily quiet, and he had time to think. On the other hand, Henry perused his time travelling on the top deck of the bus, studying a few papers. A synopsis of today's architecture would blend in once the war was over; he wondered how his life would pan out, even without passing any exams, and his thoughts returned to what the atmosphere will be like when he arrived home tonight. He closed the file as the bus pulled into Williamson Street. A half-mile hike beckoned before the Tech school.

Gyp's warning bark heralded Mr Hogg's arrival in his Austin Twelve, as he drove up to the kitchen entrance, turned, and came to a halt by Gyp's kennel. Her noisy yaps ceased, her tail wagged, she was becoming more and more accustomed to the distinct sound of the Austin's engine.

Mr Hogg slid out of the driver's seat clutching a Gladstone bag, and slammed the door. He nervously said. "Good dog-good dog." And patted Gyp who was tethered to her trailing wire.

Jason welcomed Mr Hogg into the kitchen. "Do you prefer the study, or would you rather sit here at the long table?"

"Well I prefer here, it's more comfortable, and besides so much room to spread the papers." "A cup of tea before you deliver?" Mary said, anticipating that after his journey the first thing he'd want was just that.

"Well I think it would be best left till later. I would rather get straight on with the matter in hand, and then maybe after would be a better time, in fact, you two could be celebrating." The Manilla file was placed gently on the table and the bag snapped shut and set down aside of his chair.

Mr Hogg looked straight into Jason's eyes and said, "Are you Jason Edward Smith, incumbent of Claridge Farm, Eggington?"

"I am."

Mr Hogg unfolded the file and read on. "This is the last will of Fredrick and Thomas Gunn late of Claridge Manor house Eggington. This is their last will and testament to you Jason Edward Smith the sole beneficiary of their will, with one exception of a codicil which was a change as an addition to one Henry Kneally of this address." Mr Hogg glanced up from underneath his horn-rimmed spectacles he gave a small wry smile and pursed his lips to Mary.

"Is this your boy?" he asked

"Yes he's mine." Mary replied.

Jason and Mary held hands as Mr Hogg read through the will, it was pretty lengthy; he read through probate, chattels, movables the legacy, and estate.

"What this means in layman's terms is; you Jason E Smith inherits Claridge Manor as it stands to date, the freehold of three public houses in neighbouring Buckinghamshire with adjoining land to be sold at public auction at a later date, of which you inherit all, plus monies in an account held by Midland Bank in Leighton to be transferred to J.E.Smith account wherever held; The said amount is Five Thousand Pounds."

"Strewth." Jason said. He tightened his grip round Marys hand and they eyed each other with a slight bemused grin.

"Now just one more item."

The codicil for Henry Kneally, the sale of Tom's artwork, and any residue at the time e.g. costs to be met and deducted. Monies to be held in trust, until reaching the age of twenty- one and will inherit at the said time in life. Mr Hogg retained a copy for himself, gave Jason the legal documents, and asked. "Do you want Royal and Ancient to act for you in the future?" Jason thanked Mr Hogg, but declined his offer of the firm's willingness to act for him. He would, however, use his own solicitor at Leighton for any future business.

Mr Hogg said his goodbyes and drove out the yard with dust still following the battered Austin Twelve, Gyp running excitedly up and along her trail line, knowing a release was imminent. Jason and Mary stood close at the kitchen door. He slipped his arm around her waist and tightened his grip. "You know; I wonder where all this is going to lead us? The legacy could make a huge impact on the way we farm in the future, that's providing the future doesn't interfere too much." They retreated inside, "Make us another cuppa, we'll sit and chat awhile." The grandfather clock struck half past two.

"My god" Mary said, reaching for the tea caddy," is that the time?"

"Yep. The girls and Alec, they'll all be returning, just in

time for milking."

Alec, Laura, and Jenny stowed their shovels dung forks and hard brush aboard the trailer, the pigs at the sties were bedded down, and counting two sows, were farrow to litters; one with ten piglets, the other with twelve, the rest were out in the meadow. Jason would cycle along in the late evening to usher them in for the night. Laura drove the GM tractor and trailer back to the farm, Gyp greeted them in her inimitable style. Jason had started the milking, and Mary had three mugs of tea waiting for them, which they drank with, that pleasing effect tea has on you.

Alec said his thanks and departed to help Jason complete the milking. Laura and Jenny were consigned to duties cleaning the cob's harness until being dismissed for the day before Alec left for home and Aunt Lillian had joined Mary in preparing the evening meal, Jason invited Alec to stay awhile, as he had some important news for them all, but would have to wait until Henry came home. It necessitated a compelling situation indeed.

Henry arrived home a few minutes late than usual due to a heavy concentration of army vehicles. He had never seen so many military personnel in his life, slinging his satchel and gas mask over his shoulder he alighted from the bus and ran to the farm to be met by Gyp, who by now was accustom to his returning at this time of day. She knew instinctively what time he would arrive home, she would be ready and waiting for him. Henry greeted Gyp with a friendly "Ullo". As she jumped up and down until the excitement died. He was met at the door by his mum. Inside, seated at the oak table were Jason, Alec, and Aunt Lillian, all pleased to see him.

"Had a good day?" Jason spoke first. "Sit yourself down, son," Mary poured tea for them all.

"What's for dinner mum, I'm starved?" he hadn't eaten

all day.

"Well seeing that Jason has received some good news today, I've, I should say, we, your Aunt and I have together cooked a Bedfordshire Clanger." Dotty had explained earlier how Jason loved the taste of his favourite meal. Henry frowned and the question they were all waiting for

"What's a Clanger?" He said mystified.

Jason gave a little grin. "You'll see son."

While they ate in comfort of the kitchen surrounds Jason in between his eating, slowly explained what today had been all about. Henry tucked into his Roly-Poly with relish, he found chopped beef one end, and blackberry jam the other. Another country surprise!

"I just want you all to know that the late Brother's Gunn have named me as sole beneficiary to their will." Silence reigned at the table.

"Is that all?" Henry said with a sudden show of ill humour.

"Now then Henry, mind your manners," his mum interrupted, you've been included in the will, so show some sort of respect."

"Sorry mum, I thought today was about the farm or something,"

That was what Jason admired about Mary, her understanding of the moment when he was about to become the old philanthropist to the household.

"Tomorrow," he announced, "I'll be taking your mother and myself to see my solicitor Roy Connaught at Leighton. What happened today means I will alter and change my affairs accordingly, as regards to the farm and land and monies that have now come to this establishment, I shall discuss the matter with Dotty before we leave for Leighton."

Nobody gleaned much from the conversation round the

table. It seemed Jason liked to carry his cards close to his chest for the moment, tomorrow was another day. At least they knew that their future was safe, albeit for the duration of the war.

The Rover Saloon driven by Jason reversed out of the hovel and parked outside the kitchen door. Gyp sat beneath her trail line, ears twitched spasmodically as Dotty came cycling into the yard. Gyp rose and wagged her tail as if to say, perhaps–now- I'll-be-released. No such thing, in fact for her, so she barked and whimpered a bit. "Quiet Gyp!" Jason's voice carried out of the kitchen and she settled once again.

"Mornin' all, or is it?" Dotty slipped off her coat and looped it over the hook on the kitchen door. "Where be you two off to then?" she rolled up her cotton bloused-sleeves ready to do battle with the day's tasks.

She sniffed and remained dignified. "Half a mo., "Jason cut in, "Yesterday, was a significant day for me and Mary, and the farm in general."

"Oh, that's why everybody was shoved up the swanee, then?"

"No that's not fair, Dotty, as from today, the Manor, such as it is, and property and land in the neighbouring county have been left to me in the Gunn's will, that's why Mary and I are visiting the solicitor in Leighton this morning to arrange things in order to progress changes over the next few months. Meanwhile, you will carry on with your duties and hold the fort until Aunt Lillian arrives, who will no doubt furnish you with a bit more news."

Dotty watched through the kitchen window as Alec and the land girls were off across Sweetacre with their hoes swinging on their shoulders, Alec leading the cob to harness to the land hoe, the girls alternating with one another, to lead and scuff through the rows of manglewuzels in Ten acres.

"She thought I don't want change to things."

***

Roy Connaught ushered Jason and Mary into a smartly furnished office, conveniently situated in the high street.

"Good to meet you." He said in a sharp manner. Jason introduced Mary.

"Nice to meet you. The weather's pleasant for the time of year." He said. "In fact it was extremely warm for September, and Mary threw her coat off as the secretary made her entrance just in time to catch and hang it on the coat-standby the door." Thank you." she said

He gesticulated with his right hand, "Take a pew. Tea for you both?"

The secretary departed with orders for three teas.

"Now then Jason, what can R. Connaught do for you?"

His elbows rested on the desk, his hands were clasped in front, greying at the temples, Connaught had known Jason from their school days, but he being a bright academic who went on to college at Bedford, and a short but acrimonious stay at Cambridge University something about tipping a tutor into the river Cam after a prank went horribly wrong, the story being hushed up.

The secretary returned with the Beveridge and set it down. Connaught waved her away.

"I will call if I need you"

After she left Jason pulled out the file he was carrying from beneath his jacket. "Can you read through these first, then you can say what you think, or what might be our next move should be?"

Roy Connaught reached for the file and opened it and as he flipped, each foolscap over Jason knew by his reaction that he saw the paragraph with five thousand pounds inserted. His eyebrows raised and he smoothed what bit of hair he had. He gave a low sharp whistle.

"Well. I will have to study them some more before a recommendation. It's impressive, you have landed on your feet here Jason, I must say."

Mary had her own reservations about Mr Connaught, but there again; he was Jason's selected representative, so nothing mattered. Only when everything was sorted and signed would she be happy and settled.

CHAPTER TWENTY-ONE

BAD NEWS

Jason drove home from Leighton with the knowledge that R. Connaught would administer his affairs with alacrity, and care and consideration. With goodwill and fortune and a victorious ending to the war. Jason and Mary could prosper as long as he managed his land and affairs on a strict but fair to all his employees basis.

Although Connaught administered his legal paper, he still needed someone to deal with his invoices, tax returns and other money matters that arose from then on.

As he slowed and steered the Rover Saloon into the yard, the local Bobby P.C.Benson stood with his cycle in front of the kitchen door.

"I yup, what now?" Jason mumbled to himself.

"What does he want?" Mary said Jason pulled up, allowing Mary to get out of the car. Jason parked the Saloon under the hovel

"Hi there Jason, bad news I'm afraid."

"What's the matter, Benson?"

"Well it's not been confirmed as of yet, still waiting vet's report." "Spit it out man"

"Foot and mouth over at Bunkers Hall."

"Ah, Hockliffe, Christ, that's all we need." "I have had my orders for you just as a precaution. Close all gates, no movement of cattle. Disinfectant in a tub-wash at the main gate to be maintained everyday till further notice." " Hmm, that all?"

"You'll be notified by war-ag as soon as possible. Good day to yer. I'll close the main gate as I go."

Jason slumped in to the chair by the kitchen range, slid off his shoes and moved to the sink where he gazed out over Sweetacre and washed his hands. Mary wanted to know more what it meant for the farm, this was all alien to her, and it was serious.

"It means, dearie we all abide by the rules." Said Jason. Dotty was crimping the edges to a pastry rabbit pie-dish ready to be cooked in the range." There," she said "Tonight's dinner dun-an-dusted." She slid the dish into the side oven for Mary to cook later. She wiped her hands on her apron, and composed herself for her next task.

Jason sat rubbing his chin stubble. "It also means we cannot do anything much around the farm, the cattle will be restricted to the Dutch barn and monitored day and night. I'll get Alec and the girls to collect the pigs and bring them home before the restrictions set in tomorrow." Jason straddled his cycle and peddled off towards Ten Acre to warn them what to expect of the impending disease

When Jason, Alec and the girls trudged back to the farm, the first thing Jason actioned was to sling a rope across the main gate with a warning sign of foot and mouth.

"ALL PERSONS MUST DIP FOOTWEAR IN THE TUB-WASH BEFORE ENTERING FARM; KEEP GATE CLOSED.

As Benson had remarked, war-ag signs would later be distributed covering a full fifteen-mile radius of the infected farm. Laura and Jenny washed their hands and relished their mugs of tea, followed by Jason with Alec in tow.

"Right." Jason said after tea-break, Alec and you two

hitch up the trailer to the GM tractor and collect the pigs from the rented sties." That's one piece of property I either could buy or get rid of; I'll think about that one, he thought to himself.

The GM tractor driven by Laura with Alec and Jenny sitting in the trailer chugged off to Standbridge Road, while Jason installed a soaked layer of straw coupled with Jeyes disinfectant tub-wash, plus a stiff brush at the main gate for persons to use entering or leaving.

Jason rounded up the herd of Friesians, inspecting each one as they walked unhurriedly to the milking sheds. He would later inspect them more thoroughly in their stalls, and anticipate a call from the vetenary practice.

Henry ran from the bus stop hell for leather with a sealed envelope wavering in his hand. He stopped abruptly at the main gate. Laura, Jenny, and Alec were driving the two sows and carrying their litters in the trailer coming in the opposite direction, with Gyp giving out a warning yelp.

"What's going on?" Asked Henry.

"Can't you read boy, it says what it says, you gotta wash your boots afor yer go in the farm."

They all laughed. Alec jumped off the trailer. "Foot and mouth, Henry, bad day for the farm, disease over Hockliffe, so they say. C'mon, wash your shoes, that's what it says." the girls giggled.

Henry had never heard of foot and mouth. He wanted to know more. He slid his now very wet shoes off outside the kitchen door. The aroma of rabbit pie sent his taste buds racing. "Cor mum, what's for dinner?"

"Dotty cooked us a pastry rabbit pie, Alec snared three the other day so it's thanks to him." Henry enjoyed country bum-kin dinners, that's what he called them.

"What's the letter about son?" his mum was losing a bit

of patients.

"Oh, one of my tutors has given me an introductory note to a firm of architects at Leighton." He opened the letter to reveal the name of his soon- to -be –employer, albeit for work experience of four hours a week." I can start whenever."

"Well, I think that's very thoughtful of the Tech to further your education."

"By the way, you don't seem to be doing much on the hobby of yours lately, fell out of love with it?"

Henry had to admit he had neglected his art work of late, but there was so much going on, what with the war, the farm, and Madge and her Tennis Club, he couldn't find the hours to fit it all in. Jason sat wearily down to the evening meal and gave thanks to god, but why had he let us down with foot and mouth?

"Is it serious?" Henry enquired," How can you tell if the animals have the disease?"

"It's an infection of a viral nature for sheep, cows, and hoofed animals. They develop running noses and worst of all; they'll all have to be put down and burnt on a pyre."

For the next few days the farm became static, the only real movement was for the cows to be milked morning and evening. Jason greeted vet Tony Freeman at the main gate with an unwillingness of a man about to lose his prized herd of Friesians. The vet shook hands after washing his boots.

"Rotten business." He said. He treated his profession with the utmost care and attention, knowing that at any time Jason's whole input of man-hours and devotion to the wellbeing of his animals could be lost forever. A lifetime could vanish overnight, but the vet assured him that all was not lost until the lab reports were conclusive, or not.

"Let's look on the bright side, eh?" he began with

inspecting the pigs and their litters, going about his work in a professional manner. The cows were next. He inspected their nostrils and then he surprised Henry who followed his every move, he stuck what looked like a thermometer up one of the cows bum.

"Oh crikey!" Henry couldn't contain his emotions any longer.

"Do you like doing what you're doing?"

"Of course, it's my duty." Tony Freeman retrieved a sample of blood from the next of the best giver of milk.

Jason's nerves were on edge. If there were any positive comeback it might as well be from the best, of his milking herd, it would cushion the blow if the rest of the stock had to be slaughtered. Jason bade Freeman a farewell as he drove the Hillman pickup through the cordon and said he would be in touch.

Jason took time out with Alec and the girls. He slipped his cap, scratched his head, and said, "Well. We might as well start gathering a few plums, we can't do much else; get the sack barrow Henry, and stack the boxes in the orchard, Henry loved this time of the year, there were two Victoria plum trees, one dessert Green –gage, a Denniston –tree and a lone solitary pear, Doyenne-du-comice, and six prune trees, super for making jam. In the garden, plot a row of large over ripe Gooseberry bushes needed picking. Henry shied away from these; he thought no, the girls can pick this prickly soft fruit. Sometimes, as he and Jason rambled through the orchard, he would point out the various names of each fruit tree, a legacy left over from his parents whose vision and foresight was invaluable.

Mary, Dotty, and Aunt Lillian were overwhelmed with amount of fruit to be preserved. Beetroot, pickled Shallots, Onions to string, Gooseberry, Plum, Blackberry, all in to jam, oh, and Rhubarb for crumble pie. So next, Henry was sent to Sweetacre to shake down as many Crab Apples as he could muster. His mates from High House whooped with joy when told by Gertrude they could help with the harvest of all the fruit, though Jason had mixed feelings due to the crisis that had hit the farm. He relented, so long as they abided by the rules and dipped their shoes in the tub-wash.

Sometimes their exuberance got the better of them as they ran amok among the buildings. There was so much to explore, so Jason thought up a plan to stop their little gallop. The wood that Lally chopped still lay in a big pile outside. These needed to be stacked under the shed, which acted as the wood store for the winter months to come. So, with sleeves rolled up they set about the task Jason had instructed them to perform. Jason was surprised as, by the time milking was finished so the boys were stacking the last remaining logs. He was well pleased with their effort so much; he paid them in kind with a new Florin, which the boys duly raced off on their cycles straight to Ma Leeche's shop to buy liquorice sherbet dabs.

Aunt Lillian, the land girls, and Alec had all departed earlier. Jason Mary and Henry found time to sit together at the oak table to enjoy a plate of fried egg and spam fritters each, though this food was considered to be of low esteem; it still tasted rather appealing, well to Henry's way of thinking. "It's fit for a king to eat." He said.

"Yes I wonder what the King and Queen are sitting down to tonight," Jason said

"I wonder." Mary interposed.

The phone rang as the grandfather clock struck 6.30 pm. Jason lifted the receiver.

"Ullo, Ullo, Ah Freeman. He listened intently to every word.

"So it was a false alarm, then, thank god for that. So restrictions will be lifted after P.C.Benson has called at the farm tomorrow. Right and thank you, goodnight to you."

Mary and Henry assumed that the message was good news, that the farm's ability to over- come the crisis pleased Jason. He could now concentrate on releasing his energy to the more demanding situation he faced with his newfound wealth. On Sunday morning, a mild grey mist surrounded the farm buildings, in between the patchy cloud. A few last stragglers from an overnight raid somewhere deep in Germany were droning their way back to base; at least they were safe now. Jason and Alec glanced skywards. "Poor sods," Alec said,

"Yeah, well let's hope a good breakfast awaits them." Jason reiterated.

They crunched their way across the yard, milking completed, and six churns awaited to be siphoned off by the Milk Marketing Board tanker. Both were ready for their breakfast, they caught the aroma of frying sausages and tomatoes, and fried bread.

"Just what the doctor ordered."

Jason pulled off his milking cap as Mary was serving the plate. He kissed her on the neck; she shrugged him off and smiled. "That'll be desserts!" he squeezed her waist and finally sat down and ate heartily. Gyp on her trail line barked loudly.

"I yup, somebody's about." Jason pushed his chair noisily back from the table and opened the kitchen door. Sure enough, it was P.C. Benson.

"Morning, Jason, got some good news for you."

"Yes I know, Freeman rang last night, but insisted you execute the order about lifting the ban on livestock."

"That's right." Benson handed Jason a letter, headed

from the Agriculture Ministry.

"Do you know what the scare was about?" Jason queried.

"Well, if the story is anything to go on, one of the Bunker Hall's cows ate some old ash tree seed. It proved fatal. How she found them is a mystery. Still, it's better this way, losing one cow rather than a herd, aye. You can remove your wash-tub and resume normal duties." With that said, he donned his helmet and rode off.

CHAPTER TWENTY TWO

A FRUGAL CHRISTMAS

Henry adjusted his tie, he was about to knock when he noticed an old-fashioned bell-pull. The offices were situated in the town square underneath a long row of maisonettes, a more sedate part of town. A smartly dressed woman of fiftyish opened the door, and greeted Henry with a smile and bade him enter. She enquired his name.

"Henry Kneally, Mam, I do have an appointment."

"Yes, we were expecting you." She directed Henry into a small office.

The walls were bare other than a photograph of a building that summarised their work. Two filing cabinets stood together just inside the door, a homemade planner hung on the wall behind a small desk, presumably for that person's needs.

Henry sat by the window, which looked out onto the rear garden. The lawn was neatly trimmed, as was the Laurel hedge, everything was tidy. A short-cropped haired man entered and greeted him with a handshake.

"I understand you're an evacuee and you live at Claridge farm Eggington?"

"That's right, with Jason Smith and my mother."

"Ah, I know the place I've passed that way on numerous occasions."

Henry scrutinised the man. His hair was greying at the

temples, his face had a few freckles, and he wore a copper band on his right wrist. A super gold watch adorned his left wrist. Henry estimated him to be in his fifties.

"Your name is Henry Kneally that right?" he sat down proffered his hand again, and said, "I'm Percy, Mr Wallis to you. The head of Luton Tech sent a letter, says here, "very bright student," Glad to hear that my boy."

He went on about the status of the building. Ground floor is planning and drawing office, first floor is where we model some of our structures to scale, the basement is for general office, and the room at the far end of the corridor is the boardroom. The woman brought in a tray, two cups and a pot of tea and two biscuits.

In all, Henry was introduced to five people; Mr Dillimore, a droopy-eyed elderly man who smoked shag in a calabash pipe. Two architects on the verge of retiring, and Miss Lacey, the PA. cum secretary whom he'd met at the front door. Mr Wallis went on, "as you can see, we are in need of youth who we can rely upon."

"So, what will my duties be?"

Mr Wallis shifted uneasily in his chair, and gave Henry a quizzical look.

"Well may I call you Henry?" Henry nodded "How forward are you with your studies at the Tech? It reads in the report that you are well advanced in technical drawing, and very good at drawing to scale. Hmm, just what we need of course. Two days a week are required of you, if you can manage the travelling, I know how awkward it can be, and if you are prepared to stay with us for any length of time, you will be articled and your credentials authorised by the firm."

"So what will my duties be?" Henry acutely aware he'd asked the question earlier felt a blush come on.

"As for your first job, well, have you come across

209

cellulose acetate, yet at the Tech?" Henry frowned a bit at the question.

"Ah, I thought not, never mind, we'll teach you how to trace and copy and file." He went on." At the moment, in fact, we are in the process of refurbishing the Old Rectory at Eggington for the County Council, do you know of the building?"

"I do know the council will be rehoming elderly people from across South Beds there, it's going to be used as a nursing home, so Jason told his employees; he sits on the parish council, sometimes he lets things slip." Oh does he! I know Jason from way back." Henry felt more at ease that Wallis knew Jason. Everything was coming together; the more he got to know people, the more it seems they knew one another, a very tight knit community.

The meeting over, he ran to the top of the High Street where Jason sat waiting in the Rover his mum beside him. He slid into the back seat.

"Well, how did you get on?" his mum enquired.

On the way home he explained about the people in the office, how they treated him and how he would benefit from the experience of working for Dillimore and Wallis; it felt right for him, and he got on very well with Wallis. Jason and Mary listened to his explanation and reason for wanting to join the firm. In their minds, they would not stand in his way, but to encourage and inspire him, to spur him on to greater aspirations. Henry relaxed on the leather seats of the Saloon, the smoothness of the leather he could feel with his sweaty hands.

"Enough of me, what have you two been up to?"

"Yer mum's bin spending my money, that's what. I'm only joking."

"We've been doing some Christmas shopping!" Henry

had to jolt his mum's memory, or else the single gift would almost certainly be called a combined present; he would get two cards though.

"Will the farm be hosting a party at Christmas?" Henry shifted to the edge of the seat as they approached the farm, Gyp as usual all excited at seeing the car turn into the yard. She yapped at their homecoming.

Jason lifted the boot of the car to reveal all sorts of items. "C'mon Henry, help your mother," They had shopped in Woolworths, the Co-Op, Rush & Warwick's stationers, and Jason visited the barbers for his third and final haircut of the year. Henry carried in four carrier bags while his mum carried a flat brown paper parcel tucked underneath her arm, and two carrier bags. Henry inquisitive as ever, wanted to know just what everybody was carrying. Henry knew then, what killed the cat.

It was noticeable that more and more American convoys were passing through the village, and many jeeps would pull into the yard much to the annoyance of Gyp. There were always the same question, "Where are we? And could we fill our containers with water please, Mam?" always very courteous. Henry thought the Americans were top guys because of the water, you got a handful of dimes and dollars, and packets of chewing gum, and cookies and one gave Aunt Lillian a Wampum. "What is it?" she asked, "What's it for?" the G.I. whose grandparents belonged to a North American tribe told her the pearl shells were woven into a gold and mauve fabric, a decoration they hung in their wigwam. "It's beautiful, she declared, I couldn't possibly accept." But he insisted. "I'll be very miserable if you don't, mam" she received it gracefully, and said, "I will fasten it above my fireplace and think of you boys wherever you may be," Mary kissed Aunt Lillian and waved as the Americans took their leave.

Jason drove the tractor into the yard with Alec, Laura, and Jenny in the trailer gasping for a mug of tea.

"What did they want?" Jason enquired.

"Water, but c'mon in." Mary had laid goodies on the oak table.

"Chewing gum and cookies." He mumbled.

Mary clasped his hands and counted out Ten, Dollar Bills." Uhh, what good are they to me?" Aunt Lillian calculated the sum "Well if you don't want them, I'll have them, they are worth at least four pounds in English money." To Aunt Lillian's surprise, Jason said, "have 'em, only share them between the staff, I think that's fair, any over can subsidise the farm's water rates."

The girls and Alec pulled up their chairs to the oak table warming their hands round the mugs of tea, giving them an inner glow feeling. They all sat admiring the Wampum. Who would be the first to ask what on earth is it! But before anyone could even say anything Aunt Lillian explained that it was a Native American trophy, an ornament which they all wished had been given to themselves. Aunt Lillian knew in her heart that the trophy belonged to the farm, so she placed it above the range for all to see and remember the Americans.

The weather turned from mild conditions to cold and dry, with overnight frost. Henry shivered as he went to bed; it's just three weeks to Christmas, he thought, nobody had said anything about who would be sitting down to dinner that day. He stared through the little window at the now white frosting fields. The slates on the out buildings shone, reflecting a bright moonlit night; he shivered again and slipped between the flannelette sheets, his feet embracing the woollen covered hot water bottle. Outside, the night sky belonged to Bomber Command flying out to a target whose unsuspecting souls would either die or have their life impaired. Who do you sympathize with most, them, or the boys in the aircraft? He slept until dawn, was awakened by Jason, and mum who by now was so well prepared, her presence being accepted by everyone who knew her. Jason depended on her loyalty and her consistency to the running of the kitchen, and the wellbeing of every animal he reared.

Mum was a prerequisite in Jason's eyes; without a woman, the farm could be a desolate place, but this was Jason's Place, and he would prescience any form of improving the herd or the farm in general. True, the war did not help, but after it was over, what then? He tried to project his mind forward. People needed feeding. He thought of soft fruit. If he purchased the land, he rented which the pigsties were on, there was enough acreage to grow more vegetables, and such like. Still, that was in the future. He slipped off the last suction tube from the Daisy, a good enough cow who supplied an average amount of milk. Studying the chart in the dairy, he said, "Yes" she had yielded a few gallons more than the others had. It was encouraging to note that milk production rose, especially as winter was setting in. the girls and Mary were sitting at the oak table when Jason and Alec slid their boots off and entered the kitchen. Henry thought this was a good time to broach the subject of who would be sitting down to Christmas dinner. As each sipped their beverage, Henry placed the brass candleholders on to the table just to remind people.

"Okay, Henry you've made your point," Jason quipped. The girls gave a questionable grin as they tried to follow Jason's train of thought. "He wants to know who's coming on Christmas day?" he said.

"I presume you girls get leave at Christmas?"

Jenny said yes, she would go home, but Laura said she

had nothing to go home for.

"Then you must spend Christmas with us, that's an order." Jenny would have company of four other girls going home; she wouldn't be travelling entirely on her own, which would take all day.

"So Laura, does the hostel close down?" Mary asked "You can stay here, there's a spare room next to Henty's little room," Mary loved the idea, she would have somebody to confide in, be it little worries or just simple things, and besides, laughter was in short supply at the time the house needed companionship.

Alec, Dotty, and Aunt Lillian would join the sit down. "So the company is complete, happy now Henry?" Mary beamed.

Henry used to love Christmas in London before the war, his class mates would come round to show off their presents, he likewise, then maybe invited to tea. He loved the lights and the bustle of six wheeled trolleybuses, the taxi cabs honking their horns, the shops illuminating their windows displays and reflecting out on to the pavements, you could smell Christmas coming, as he was about to find out very soon, when Dotty began to steam the ingredients for the pudding. Last Christmas had passed by all too quickly, but he reckoned he had conquered all his fears; in fact, he almost had that feeling of being a villager.

During the few weeks leading up to Christmas Jason sat in his study contemplating his next move as to how he would tackle the problem about Claridge Manor. He would engage a surveyor. A thought occurred to him, he could approach Dillimore & Wallis with a letter hand delivered by Henry. He called Henry into the study and revealed his intentions.

Christmas day arrived, frosty but clear; Jason and Alec were finishing the mornings milking. Henry made his way down the wide stairway. Cold air and the aroma of breakfast and steaming Christmas pudding wafted along the corridor.

"Hmm, that smells good mum." She was moving pots around on the range as Dotty and Aunt Lillian arrived to give her an extra hand.

"Anything I can do?" Henry said, trying to be a good soul on this special day.

"Yeah," Dotty said. "Get the hand cart and bring in a load of logs for the lounge fire, it needs to be warm."

Henry was crossing the yard with the load when Laura arrived. She had cadged a lift with the Milk Marketing Board tanker. "I knew if I were ready in time I could save the walk." She called to Henry. All she carried was a brown leather suitcase.

"Do you want any help?" Henry said.

"If you don't' mind" after all the salutations were over he showed her to her room.

"It's been a time since I climbed house stairs," she said. Henry was puzzled, he asked why.

"My parents lived on a barge on the Liverpool and Manchester canal but they've since passed on" "Oh sorry to hear that."

"Don't feel sorry, Henry, they were never really close, though I was the only child."

Henry was surprised to hear her story. Laura to him was a warm loving person, he felt sympathetic towards her.

"What are your aims in life?" she asked, if it's not farming for you?"

"If I knew, I would tell you. Up to now, I am being taught the basics in architecture."

"How's that coming along?"

"Well to be honest, I'm in two minds."

"Does your mum know?"

"I have spoken about it to them both, they say I should wait and see how I feel in a year's time."

"You shouldn't give up," she said, "I think you have a bright future ahead of you." They walked down the wide staircase together.

The old decorations adorned the lounge giving a feel of pleasure and satisfaction. Dinner would be served in the lounge, as this was a customary event at Claridge farm. Jason had never altered this long established habit. Outside the animals were fed and watered; the hens were kept in for the day and had plenty of feed. The eggs would be collected early on Boxing Day morning. Jason and Alec would turn out at teatime to milk the cows, and bed down and feed the pigs.

The cob was stabled with new straw, Christmas dinner would be served at one o'clock, no later. Dotty carried in the cockerel that had been seriously fattened in a cage on his own; he weighed in at twelve pounds, enough for any large family. Laura entered wearing a figure hugging red sweater and black skirt, and flat black brogues. She looked a million dollar. Jason drew breath, Alec clapped. Mary admired Laura for being herself. Just what I would have worn if I had been her age, she thought. All eyes were on Laura. Aunt Lillian congratulated her for being lovely and having sensible judgement, only Dotty gave a hint of being a bit envious. "Fine hussy you've turned out to be."

"C'mon Dotty, don't spoil the day, she's all what we need, give youth a chance." Alec blurted out, losing his green glass eye in the process. It rolled along the table only to lodge under Dotty's plate.

"Well I never," she said, her feelings showing to be indignant. Henry was surprised as anyone that Alec had only one eye. They pulled homemade crackers and wore silly hats; Christmas in wartime wasn't so bad after all.

"Think of all the soldiers and what they are going through," Jason said the toast was made to them, with Dotty's homemade Dandelion and Burdock wine. Jason flicked on the radio for the Royal Speech, but the home service was reporting rumours Dwight D Eisenhower would become Supreme Allied Commander over the British forces.

"Not Monty then." Alec said in dismay.

"Let's toast whoever gets the job and good luck to him." Jason raised his glass and they all clinked together.

CHAPTER TWENTY THREE

CHANGES

Jason was determined to bring changes to Claridge Farm come what may. He had the resources of unforeseen wealth at his fingertips. His awareness of restrictions and controls only made his determination to forge ahead with restoring Claridge Manor sooner rather than later. The insurance would cover the restauration, and Henry's position at Dillimore &Wallis proved to be the link. He would invite Henry to be more involved with the project. There were times when he would have chucked farming in altogether, especially after Kathy died. He was glad that common sense prevailed, and gradually the farm and ideas would come to fruition.

Midnight Mass at the village church was well attended, the Christian faith defended at all times, his belief unwavering. Reverend Stefan would call in on his way home, no doubt remembering the last time he called in, and the consequences that followed, a repertition he could do without. He was mindful of Dotty's Elderberry wine; one sup and he would be on his way. Gyp had made certain of his getaway into the night, but four hours later the Reverend was found yet again in the ditch, this time, with more sinister overtones. Deep lacerations were found all over his head; the blood had dried and caked his eyes shut. He'd suffered a mild concussion due to the cycle plunging to the bottom of the ditch. Unbalanced, he'd flown over the handlebars and hit his head. The doctor examined his neck for whiplash but nothing was broken. "How come you ended up in the ditch, Reverend?" he asked.

"Well it's not the liquid, I saw the ghost."

"The ghost?" a Barn Owl, more likely, these are bird claw talon scratches, if I'm not mistaken. "I can see the headlines now, Bird Attacks a Defenceless Vicar."

"Thank you, doctor. I'm glad you can see the funny side of my demise."

The very Reverend ventured into Leighton High Street, without his usual Homburg hat, but instead a bandaged head that resembled a beehive. Curious glances were directed and little nods of a sympathetic nature ensued.

***

Jason wrote with a steady but slow hand, he very rarely put pen to paper; he would give the letter to Henry to pass on to Mr Wallis, of Dillimore & Wallis when next he attended.

Would he, Mr Wallis, in all correspondence allow Henry to be go between he wanted Henry to be committed and informative. The instruction was for them to come and assess and evaluate the reconstruction of Claridge Manor and restore the building for future use; any modifications to enhance the character would be most welcome.

Henry's first day began at Dillimore & Wallis after he handed the letter, which he was entrusted with by Jason to Mr Wallis. Miss Lacey escorted him to each section of the establishment and introduced him once again to his fellow artisans. His very first job was in the tracing department; three copies each had to be traced of the Old Rectory at Eggington. He knuckled down and produced some fine work which, when inspected by the senior tracer, was faultless and he recommended this accordingly to Mr Wallis.

At break time, Miss Lacey came and sat with Henry. She wanted to know more about his life, not that she was a nosey parker, but somebody who was trying her best to make Henry more comfortable in his strange surroundings. Henry toyed with the idea that Miss Lacey was more vulnerable and emotional than he was and they gelled instantly. Henry liked Miss Lacey for her sincerity and candour, and by the time to pack up and go home, everybody had welcomed him as a bosom friend.

Henry arrived at the farm just in time to say cheerio to Aunt Lillian as she was leaving for Rose Cottage. "How was your day, then?" She called. He raised two thumbs; she could see his enthusiasm all over his face. Mary met him on the doorstep to heaps more appraisals.

"I'm starved, what's for tea mum?"

Jason popped his head in. "See you later."

A week or so into the New Year the weather turned nasty. The household awakened to a blanket of snow covering Sweetacre and all the surrounding meadows; the only thing that wasn't covered was the dung heap, which steamed profusely. Later that morning before Henry set off to Luton Tech, Laura and Jenny would have to make ready the cob, hitch him to the undersized Tumbril cart, back him up to the heap ready to load the manure bound for the Dinges, where hopefully, this year's Manglewurzels would be sown, alongside Swedes and Onions, and field Beans, the perfume of which Henry thought was exemplary. He thought about himself standing in between the rows of last year's crop, and the scent they gave off was unbelievable, but come the time when ripened, it was a different story. The Beans were harvested the same as the corn, they were really rough to the hands and arms, but to hear the beans being thrashed was something else; they made a thwacking noise against the drum in the machine and one had to shout to hear one's own voice above the din.

Henry had waited over an hour for a bus. Obviously, the weather had proved too much for them to operate, Jason came by with the new GM tractor and trailer, off to Leighton with a dozen porkers for slaughter. Prices were reasonable, even if the war had taken its toll on farming in general.

He pulled up aside of Henry, "No buses running today? Hop aboard, come with me to the Abattoir." Henry squatted his backside on the side-wing of the tractor. As they moved off the wind cut into his face.

"Cold? You'll get used to it" Jason was a battle-hardened countryman. They steeled themselves against the elements, the snow lay up to a few inches deep, and starting to drift. The tractor made easy work of the conditions.

Jason drove the tractor to the abattoir, which was situated on the edge of town, unloaded the porkers, one of which decided it would rather run around the knacker's yard for a last gasp at survival. The porker was caught by Henry having to throw the pig net with the encouragement he received by the employed staff, who clapped and cheered as Henry slipped and slithered in the snow. He regained his balance after the porker nosedived between two barrels of stored blood. Henry hadn't had so much fun since the time he tried to catch a lone hen in the meadow before locking up the arks for the night. There was something to be said about farming, you never know what's round the next corner until it happens.

Jason roared with laughter at the antics; flashback of his own youth, recalled the day his father borrowed the hay-rake and horse from the next-door neighbour's farm and instructed him to get up into the seat and work the lever, criss-crossing the cut hay into straight lines, ready to load on to the Tumbril cart. The horse had other ideas, bolted, only to end up in the Mangel-wurzel patch, flinging the beet twenty feet into the air.

Soon after, they ventured next to the cattle market in Leighton High Street, where Jason purchased a Jersey cow and six Geese, and a Gander to boot. Henry questioned the wisdom of these purchases.

"They are an investment, an addition to the livestock." Jason retorted.

Next, they called at Moorland & Tompkins Auction rooms where surplus farm implements were being sold. "What are we looking for now?" Henry interrupted.

"You'll see. I know what I'm doing, just follow, and observe."

The auctioneer called lot number thirty-two, a very well preserved copper hand cranked revolving churn for turning cream into butter. Jason's bid was accepted, the gavel thumped the block. "To Mr Smith." The auctioneer called, knowing him of old.

"C'mon Henry, it's getting late, must get home. The snow's closing in." The trailer was loaded, the geese who's necks protruded through the pig-net cackled as they moved off, and the Jersey cow expected later by licensed carrier. Jason had earned his day's work; Henry felt very elated, also very cold. His hands were numbed to the bone, his eyes watered as Jason drove the tractor and trailer, lumbering into the yard. Gyp practically stood on her two hind legs to greet them, yelping madly, Henry jumped down and ran straight into the kitchen, he stood shivering with his hands resting on his bottom against the range, his mum surprised to see him.

"I thought you were at tech?" she said

"The bus never came, Jason persuaded me to join him on

a trip to the abattoir and the auction market. You should see what he brought."

"Yes, I know of a sort, for some week now. I knew he was up to something, scouring the local paper and the ads, well, tell me?"

"A Jersey cow, six Geese and a Gander, and a Butter maker."

"A what?"

"A Butter maker, you've to crank it by hand."

"Oh yes, not mine. Dotty and the girls can do that job."

Jason removed his flat cap and stood legs apart in the doorway.

"You've told her then?" he said to Henry.

"She's not happy about the Butter maker."

"Oh dear, tut, tut. Don't worry my love. It's easy once you get the hang of the thing." Jason loved teasing Mary.

"It's alright for you, you know how it works." Mary sidled to the kitchen door to have a peep at the antiquated contraption, which she was expected to work.

"If you're worried, Dotty will show you and the girls the ropes on how to make butter. I know, she's an old hand at it, when in her earlier days she worked for old Yirrell over at Briggington."

Mary wiped her hands on her apron. "How come Dotty was able to work for you?" she asked.

"By pure coincidence. Yirrell died, his farm was sold up, Dad gave her a lift one day in the trap into Leighton; said she was looking for work, it just happened."

Laura and Jenny dropped the trailer tailboard and lifted the pig-met from over the necks of the Geese. They would not hurry them, let them find their own way down and into the yard, that's what Alec ordered. Laura herded them forward, Gyp still with her head down, her eyes following every movement of their waddle. These strange creatures with their disyllabic Gag, Gag, Gag, with every step, a sound she would become very familiar with over the coming months.

The geese found themselves in a disused pigsty. Fresh straw had been laid, the lock with a sliding bolt slammed shut by Alec.

"There you are girls. Your job now is to look after them, keep them shut in for three days, just feed with mash and water, let them get used to the sounds of the farm, then you can let them out and drive them through Sweetacre to Thedeway Brook. A stretch and a paddle, then drive them home to the yard. In time, they'll get used to their surroundings. Alec's knowledge was of great value.

A large cattle carrier came rumbling into the yard, it was swung round by its driver, who leaned out and shouted. "Where do you want her, Gov?"

Alec pointed, "Right here, mate." Alec and the girls were satisfied the geese would settle in and behave themselves; they could be noisy if they wanted too. The farm will know it when they do start their chorus.

No sooner had the geese been domiciled, another job of unloading beckoned. The driver let the large tailboard down. Inside was the prettiest Jersey cow the three of them had ever seen. Laura almost swooned, Jenny coo'ed. Alec had seen it all before.

"C'mon, no time for sentiments you girls, go on Jenny take the halter and lead her down."

"What's her name I wonder?" sighed Jenny.

No sooner had they unloaded the Jersey when Jason cycled into the yard.

"What shall we name her?" Jenny being affectionate as ever over the Jersey who gave a little murmerous moo, wondering where she was, and what sort of farm she had been transported to.

Mary and Aunt Lillian appeared at the kitchen door to see what all the fuss was about. Jason propped his cycle against the kitchen windowsill.

"There you are, a nice little earner if I'm not mistaken." He boasted.

"Oh yes, while we do the hard work turning the churn," Mary said.

"Don't worry, Dotty and the girls will make the butter; if you think you're not up to it, you Lunnoners will never learn."

Mary felt she'd let Jason down by not showing more enthusiasm over the making of butter, but Jason should understand how difficult it was to adjust to country ways if you're born outside what the culture demands of you. The transition takes a little longer to grasp.

Jason quickly realised he'd spoken down to Mary, which made her feel uncomfortable.

"Sorry, me and my big mouth." He strode over and put his arm around her and kissed her lightly on the cheek. "Sorry", he whispered gently, she gazed into his big brown eyes.

"You're forgiven," and gave him a little push, "Fool" she said.

"What name shall we give her?" Jenny shouted across the yard to Jason who turned and strode over to inspect his purchase. "What name shall we give her?" Jenny said again, becoming impatient.

"You'll think of one between you all."

Laura and Jenny's minds went blank, until Aunt Lillian called out "Aubyn"

"Why Aubyn?" they called.

"That's where my honeymoon took place on the Island of Jersey before war broke out."

"Right Aubyn it is" the two girls loved Aubyn. Mary wanted to know where all these extra animals were going to be housed as she poured out tea, for themselves.

"It's all the more work," she protested. Jason sipped his tea, sat back, and announced "I'm not finished yet, with buying livestock as you put it. I'm thinking of some thirty Turkey chicks to fatten and sell for Christmas."

"The stall is ready for the Jersey; the geese and gander we'll keep in the end sty for the time being. I shall purchase a second Ark for them later; I know where I can lay my hands on one, that's no problem. The Turkey chicks will be kept under a warm heater lamp for a few weeks, then, transferred into a long upright breeder cage."

Henry and his mum listened to Jason ramble on about how the farm would come alive over the next few months.

"You'll find you'll have to engage more staff if you continue to build up more stock." Mary expressed her concern. Jason lifted his cap and scratched his head. "I know, I know. let's hope another POW, walks into the yard. If he turns out to be like the last one I shall have no complaints love." Jason slid his mug to the end of the oak table.

"Must get on, I'm off on my cycle, shan't be long."

The snow had eased; there was just enough time to broker a deal. He rode out of the yard, with Gyp yelping as he peddled through the main gate. He knew of someone in the village who had discarded an old upright chicken cage, he'd offer him next to nothing for the cage, he'll be glad to get rid of the blessed thing.

Jason had often passed the smallholding of Matty Tibbs, and knew of his own ability when coming to an arrangement. Jason bartered a dozen eggs and a basket full of Bramley apples. They shook hands, deal done. "I'll collect tomorrow," he said. He did not say how big the basket was.

The next day the girls were excited about who should milk the Jersey. Jenny volunteered. Aubyn was very docile, but the Alpha Laval milking pipes were short of Aubyn's stall. Jason said, "Might as well milk her the old fashioned way by hand," an hour it took Jenny to milk Aubyn. Jason allowed time as none of the girls had experienced hand milking before.

"What's the first part of making butter?" Jenny enquired. "Where you let the milk stand till ready for the butter churn?"

"Good question, Jenny. Have you finished her?"

"I think so."

"We'll take the milk over to the dairy, while you find a large earthenware dish. Pour the milk in and let it cool in the darkest place you can find, let it stand until the cream settles before we skim and pour in to the butter churn, then you crank to your hearts content."

So the farm entered a new phase of producing something the villagers didn't expect, not during wartime. It would eek out the meagre rations they had all come to accept as part and parcel of everyday life. Jason knew that some of the people were on the breadline, he'd do anything to help those who were suffering, and by trying to put something, a little extra on the table meant a lot. Digging for victory had been promoted over the radio by the Government; so likewise, he'd extended his very own garden into part of the orchard and let plots out to the villagers who wanted one. This proved very lucrative, and in many ways to Mary of more company. She got to know quite a few of the inhabitants and wouldn't have done otherwise.

Dotty waddled over to the dairy just to make sure that Jenny had left the milk in a state of calm; timing to perfection was the key for making butter.

The war effort was going well. The farm was producing as much as Jason could manage. To necessitate any further production meant he would almost certainly need another hand. Where could he find one? He thought. Everyone else was doing their bit; at least Dillimore and Wallis had kept their word and duly arrived to survey Claridge Manor.

Jason shook hands with Percy Wallis and his associate, and escorted them through the yard to the Manor. Months of cruel weather had left leaves, bits of branches, dust, and an accumulative assortment of bric-a-brac that had been blown around from winter storms. The manor appeared to be in a sorry state. Wallis spoke of the Gunns briefly, but stopped short of any discussion about their untimely death.

"Where shall we start?" he muttered. "Do you want the Manor to be restored to its original state, or do you want simply a tidying up job?" Jason had already thought about that question he knew would surely be asked.

"To be honest, I think it should be restored to its original state, I'd like that. I know there are shortages, but I'm sure you'll think of something on how the Manor can be improved without changing too much. I know one thing that must be done, that is connection to the main drains." He left Wallis and his assistant to get to their work.

"I'll be in my study if you need me, some invoices need my attention."

Percy Wallis endeavoured to achieve a scale drawing and a set of figures that would satisfy Jason and Mary. He knew also of a derelict building that housed some oak beams and rafters, which Jason could purchase at a reasonable price to replace the charred remains of Claridge Manor.

CHAPTER TWENTY FOUR

NO RESPITE

Jason's figures did not add up. "Mary," he called, "Is Aunt Lillian here yet?"

"She's just walked into the yard!" Mary called from the kitchen, still washing the remains of the eggs that were collected this morning. Two Geese eggs were found, which caused a surprise for everyone. Jason met Aunt Lillian in the kitchen. "You're the lady I'm looking for."

He smiled at Henry's Aunt, the smile that says, help me!

"What do I owe you for now?" she slipped off her coat and looped it on the peg behind the kitchen door.

"I'd like you to come to the study, I've come to the conclusion I need someone who I can rely on to re-organize my documents, you know, like office work. You're good at sums, cos mine don't add up. If you could spend some time in here each week, would you?"

Aunt Lillian glanced around the study; she'd never been inside the study.

"First thoughts?" he said

"When do I start?"

"Right now. He fiddled with some letters and invoices. Here, look at these, I don't know how I've coped before, it's a mess."

"Where's you in-tray?"

"My what?"

"In-tray, you start with the in-tray. When you have completed that transaction, it goes into the file-tray, there to the right of the desk. Where's your filing cabinet?"

"Err, I dunno. Look, just write a list of whatever is applicable to an office, let me know, and I'll drive to the stationers at Leighton and order whatever you want."

Aunt Lillian wrote a list and presented it to Jason. The list comprised of three wire trays, paper clips, and a three-draw filing cabinet complete with folders, a diary, blotting pad, some blank notes, and a decent pen. He scanned the list.

"Three wire trays?" he said to himself. Lillian read his lips.

"Yes. One in-tray, one pending, and one for file."

"Right, I'll get on this straight away,"

Aunt Lillian returned to the study and made a start on the collection of letters, invoices, and whatever needed to be questioned. She was very methodical in the way she worked; sifting through the paperwork, she collated a neat pile in alphabetical order. She came across an envelope unopened, ran the opener along the top of the envelope, and opened it to reveal a letter from Mr Hogg of Royal Ancient Liverpool. She read the letter to Mary in the kitchen. Its message revealed the non-sale of the paintings by the Gunn's, which were still stored in the small loft above the outhouse. "Perhaps he's waiting for the monies to be arranged into trust for Henry." Lillian pondered.

"That's not like Jason to forget something as important as this," Mary uttered, frowning. "Before he returns with the office requisitions I'll slip it in my pocket."

Aunt Lillian retreated to the study and waited patiently for Jason and his purchases. She thought also of it being strange, he chose to leave it unopened, there must be an explanation!"

Jason had bought everything Aunt Lillian requested, and unloaded the Saloon with the help of the girls. In no time, at all they had the study shipshape for office duties. Afterwards, they all sat around the oak table waiting for afternoon tea break.

"I'll chivvie Henry to devise a wall planner showing which fields are planted, laying fallow, and yes, I can for the future. You lot, I shall be giving work related duties from the office starting from tomorrow." Jason said proudly.

Next morning he couldn't wait to use the reformed study. "My own office," he sat proud.

Installed in his green leather chair. Aunt Lillian had arranged and displayed the contents on and above the desktop for his attention; six opened invoices and two letters lay in the in-tray, one opened letter in pending, and none for filing. He leaned forward, retrieved the letter from the pending tray, and opened the letter. He had guessed right, it was from Hogg. The day it arrived his instinct told him the letter could be from him. The paintings would revive old memories of that fateful day he'd tried to erase out of mind and sight, but he and Mary were planning to live in the Manor. Well. The sooner he could arrange the sale, the better. He'd ring Roy Connaught, let him deal with it, that's right, he thought.

With breakfast over Henry was off to Dillimore and Wallis with Jason's request to sneak home a roll of squared drawing paper to install his planner, an innovation to catapult the farm into a forward mode of producing. Jason was proud of his achievement; the team filed into the study where Jason told them of his ambitions to lift the farm to greater production, and if they had any ideas, to come forward and say what they had to say.

Alec belonged to an older generation and bleated on and

on that, it wouldn't work. "Too much talk and not enough doing." He said.

"But that's what it's about, Alec, don't you see? We are living a day-to-day existence. We need to change, we need to change, we are a diverse farm, a mixture of arable and dairy."

"What about a field of sunflowers?" Laura quipped.

"What about a herd of Beef cattle? Alec often had dreams of this.

"Jenny?" Jason said.

"Oh I'm happy with Aubyn the Jersey." They all laughed.

"Good lad," Jason said as Henry unfolded the roll of squared paper on to the oak table, unconcerned as to how Henry had procured the graph paper for him.

"I hope you're not going to be too long on there?" Mary said

"Shush, woman, can't you see this is important?"

"Well where do you want me to lay dinner then?" she said indignantly.

"Give us ten minutes; I want to explain to your son my plan to give this farm what it deserves, a better way of managing. I'll show Henry how and what to do, he can lay the drawing paper out in the study after, and create rotation cropping, which fields are expected to grow different crops, and so on."

"Then I can serve dinner?" she said, sounding more impatient.

"Yeh, you may, so what have you prepared today? Smells good though, eh Henry."

"I've cooked minced meat from the weekend joint, so you'll be eating cottage pie, does that liven up your taste buds?" Jason nudged Henry.

Mary was proud also of having to cope with rationing.

Nobody gave her a planner or much of a thought, she had to carry on as thought they were living in the land of plenty. The worry of the next meal always challenged her to the extreme, but she carried on regardless, and Jason knew and respected that times were tough on everybody; he was trying his damnedest to alleviate any pain or suffering of the mind and soul. Then Jason made a shock announcement.

"Tomorrow, we'll kill a pig!" that shook them both.

Mary felt quite sick. "Don't worry," Jason, added, "We kill, hang, bleed, cure, in that order. I'll show you how it's done. We get the Burco boiling, lay the pig in the bath, and use a stiff brush and scrub all of its hair off until it's smooth. Then we'll tie its feet together and hoist it over a beam, slit it's throat, and bleed the animal. I'll show you how to trim and cut and cure for bacon." Mary shuddered at the very thought. Henry was gradually coming to terms with country habits and customs. The team were taught all about the killing of the pig. The girls were apprehensive. Alec and Dotty had seen it all before, no remorse there then. Mary wanted to hide. Henry as brave as ever, filled the Burco for boiling. Aunt Lillian would wait as long as she could before venturing out to the farm; in fact, she'd ring Mary to say she felt a bit under the weather and not go in today.

"I don't blame you, Aunty." Mary replaced the phone and retreated upstairs, leaving Dotty to wash and prepare for break time and dinner tonight.

The gunshot reverberated all over the farm. A deathly silence ensued, not one animal made any sort of noise. Strange how animals react to the sudden impact of a shot, instinctively they sense a knowing of death. It took a full ten minutes before the Cockerel began crowing, a sign for others to resume normal continuance. The Burco boiler had reached its temperature, and the girls acted accordingly, pouring the water into the bath. The pig was carried by Jason and Alec who gently slipped the porker into the hot water.

"Right, let the sow soak for a while, and later we'll start to rub the hairs off with a scuffing brush." Jason said

They took time out in the kitchen. Dotty having prepared five steaming mugs of milk cocoa, which went down well with the girls. Mary plucked up courage to join them.

"C'mon, love, it's all over bar the bleeding." Jason loved to create an atmosphere of human clumsiness.

She sat down with the others. "Would the pig have suffered?" she said mutedly.

Jason held her hand. "Why don't you come with us now and see for yourself how the pig is having her bath." They all laughed. How thoughtless, she thought.

Jason and Alec turned the pig over to start the rubbing down procedure.

"You can all take turns in the curing process, Alec will supervise." Jason clutched Mary's waist as Alec began to scuff at the hairs. They fell away quite easily and in no time at all the pig was smooth white. The next job for the team was to slide four poles under the bath and roll it to where the pig would be hoisted over a crossbeam. Alec tied a rope around its hind trotters so the lift terminated in the shed next to the dairy. Once in place, Jason prepared the knife and cut the pig's throat, blood drained into a churn saved for the event. The blood would be sold to the butcher to make black pudding. The pig would drain for the next twelve hours before the cutting of sections could begin.

The team dispersed to attend to their normal duties. Mary did not stay to witness the slitting of the throat; she would steel herself to come to terms with farm life. In some ways, life on the farm was pleasant and idyllic and other times it could be cruel, but that was country life. In times like these, it's a question of survival of the fittest or go under, and she aimed to stay above the waterline.

Jason and Alec assembled four large pans for curing of the hams. Each day for four weeks, somebody or whoever was free would rub salt into the hams, by utilising both of the pig's ears to rub the salt in, this way stops fingertips from getting sore. Most times, it fell to the girls, but they didn't mind, they were only thinking of the lovely bacon sandwiches they would eat at break-time.

To cure and hang hams took a great deal of time and effort.

Jason's planner as almost ready for the wall in the study. Henry suggested pencils to use on the plan for easier rubbing out for next entrants. Jason agreed, as the last day of March approached and incidentally ended like a lamb, spring beckoned and heralded more work.

The phone rang; Jason took it in his study.

CHAPTER TWENTY-FIVE

A NEW UNDERSTANDING

Jason replaced the phone and walked into the hall.

"Who was that?" Mary called

"Just what the doctor ordered," he said, "We are employing another POW, starts on Monday."

He rubbed his hands together. Alleviated a whole lot of problems, knowing it was labour on the cheap. Hey, you know whatever I think, who cares so long as we get the work done. He sat down at the oak table and issued a big sigh of relief. "We'll try and keep him for as long as they let us, and Alec's not getting any younger, I detect certain signs of fatigue the other day. I think I ought to have a gentle word, instruct him to come to work only if he feels like it. I don't want to be classed as a slave driver!"

"None of us are getting any younger. What about Dotty? I mean, how old is she?" Mary felt very concerned for Dotty's welfare. "Shouldn't we let her off a couple of days a week? I can manage, and Aunt Lillian wouldn't mind standing in. Besides, Henry always helps out at the weekends."

"I think that with the forward planer now installed we will know in advance what to expect of everyone. I can deploy my labour accordingly with far greater results. The only thing I cannot predict is the weather," Jason ever the pessimist as usual. "I wonder what sort of character the POW will turn out to be?" he was full of apprehension " I just hope he's as good with language, if not we'll just use hand signals."

The weekend passed quite quickly. Henry experienced his first dab at curing the hams his pig's ear was wearing a bit thin, leaving him with a couple of sore fingers after the rubbing of salt. Jason prepared the hams for hanging, and smoking with woodchips, that Henry collected from the carpenters woodshed in the village. Jason would teach the team how to smoke the hams.

The early part of April shone bright and clear. Dotty as usual was busy about her chores. Mary fussing about the kitchen and humming a tune to herself. Jason and Alec were rolling out the churns for the co-operative tanker. The news that came from the BBC Home service, the radio crackled with static, announced that the bombing of German Cities was having a devastating effect on moral. The war was swinging in our favour. The news also gave way for the shipping forecast was not looking too good either; South coast cones were being hoisted.

"Looks like we're in for some bad weather," Dotty remarked.

Mary threw Gyp some scraps for her to chew on. The noise and sight of two vehicles made Mary look up as they followed each other into the yard Laura and Jenny jumped out from underneath the canopy of the smaller vehicle, while a much larger vehicle swung round to park alongside. The opening at the rear revealed German POW. The girls stood back and watched as the figure of a young POW. Dressed in a grey-green serge uniform, his trousers tucked into black leather flying boots, emerged from the canopied lorry. As he turned and faced the group so Jason and Alec joined the curious watchers. The German POW slid off his side –cap to reveal a fair-haired young man in his mid-twenties. Both vehicles drove away, leaving the group to the spaciousness of the yard.

Jason spoke first. "How do you do?"

Alec just nodded at the newcomer, everybody felt ill at ease. It wasn't like this with Lally, maybe because he was older and wiser. Anyway, the young German introduced himself as Hans Maher. He'd been ordered to the farm by the camp commander, his willingness to buckle down and abstain from being recalcitrant led to a reward by a little freedom working on the farm

Was it a passing glance, or fleeting moment, a casual eye-to-eye contact?

Certainly, Laura felt it was so, there was something there. Henry felt a little morose at being left out of the meeting, for his departure to Luton Tech somehow always coincided with anyone joining the farmhands. He was wretched with himself, knowing that by the time he arrived home, they, the girls, and Hans would have been collected, and it would be Saturday before any real contact could be made. By that time, everyone except himself would have either spoken to him or maybe his English wasn't so good that their understanding of him would mean nobody actually gained any knowledge about his affairs. Rightly, so there should be no fraternisation with the enemy. Henry would bide his time, let the information come to him.

Hans refused tea; a glass of water would suffice his needs. Jason indicated to Hans to sit at the oak table, Dotty and Mary busied themselves about the kitchen readying the break-time refreshments before the hired hands went about their daily tasks.

As Mary gave Hans the glass of water, she noticed how scabrous the back of his hands were; he withdrew his hands into his pockets until Mary moved away.

The girls and Jason were inquisitive as to his knowledge of English, if any at all. He spoke in gentle tones of good broken English.

"What will my duties be today please, I must know and where are the err, what do you say, toilets?"

The girls giggled a little, but realised that he'd got his priorities right in the first question.

Jason thought, at least we can understand him; we don't have to start waving our hands and arms around.

"You mean lavatory," Jason said, "I'll show you where when we start work." Mary sensed a sadness in Han's tired blue eyes. Dotty could not understand why we needed foreigners, especially Germans who hated us, and to encourage them into our houses. It's unreasonable and unfair. "I'll bet our lads aren't getting the same treatment as these fellows." She spouted indignantly.

Mary whose own life had been subject to jeopardy over Bert, left her feeling no more prejudice and holding lesser opinions of harm against those who sort to destroy our whole existence, but she had learnt compassion and couldn't wait for the day war ended.

Jason beckoned Han's and the girls to follow him into his study.

"Do you understand what this is?" he said to Hans pointing to the wall planner.

"Ja I think so," he smiled.

"Today, my plan tells me we shall be spreading ammonia on the Big and Little Dinge fields, Laura will drive the tractor, and you Hans will feed the spreader from the pile of bags Alec has already stacked for you. You understand?"
"Ja I understand."

"Laura will show you what to do." Jason held a lot of trust in Laura. "Jenny, you can help me, Alec's having a day off today, he's seeing the doctor, bit of a breathing problem."

Laura reversed the tractor and Hans guided her to the spreader. Jason and Jenny oversaw the unit across the road opposite the main gate. Big and Little Dinge were two fields away beyond Greenacre and Pitfield. Hans would open the gates for Laura and see her through, with widths being very tight.

Dotty pegged out the last of the washing; A southwesterly was blowing, a drying day to behold. She couldn't get it out of her mind of Laura being alone with a German.

Really, the men should have worked together on that job. It unsettled her.

As Jason and Jenny walked back through the yard, Roy Connaught, Jason's solicitor, pulled in behind them, "I yup" said Jason. Roy Connaught greeted them with a casual "Hello, How are you all, and where's your lovely wife, Jason?" Connaught said this with a certain haughtiness, which Jason just shrugged off, but Mary who was standing at the kitchen door could see right through him; she didn't care for him too much.

"Come to collect the paintings, just hope that I've chosen the right auction house." He said with a cocky grin.

Jason rubbed the stubble about his chin, through lack of razor blades, they were truly scarce.

"C'mon Jenny, follow me." He slid the ladder from two brackets, which held it in place under the hovel. Here catch hold of the small end, we've to open the trap door above the outhouse where they are stored." Jason climbed up first and handed them down one by one to Jenny who, in turn, handed them to Roy Connaught who then loaded them into the boot of his Humber snipe, taking great care not to damage them.

Jenny was surprised to find herself involved with

something quite personal other than farm work. "Where have these come from, if you don't mind me asking?"

Jason replied, "It's a long story, you're not to bother you pretty little head. In the meantime, just keep handing the paintings to Mr Connaught."

An hour had passed as Connaught carefully packed the last picture frame on to the brown leather seats in the back of the Humber." Fifty, in all." He said.

"Fifty," Jason said. Jenny copied. "Fifty." I haven't been counting; it's quite a lot of pictures." She dusted herself down. Mary entered into the conversation, she whispered into Jenny's ear.

"It's Henry's legacy you've been handling, they were saved from the Manor when it burned down."

Connaught greeted Mary with his usual cheeky self. Jason stood off the last rung of the ladder, thanked Connaught, who I turn bade him farewell. He'd be in touch on the phone, after the sales.

***

Hans jumped down from the back of the spreader and ran to stop Laura. He waved as something was jamming the mechanism; he waved his arms frantically, begging her to stop. She braked, turned the ignition off.

"What is it?" she called

"Something's wrong inside the spreader!" he called.

Laura clambered down off the GM and went to investigate.

Hans lifted the long lid of the spreader. "See down there?" he said," the worm screw is jamming, not letting the crystals through."

Laura peered inside. "How do we fix it?" she said, in a

not too confident manner.

"I'm not dipping my hands in there until you disengage the coupling first." Laura thought Hans is no mug; he knew how to take care of himself. He threw his side cap and serge green tunic to the ground, rolled up his sleeves, and deftly sunk his hand and arm through the crystals, heaping them to one side, allowing him to see a piece of hard wood that had jammed the worm screw to the cog. "There, you see?" he said, struggling to free the offending piece, but without success.

"What if I couple up and reverse the whole lot, will that release it?" Laura said now with some authority. "It might do, try it."

He held the coupling to the power take- off as Laura reversed the GM, Hans directing with little hand gestures. Laura was very close to him. As the coupling snapped, their eyes met and held for, it seemed like eternity. She felt it, he most certainly did. She moved the GM a little closer, all the time Hans waving her back a little. "That's it!" he shouted," turn the ignition off" Hans removed the offending piece of wood. Just then, Jason appeared on his trusty cycle grinning to himself, "What's up?"

"A piece of wood jammed the mechanism, but Hans has fixed the problem, haven't you Hans?" Laura said.

"Ya I've fixed the problem, haff done this many times back home on my folk's farm."

"So you are a farmer yourself?" Jason said with an ever-increasing like-mindedness towards the POW. He waited till the fertilizing was complete, then oversaw their way home.

Alec had been ordered by the doctor to have at least seven days off, even Hans didn't know it would leave Jason very short-handed, with just two girls. They would between them manage to keep the farm ticking over with Big and

Little Dinge spread with fertilizer. The rain overnight came at the right time. The girls left the study with strict orders that the dairy herd were to be allowed only thirty minutes in Dings fields when the time for them to chew the cud came in two months.

"From now on we should see milk production increase from three churns to at least five." Jason was feeling much more secure, what with the legacy and the purchasing the rented field, which for its first season would be a crop of winter oats. The field would join the rotation system.

Today and the next, while being short- handed, the girls would make butter, turn the hams, dig the garden, and sow seeds. The Friesian herd were being let out into Sweetacre now that spring had arrived; in fact, the farm was in good shape. Jason wandered over to the Manor in time for the first replacement oak beam to be inserted across the bedroom. As he stood in conversation with Wallis, the hooter sounded, and Gyp barked louder than ever. Jason excused himself and trotted back to his study. Breathless, he answered the phone.

"Who was that?" Mary asked.

Jason sat himself at the oak table, at the same time thumping his fist.

"It appears there's been an unsuccessful attempt to breakout at the POW camp in Wales. All POW have been confined to their huts. Damn, Damn!"

Mary, meanwhile, had prepared four stuffed pigs feet with breadcrumbs, frying fat, onions, and sage from the garden. The stuffing would be inserted after three hours of simmering. Dotty showed Mary how to make brawn from the pig's head, the larder being filled with an aroma to excite anyone's taste buds.

***

Henry gazed at the endless fields of new growing corn, freshly mole-boarded rows for new potato seed to set. The criss-cross pattern and different shades of colours as the beauty of the sun's rays shone on distant fields after the rain, made a brilliant collage.

The bus on its diversion route through the village moved the passengers unevenly from side to side due to the unexploded bomb still not recovered from the night of terror. Henry wondered what progress the bomb disposal team had reached. Nearly eight months had passed without any signs that the bomb had been located, or defused. When he finally arrived home, to his dismay he learnt of the breakout, and Hans's confinement. "Agh, well." There would be another time! In the meantime, he consoled himself perusing over whether to sketch Jenny milking Aubyn. He had sketched many different scenes in and around the farm and village, and this particular one had caught his imagination.

"Do you want a smile, Henry?" she said. Her fingers and hands caressing Aubyn's teats, the stream of warm milk ping-pinging onto the bottom of the pail in an incessant beat; one teat, then the other, alternating on each teat, she squirted a stream of milk that just missed his head. He ducked, then a blush crept up his neck, knowing Jenny was always the fool, her sense of humour never wavering. He perched himself on the old chopping block and sketched her and Aubyn.

"Don't be too long I'm nearly finished, can't sit here all night you know, other jobs need attention, besides, my time's nearly up for today." Jenny extracted the pail away from Aubyn. Henry thanked her for being such a good sport and model.

"You can draw me anytime you like." She marched off across the yard to the dairy cooler, and readied the milk for making butter, which Henty loved on his toast in the mornings at breakfast. A lot could be said of girls; without them, the farm would be hard pressed to function.

Later over tea, Jason, Mary, and Aunt Lillian deliberated over the day's accomplishments.

Two weeks had passed before Hans was allowed back to Claridge Farm. Alec had done his best to fill in, but Jason knew sooner or later, in Alec's case, he would ask him to retire for his own sake. To be fair he had worked longer than anyone Jason had known. Alec had aged quickly over the past months. After all, he was already halfway through being a septuagenarian, albeit seventy-six. Jason knew it would hit him hard, but he could always toddle along to the farm to find companionship, to have a chat and a laugh. Alec would understand the score; he knew there would always be a chair for him.

Henry's break from Tech for half term gave him time to reflect on past studies, and a time to get to know Hans, if allowed. Jason issued orders to Laura and Jenny, with Hans now back to full time. Their first task of the day was to harness the cob into the small Tumbrel cart, traverse through Sweetacre to where the last remnants of hayrick were to be cut and loaded as some of the hay had mould. This would be spread under the Dutch barn ready for a new intake of young Shorthorn Bullocks to be reared as beef cattle. Jason would bid for these at the next market.

"Henry, are you joining us today?" Laura said. He was introduced to Hans by the girls.

"Well kind of, for a little while," he replied.

He walked with Gyp at his side behind the cart, which creaked and squeaked over some molehills. The girls rode seated on the fore-rack, while Hans led the cob. Henry soon realised that Hans carried an injury or something was bothering him. The limp was noticeable in his left leg;

perhaps a war injury, Henty thought. They trundled on, Laura giving Hans the direction to the now sorry depleted hayrick.

Hans brought the cob round to halt parallel with the cutaway part of the hayrick. He spoke in a soft broken English accent.

"Whoa," he said. He stripped off his tunic top and rolled up his sleeves. The shirt had been roughly ironed; his trousers were neatly creased into his flying boots.

"I'm ready." He said.

CHAPTER TWENTY SIX

THE ENIGMA SOLVED

Henry's job was to stand by the cob's head while Hans and the girls worked in total silence. Not a word spoken.

Three American Mustang warplanes flew very low, shattering the uncomfortable atmosphere Hans, startled momentarily, stared in awe, he shook his head, and carried on cutting the remains of the hay, while Laura and Jenny pitched and loaded. The planes unnerved the cob; he threw up his head, and pulled out of Henry's hands. The girls screamed, thinking the cob would bolt, but Hans, quick to the rescue of the unsettled animal, threw himself off the in-cut ledge of the hayrick and grasped the harness and bridle. He quietened the cob with strokes to its forehead, speaking softly into its ears. Whatever he conveyed to the cob worked instantly, Hans all the while stroking its mane and forehead, all the time pacifying the cob with whispered words.

Laura, bemused and looking on, admired the way Hans handled the situation. Henry, on the other hand, picked himself up about to give the cob a slap, but Hans held Henry's arm and shook his head. "Nein, Nein, Nein, always console the animal, always!"

Laura saw the compassion in Hans way of dealing with the cob, their eyes met again, this time Laura smiled and acknowledged his commendable actions, and Hans resumed his cutting of the hay. The girls and Henry knew Hans had saved what might have been a nasty accident. Laura would see to it that Jason would be told about the incident, how Hans had reacted, Henry and the girls knew fraternising with the enemy was forbidden.

How can one work with somebody and not talk? Henry was curious. Should he thank Hans or should he keep silent and let the moment pass? Henry and Gyp walked at the rear of the Tumbrel cart back to the farm, while Hans led the cob with the girls buried in the hay on top, having a giggle to themselves. Henry, with second thoughts, hurried to the side of Hans, clutching his tunic top he'd discarded at the hayrick. Henry handed it to him.

"Danke schon." He said the ice was broken between them.

Jason opened the gate for the tumbrel to pass through, at the same time directing the group to the Dutch barn where the hay would be unloaded and strewn about to be readied for the Bullocks.

Dotty sounded the hooter four times, which made Hans laugh.

"Vot was that?" he remarked, surprised at the noise.

Laura was first to answer. "That, as you put it, is the sound for tea break.

"Ja, good."

Henry waited to see if Jason would allow Hans into the kitchen. Of course, he would. Hans by now was part of the furniture. It would be taken for granted.

Mary and Dotty, both with their arms folded and leaning themselves against the kitchen sink, sipped tea and listened to the chatter from the girls, quite oblivious to anyone else. Hans sat at the end of the solid oak table admiring it and stroking his goatee beard, alone and unprepared for this gathering. Jason entered with Henry in tow.

"Where on earth have you two been hiding, your teas practically stewed," Mary said.

"Yes, and cold," Dotty added.

"You see what I have to put up with, Hans." Jason gave a little grin and sat down next to him. Henry likewise. They sipped their tea. Jason rested his mug and asked Hans where he lived in Germany. Dotty quick to chip in, reminded them of her forecast of the weather earlier, had come true; a weather front had hit the area the likes of which they had never witnessed. Gyp slunk in to shelter by the stove; Jason peered out the window and really gave up on the day.

"Sorry Hans, as I was saying, where about's did you live?"

"Hav we time?"

"You have time."

Henry shifted in his chair a little closer. The girls stopped nattering, surprised that Alec entered and joined Mary and Dotty, who were not at all happy that Jason was allowing Hans to evoke a Freudian slip. Even Gyp cocked an ear, herself spread-eagled on the mat in front of the stove. Hans was having Second thoughts about telling his story, but he ploughed on.

"My family lived on a small homestead at a place situated on the outskirts of Darmstadt just a few kilometres from the city of Frankfurt. You know Frankfurt?"

"I've heard of it."

"My parents owned their smallholding but rented fields, about hundred and fifty acres in all. They grew Maize and Linseed, and kept twelve head of Friesian milking cows."

Jason nodded approval. "Ah, about the same as we have here. Go on."

"My life as a boy in the late twenties became obsessed, not by farm life, although I was expected to help and do certain chores about the place, but my mind was elsewhere, my passion to become a glider pilot intensified as the club for gliding activities joined our boundary on the farm. Every day through the summer months of my youth, I would look up and see the silver wings soaring above the farm trying to find thermals. I thought to myself, one day I want to do that, my father knew of my secret passion for gliding and on my seventeenth birthday a surprise awaited me at the breakfast table, a letter which I opened and found an entry form to join the gliding club and monies for six lessons starting on the very next day. Henry sat wide eyed and thought he would have loved the opportunity.

"Carry on." Said Jason.

"I must have been a natural because after five lessons my instructor said I could go solo. He had that much confidence in my ability,"

Jason and everybody were so absorbed in the story that time was forgotten. So much was their curiosity that when Aunt Lillian arrived for her stint, shaking her umbrella and cursing the rainstorm, she surprisingly stumbled in on an intense gathering who had rejected the day and weather, "Shush." They chorused. The girls pulled a chair out and gestured Aunt Lillian to sit down and listen. Dotty made fresh tea for all, for she wasn't in a hurry to leave either.

"Give Hans a glass of water, he must be parched." Jason said caringly. Hans sipped the water and carried on.

"During the following year I had become an experienced competition contender for the title "Glider Pilot of Nineteen Thirty-five"; I was invited over to fly in England at the London Flying Club at Dunstable."

Jason and Alec raised their eyebrows at the statement Hans had just made. At this point Jason reacted. "Do you know you are just six miles from the very place you have mentioned?"

"I know where I am." He said.

This surprised everyone to think a German would be aware of his surroundings, Hans carried on with his story. "As the years went by, it was obvious that Germany was heading for war. After everything they had worked for his parents knew, their lives would be turned upside down. They were devoted Lutherans and hated the very essence of the word war. The day came when Hans received his papers to join the Luftwaffe. The authorities in Berlin knew of his exploits as a glider pilot and so sent him to an airfield just outside Augsburg. When I arrived. The perimeter bays were full of camouflaged aircraft. Now I understood the full extent of the war that Hitler was to vent his extreme views on other nations. I thought he teetered on the edge of lunacy, still I was ordered to do a job and become a bomber pilot. The first year I was assigned to bombing Slovakia and Polish towns. It was only when Hitler changed his mind and invaded the Eastern countries and widened the war I knew in my heart of hearts we were destined to failure."

"How come?" Jason asked.

"Because Napoleon tried and did not succeed, you can only take so much, that's why."

Laura could see the sadness in Hans blue eyes. Just as it's terrible for them, it's the same for all of us, she thought.

Hitler now had two front lines to fight, his forces would be stretched to the limits, but there were some misgivings within his own ranks and he knew it. Hans took another gulp of water. Jason reminded himself of the time but this was too good a narrative to let go by.

"What happened next?" he said, trying to hurry the story along. Hans took another sip of water, and continued his story.

"Since Dunkirk, most of us were assigned to fly day sorties far in to Poland and Romania. It was after one of these sorties when I and my crew returned and were debriefed I was ordered to the Flight Commandant's office. He had received an official communique from none other than Herr Goering of high command. It seems that one of Hitler's closest, no, I should say his right hand man, had requisitioned a Messerschmitt 110 light aircraft to fly to Scotland, and seek political asylum," Hans rubbed his brow, "Hopefully through a titled person who owned an estate."

"Ah he knew he would be well looked after, that's what we English people are renowned for." Dotty said with such fervent intensity.

Hans couldn't help noticing Dotty for her loyalties; she was a good woman in his eyes.

Hitler wanted retribution in some way or other, so a plan was hatched to assassinate the traitor.

"Who was this traitor?" Jason asked.

"Rudolph Vonn Hess." He shot back.

"Hmm. I'm sure I read about him in the newspaper when it happened, made headlines but then people tend to forget about the story, so what was this plan?" Jason became more intrigued.

Hans was trying to convince himself that this was the right thing to do, explaining to these people a plan that was so confidential that even Hitler's most senior commanders did not know what was about to happen. So what, he thought, I'm well out of it, and I'm fond of England.

Another round of tea was served. The hall clock reminded Jason that it was two o'clock. The rain began to ease, and there in the distance he could make out the clearance of the clouds beginning to thin and break.

"Go on Hans," he said

His audience began to fidget in their chairs but nobody was going anywhere.

"August last year my crew and I were posted to an airfield just north of Paris for a month. We practiced night flying in and around the airfield in a Dornier 217 conversion. We practiced with Dummy bombs at first. A pinpoint of light was the only thing we had to aim for. Then, we perfected the manoeuver, the last task being a live run, a shed in a disused quarry to be the target. A detachment of Wehrmacht shone a beacon of light from a searchlight on the target and whumsh. We demolished the shed."

"Then what?" Laura said.

"Ten months ago, I and my crew were briefed for a secret mission to a position over South Bedfordshire and rendezvous with a searchlight battery squad, who also were picked for special duties. We knew in advance from our agents who operated here in England that at some time the traitor Hess would be transferred to a safe house in the Home Counties. The plan, if successful with favourable weather, the operators of the search light would swing the beam out of the sky to a predetermined stop; the escort would have bivouacked, which made our job and target a lot easier to find and assassinate Hess."

Jason could not believe his ears at such a bizarre story, and yet something told him Hans was telling the truth thinking back to the night of the bombing around the farm, it all fell into place. Of course, of course, Jason repeated over in his mind. He asked, "Hans was there any collusion with our government?"

"If there was, then I wouldn't hav known, we just follow orders."

An assassin here in my house, the pilot of the plane that nearly killed us all. Jason was bewildered by it all; he was angry, and yet sorry for Hans. Jason thought for a moment before he asked the next question, he had to know for sure.

"The night in question, Hans when you knew you had reached the point for this so called assignment, did you circle three times before the searchlight beam illuminated the night sky?"

"Ya, on the third run the beam would have swung round and down to ground level, giving me and my bomb aimer a precise fix on where the convoy would have halted for the night."

"Christ, that's right!" Jason hit the table with his fist, startling the girls and Hans. The household were taken aback by his aggressive response to Hans's storyline.

He grimaced at Hans, and thought, he wouldn't have known what torment he put us through that night. Of course, not, he wouldn't have known anything other than trying to hit the target they were supposed to have destroyed.

"Why all the questions, Mr Smith?" Hans asked.

"Because," Jason glanced at the kitchen clock," at this precise moment in time, one of your bombs you supposedly dropped did not explode. Not two fields from here the bomb disposal team are trying to dig and locate the damn thing. It's soft blue clay here, Hans, very difficult to dig anything out."

"How was I to know?" he spluttered, it wasn't delayed or anything like that."

"Well you missed your target by at least three fields. After the bombing, the convoy moved on its final leg of the journey. I'll bet to a safe house somewhere in the next county, or maybe near here, who is to know what's being decided?"

"So how were you taken prisoner of war?" Laura wanted to know the whole story before everyone made a move to start milking.

The girls and Henry restless again on their chairs, Dotty prepared herself to leave, Aunt Lillian and Mary bustled about with their chores. The rain had eased to a fine drizzle, the sun trying to break through.

Jason checked the time again, nearly half past two, he pointed to the timepiece on the sideboard, "Sorry," he said," but we'll have to finish this another time, we must get on."

They all moaned.

"Just a little longer," Laura said

"Well alright, but make it short, Hans.

"After the mission, the task completed, our flight plan was to carry on flying in an easterly direction, our luck held, and I knew we could reach the coast, and once there we would follow the coastline until the Thames estuary came into view. Then a port turn towards the French coast, our job done. But unfortunately, the the right starboard engine spluttered and caught fire. The only choice was to ditch and absprigen. Eh, how you say bail out. We could see the coastline and sea, my navigator's last words....." Our position over island of West Mersey Essex", we bailed out throught the bomb doors, that 's where I slipped and caught my ankle, and not knowing I had a stress fracture, I jumped it was very frightening, as I drifted down I saw my plane hit the water and burst in to flames. My only thoughts were I didn't want to hit the water, please God, I knew my war was over.

"So, where did you end up?" Laura seemed the only one concerned.

"I crashed in to a chestnut tree. I must have passed out. When I eventually regained my senses I found myself dangling thirty foot from the ground, I was helpless, and my ankle was giving me such pain. I was just hanging in my fallscirhminger..."

"Your what?" Laura asked

"As you say, parachute." Hans corrected.

There were times in Hans's life that had been full of uncertainties, but sense his capture one thing he was certain of, was that the people around him now bore no ill feelings towards him. Quite the opposite happened; they were very friendly people. After everything that Germany represented and inflicted on other people, Englanders were reasonable and moderate human souls, he respected them for that.

"So who rescued you?"

"I must have dozed off, thinking nobody's going to find me. The dawn broke, and vogals awoke me. I considered my position. It was hopeless, the more I struggled, the more the harness tightened. I imagined I had landed in some sort of obstgarten, I looked up, then sideways, and then down, and noticed a dog staring up at me, growling a little, a dog not unlike your dog Gyp." Gyps ears twitched upon hearing her name; "I made myself believe into thinking someone must be with the dog. I spoke to the dog and thought, I'm going insane, here am I helpless in a tree, talking to a dog, and I laughed. How I laughed, the tears ran down my cheeks and then I heard a man's voice calling the dog, so I shouted at the top of my voice, "Help please help me," the man came and looked up at me and said, "what are you doing in my garden?"

"Your obstgarten?" I said

"Yes, my garden" the man said

"Please get me down, I am a German pilot and need help, I've broken my foot. He and the dog walked away, don't leave me I cried, later, I found out he was a retired Royal Navy man and lived in a very small house nearby. I checked my watch. The hands had stopped at four forty two, almost four hours ago by the sun; it must be nearly nine o'clock by now. I waited and listened. I heard a car engine; no, it was much heavier sound. Then I heard men's voices, two men in Police uniform arrived, Fire servicemen with a ladder, accompanied by an Army officer and Guards. They rescued me and carried me to the Navy man's house where they bandaged my ankle, and then I was escorted to the police station where I was formally charged as being a prisioner of war. From there, I was driven to an Army prison and interned into hospital."

CHAPTER TWENTY SEVEN

FAIR GAME OR FAIR PLAY

Jason pushed his chair from the solid oak table with the noise that usually sets your teeth on edge. Dotty prepared herself to leave for home on her trusty cycle, and Gyp followed her out, accompanied by a soft plaintiff whine. Henry was bewildered, was the story true? Jason shook his head in disbelief; the girls and Mary, and Aunt Lillian reserved their own thoughts for another time.

The sun had at last appeared and threw some warmth around the farm. Everywhere sparkled, even a rainbow took a bow as the cloud rolled and billowed away to the east. Hans yawned and stepped outside, stretched his arms and broad shoulders, and surveyed the scene, marvelling at the greenery and sparrows chirping happily.

Jason followed him out and gave some orders of jobs to be done.

"Laura and Jenny" he said, "hitch the GM tractor to the trailer and go and collect the wood from the carpenters store in the village, there you will find a load of two by four cut lengths of timber rails and posts already cut to size by the carpenter. Load them up and return them to the Dutch barn. You Hans, with me."

Henry followed, but Jason directed him him to feed the hens, and collect the eggs for the last time that day, and after, to round up the cows and herd them in for milking from

Sweetacre.

"Right Hans, are you ready for a bit of digging? I want post holes dug every eight feet in line with the stanchions of the Dutch barn. The tools are over there under the hovel near my car, yes?"

"Ja, understood, Mr Smith."

"Jason please." He said to Hans. While he fetched the spade and shovel, Jason measured out where the holes were to be dug, tapping in a peg at each spot. Hans indicated with his hands at what depth Jason wanted the holes dug, "How deep?" he said

Jason had prepared a template, a cane with the measurements marked, he held his hands apart. "Two feet under, four feet above the ground, right?"

"Ja, I understand." He lifted the spade and struck the first downward dig. The spade hit some chalky clay. It would be a hard slog, but he felt elated at being free.

The following day was bright and sunny, the girls Laura and Jenny were to stack the posts and rails under the Dutch barn ready for Hans to fix, but first there was the matter of mixing the cement for the first two postholes when dug.

Hans stripped down to his waist. His muscles rippled in the sunlight; after a few minutes of digging, he turned to find Laura and Jenny watching his every move. He knew he could not be seen to be fraternising, especially with the opposite sex, so he just smiled and carried on working.

Laura admired his muscled torso, and wished his arms were around her. How could she explain to him how she felt? He was always on her mind. She lay awake at night in the hostel thinking of him, and the hurt she would cause among her mates and friends there on the farm. Thinking of the hatred, she would encounter. She mulled these thoughts over again and again in her contorted mind until sleep overtook her aching body.

***

Dotty tut-tutted as she rode her cycle across the yard. "Hello" the girls shouted. Her reply was more clinical than they expected. "I hope your dreams don't come true."

"She must have a sixth sense." Laura said under her breath. "The madam she is, don't miss a thing, eyes like an eagle, and a tongue as ferocious as a dragon." Laura was trying to work out in her brain how she could communicate with Hans without drawing too much attention. Would she be angry? Laura decided to let Jenny into her secret. She waited until they returned to the hostel. If Jenny was miffed by the affair at least if there were words, the farm people would not be involved. Laura waited until she and Jenny were alone washing each other's hair, and blurted out. "I think I'm in love with Hans, and don't know how to tell him."

"I had designs on him." Jenny said," but then I thought, it wouldn't be fair on our boys fighting on the front line and maybe all the discord here on the farm, and the villagers, what they would think, so I said no, I don't want no part of it. You can have him, but I'm not angry, Laura in fact I think Hans would make a good husband for anybody. His whole attitude and thoughtfulness towards us are by no means hostile, he seems a gentle person, but I'll give you my blessing. If anything comes of it, there I've said my piece."

"I'm really grateful, Jenny, but I've a problem, how do I communicate, how do I let him know my feelings for him?"

Jenny hung out the towel to dry on the line provided. As she stowed the combs and brushes into the locker, she said, "How about using Henry as a go between, you write a letter, he'll hand it to Hans discreetly, tell Henry to say to Hans, to return, write and use the same envelope if you wish to correspond, oh, and make sure you use a brown envelope, that way it does not show up so much."

"I'm glad you're not angry with me, Jenny, it helps to ease the awful thoughts that are running through my head as to what people will think once they discover I'm courting a German."

"I don't think you'll have any trouble once the Allies land in France, and start pushing them back towards their own country. People will feel less anti, aren't the Royals from German blood, that makes us cousins, don't it?" Jenny pondered a bit more.

"Laura." She said, "Have you really thought this through what if Hans is transferred to another prison camp further away, say up north somewhere, what'll you do then?"

"I dunno, I haven't thought about that happening, but I now know when I write my first letter, in the event of that happening and we no longer communicate, and if he survives to be repatriated, to write to the farm to me c/o Mr and Mrs Smith. I shall let them know of my forwarding address before I leave.

Laura lay on her bunk bed propped up against the headboard, her legs pulled up, providing a rest for the notepaper and pad.

She wrote not of a sloppy letter, but a constructive one, setting out her thoughts and feelings for him. She wrote not about love, but of a friendship, she wanted so desperately to last. She told of her own anxiety of not having any family as such, just one or two distant cousins dotted about somewhere who did not correspond or they were too busy with their own lives to care about her. However, I'm sure I could reach them in times of importance if my friendship with Hans turned in to something more serious she thought. How would they react? It would be for them to decide. She then wrote of how he could reply, and what method they would use to communicate with each other. I don't like using a third party, but at this stage, I can't think of anything other than using Henry to find a secret place for us to exchange our thoughts and feelings.

I am sure you found yourself wanting; I thought I saw something in your eyes when ours met on a couple of occasions. P.S. Use the same envelope for reply. Henry will point out the location although I've still to talk with him, and for him to agree to our liaison with each other. I think he'll understand and not be aggrieved, even though he lost his father through the war.

Henry came through the gate from the orchard just as the vehicle carrying the land girls pulled up into the yard. Laura waved to Henry and called him over. Hans already stripped to the waist and digging the firth posthole, remained pre-occupied and unaware of Laura's actions.

"What do you want?" Henry called

"A minute of your time, that's what." Laura said with a charm and smile he couldn't resist. Laura ushered Henry to a secluded spot under the hovel out of sight.

"What do you want?" Henry said again.

"l want you to be a real friend, Henry." She said, "it's nothing serious, it's "she paused." I want you to give Hans this letter and, will you find a secret place on the farm for future exchanges, somewhere out of sight but convenient for us to collect without being seen?"

"Has Hans any idea?" Henry said, with mixed thoughts of his own.

Laura showed him the envelope. "It'll always be in a brown envelope," she said, until worn out, and then I'll replace it with a new one. It won't be sealed, so no spying on me, Henry, do I have your trust and will you find a secret place for me?"

Henry nodded, "Of course I will, in fact I've the very spot for the exchange." Henry couldn't hide his delight to be on an illicit tryst, maybe in the future, who knows?"

Henry led Laura to the front of the hovel, making sure no one was about. Gyp twitched her ears. Henry pointed, "See the dividing wall of the yard and the orchard? If you open the gate, to your left, there is a disused old rabbit hutch Jason used in earlier times, perhaps for ferrets, who knows. I'll place a brick in behind the door; you can slip the envelope underneath. Nobody will be any the wiser."

"You are a little pal." She said, and went to the back of the hovel and wrote another postscript, outlining what Henry had just told her. She did not write any kisses but signed her letter as a faithful friend.

In the beginning, Henry had to get the letter to Hans without compromising Hans or himself, and for the sake of Laura, which wasn't easy, for at the moment everybody seemed to be in the yard. First, the postman, then the milk collection tanker drew up, and then Jason and Jenny strolling towards the kitchen, and to top everything his mum began calling him.

"Where are you Henry with those eggs? Laura called quietly, "here, I'll take the eggs, now's the time to slip round the Dutch barn and give Hans the letter. Look, we know where everybody is at the moment."

"Thanks Henry, I'll make an excuse for you."

"Where is that boy?" she kept calling. Before Laura set off, Henry hesitated. "Just a minute, Laura," he said "Don't forget the villagers who come to dig their gardens, look out for them." He added in a hushed voice.

Henry approached Hans, making sure that nobody

except himself was around. Hans had his back to Henry, using a pickaxe to loosen the chalky clay. He stopped for a breather. Henry, who stood behind him, was hesitant and a little apprehensive. Hans turned and threw the pickaxe on to the heap he had just dug out, wiped his brow, and saw Henry.

"Schwierig" he said, "you come to help me with der digger?" Henry shook his head, slid his hand into his jacket pocket and handed the envelope to Hans.

"Vots this?"

"From Laura, for you to read tonight. No one must see you read the letter. You'll know what to do. She told me to tell you that she has explained everything and that you must follow her instructions to the letter."

Hans folded the letter in to the inside pocket of his tunic. "Yah I understood."

"It's understand." Henry politely pointed out.

"Yah, I u-n-d-e-r-s-t-a-n-d." Hans gave a wry grin, thanked Henry, and returned to his digging.

Laura couldn't really explain to Mary as to why Henry went missing; only that she had to tell a rather large white lie. Her first job that morning was to milk Aubyn, the jersey cow, and that one of the legs of the stool had come loose," I asked could he fix it, as Jason and Jenny were on duty in the milking parlour." She said Henry had made a good job of repairing the stool, and Laura remarked, "If you are training to be an architect then you must know how to fix a leg into a stool." They all had a jolly good laugh. Henry's face coloured beetroot red.

"What's so funny?" he said.

"Oh nothing, his mum replied." Your face, go take a look in the mirror."

Henry frowned. Laura coughed as she sipped her tea.

CHAPTER TWENTY EIGHT
OPENING OF LETTERS

During the past few month's troop movements on manoeuvres intensified so much that Jason's eggs and milk were in great demand. Jason also knew that these conditions would only last for a couple of weeks before they all moved on. The surrounding area had become a holding region; soon it would be Armageddon on the continent.

The fence, which the girls and Hans had erected around the Dutch barn, was all but finished, and Alec who had stolen into the yard with his impaired eyesight, was allowed to make a critical judgement on the straightness of the fence.

"It needs to be sturdy to hold them there Bullocks in." he exclaimed. "I recon you should have had a least eight inch round posts to hold them buggers back." But Hans stood by the four by four and gently pulled and pushed as they resisted the test, and were as solid as a rock.

Jason joined the party to give his assessment. " I think you've done a good job, the animals should arrive by tomorrow morning," Laura and Jenny were given the task to make sure the drinking trough was filled with water; also to maintain and feed and be responsible for the wellbeing of the Bullocks while in the Dutch barn.

Jason gave a nod of satisfaction that the job on which the girls and Hans had worked met with his approval. All that remained was to clear the site of debris and make the surrounds tidy. The bullocks would stay in the barn for three days before being turned out into Little Dinge. They would stay for the rest of the summer to gain some sort of weight before being sending to slaughter. On any account, they should sell for a decent price considering that an invasion of Europe was imminent. The Armies would need all the beef they could get to sustain them on their quest for glory.

The bullocks arrived in two cattle wagons contracted to a company from Leighton to load them on at Dewdrop Farm, Ashton Abbotts, and transport them to Claridge Farm a distance of some twelve miles. Jason had thought about turning drover and walking them, but thought better of it; due to the inclement weather that had prevailed all over the country, he decided that transport was the better option.

Henry, on the other hand had become a little unenthusiastic about journeying to Luton Tech. he thought it would be more beneficial if he were to approach Dillimore & Wallis about an apprenticeship with them full time, seeing that his fourteenth birthday at the end of the year could see himself out of high school. He would ask his parents what they thought of his proposal at dinner tonight. Little did he realise that the very same day the Postman would deliver a letter titled him as Master Henry Kneally c/o Claridge Farm, Private. To be opened immediately.

Mary tucked the letter in the brass rack beside the kitchen dresser. She had an idea what the contents might be. As Jason approached the kitchen door, she waved, pointed to the letter, and smiled.

"I think Henry's legacy has arrived, he'll be pleased." — But were they?

After Henry delivered his thoughts about leaving Tech and broached the subject of full time work with Dillimore & Wallis at the dinner table that night, the atmosphere became a little tense. "Then there's your national service to do," Mary repeated the question, and he held his plate out for her to ladle steaming stew on to it, that she and Dotty had concocted that morning.

"Aren't you going to open your letter?" Mary couldn't contain her patients any longer.

"After dinner." Henry said, "I'm hungry."

Jason made a self-deprecating gesture as if to say it was no big deal.

He pondered on why Henry decided to release himself from Luton Tech. "Well, son, I think you are making a simple error of judgement, I recon you should stay at the Tech till you get some sort of grades then consider the offer at Leighton." On numerous occasions, Henry felt a little rebellious about his life, sometimes he wished he could be with the armed forces. He was in between ages, not old enough to fight, and too young to work, he felt frustrated and in limbo.

Henry sauntered to the study. Opened the letter with Jason's steel letter opened and ran his finger along the inside of the envelope pulling out the headed letter; he flipped it open and read its content. It listed all Thomas Gunn's paintings, which had been sold at auctions or privately; each one was categorised at sale price, to each one was inserted in parenthesis. He meandered back along the hall, still reading and sat down at the oak table. His mother and Jason looked on bemused and with anticipation, waiting for some sort of reaction from him.

"Well." His mother said, "Are we to be let into your fortuitous gifted life?"

"It's my legacy!" he said proudly, "and you knew, but checking through the list the Zulu Warrior doesn't appear."

Jason gave a little cough, and pulled his chair from

underneath himself. "Must get on, lots to do."

"How much? The total, Henry," his mother continued to press him.

"In all, two thousand and fifty pounds, cheque to follow unless otherwise to be instructed. Yours Roy Connaught," he read.

"You lucky old thing." Mary planted a kiss on Henry's cheek." How our fortunes changed, I'm pleased for you."

Jason stood in the doorway. "If you want my advice lad, you'll do well to let Roy invest the money for you, he'll think up some sort of savings account, maybe a building society, or national savings certificate's. Would you care for me to have a word?" The latter part of Jason's statement was taken up by Henry who considered Jason's wisdom more than anyone did. Who else could he turn to other than his mum or Aunt Lillian; all options open he would let Roy Connaught deal with the monies and Jason would telephone him to set up a meeting at a later date.

A month later the cheque was deposited at the local branch of the Co-Operative Society for which Henry had been granted a passbook with an identity number, and the said amount of two thousand and fifty pounds typed across the blue inserts, very neatly and precise. He printed his name inside the front cover and signed his signature thus with a flourish. Henry felt very fortunate to have inherited such an amount of money at his age; it would be up to him not to squander it but to make good use of his fortune. First, he needed a new pair of grey trousers, and a gansey. Next, he would buy his mum a new dress, and Aunt Lillian a set of garden tools, and Gyp a new collar. He dreamed of what might have been only to be brought back down to earth by rationing and clothes coupons. He would let the money accumulate until after the war when things got hopefully better.

His status went up when news of his legacy filtered out among the villagers. It took a while. He noticed that Madge became more sociable towards him, even Dotty started call him "My little darling." And all silly names, which made Henry all the more shy and a little embarrassed with himself. He tended to make himself scarce, but soon found that the only way was to face the people fair and square, and enjoy the plaudits that came his way. His fame would soon be forgotten and life would resume as normal and sanity would prevail.

***

Hans returned to the prison camp full of expectations of reading that Henry had passed on from Laura. The prison encampment comprised of twenty wooden huts with corrugated oval roofs holding ten prisoners to a hut of all descriptions from Luftwaffe crews, and others bearing the badge of Wehrmacht, and some Submariners; in all, two hundred men were held amongst the tall conifers and larch trees, a wooded confine some twenty miles from the farm. After eating his rations for the night, Hans retired to the latrine house at the rear of the wood. Here he wouldn't be disturbed, as the light from the evening was still quite bright, and being on the edge of the wood, he could read without any interference. He wouldn't forget either that the camp concert volunteers, he being one of them, rehearsals would begin at eight o'clock on the dot. The prisoners of hut 1 were attempting to re-enact the Shakespearian play, Comedy of Errors. The camp commander agreeing to speak the female parts owing to the fact he came from a classical theatre background and had quite a repertoire of actual stage appearances in London before war broke out.

Hans was to act the character of Solinus, Duke of Ephesus. They were expected to learn the parts of act one, scenes one and two to start with. Owing to the lack of space in the huts, they would read the script sitting round the stove. Not giving heat at this time of year. Each in turn would hold a candle and read his part aloud, directed by the commander who could speak fluent German and had all the scripts translated to German. Hans being clever, had taken his to the latrine as a cover, the earth closet being the perfect place to read Laura's letter.

He sat down on the wooden seat and opened the letter, which Laura had sprayed with Eau-de-cologne. Hans gently raised the paper to his nostrils and drew in the perfume, not forgetting he also was in the latrine.

Dear Hans, the letter began with Laura's prefect handwriting, *since your arrival at the farm I find your overwhelming charm and thoughtfulness very commendable. Your generous input of selflessness and attitude towards us every hour of every day, even more so when we met the very first time, our eyes met and something happened. I'm sure you felt it as I did, can't explain why, just wondering if you feel the same way? I'm not writing of love, it's important we keep our feelings and friendship at arm's length at the moment, besides the locals might not approve of our liaison. I know it will be difficult for you to reply but follow my instructions and nobody will be any the wiser. Only Jenny and Henry know of my writing and they have sworn on oath.*

Hans sat pondering his thoughts. He hadn't heard or received any letters via the Red Cross as to where or what happened to his parents; were they dead or alive, or moved on somewhere? He had never looked at, or had any intentions towards a German girl, but with Laura, it was different. It was a meeting of two souls trying to find peace and happiness. He dwelt on these thoughts for a while until he heard his name being called softly, "Hans, Hans, Der Commander warten?" Hans shifted his body off the seat and spied through a now defunct knothole in the door. Sure enough, one of the would-be thespians was tapping and whispering along the row of latrines.

"I'm here. I'm coming." He whispered. He shoved Laura's letter quickly into his inside pocket, opened the door, and waved his script to his trusty comrade.

"See, I've been rehearsing my part of Solinus.

CHAPTER TWENTY NINE

THE MOVE & ALLIED LANDINGS

Dillimore and Wallis confirmed that their association with the contracted house refurbishment company had all but finished. Jason and Mary were invited to inspect as was Henry, Dotty, and Aunt Lillian. Together they were shown with a good deal of pride by Mr Wallis, around the new and polished wooden floors of the old Manor. The kitchen, dining hall, a staircase, small bedroom, and new oak rafters, had all been renewed to Jason's satisfaction.

Mr Wallis had overseen the whole project, subject to Jason's approval. Everyone "oohed and aared" at the work the refurbishment company had achieved; from the rafters, the staircase and the floor in herringbone style to kitchen cupboards, were all solid oak.

"This must-a-cost-a-fortune." Dotty said in amazement. She thought the kitchen captured the mood of the manor. Aunt Lillian could see long dark draped green velvet curtains edged with gold in the dining room; Mary could see a four-poster sitting comfortably in the main bedroom.

"Is this where we are to live in future?" Henry asked in a more subdued voice.

"It is" Jason said, "I guess it's very congruous. We will move here in the next three weeks. That's right Mr Wallis. The girls will help us move and Hans can shift the heavy stuff."

To Mary's surprise, he mentioned buying some antique furniture, "There's some good items to bid for at the sales, aren't there, Mr Wallis?"

"I suppose so, you might find a Queen Ann bedstead at the sales, I could let you know when a piece comes on the market."

Mary visualised the scene preparing for bed, Jason in his long gown and nightcap, her in a billowing pink gown and bonnet. She laughed at her own silly thoughts.

"What's so funny mum?" Henry asked.

"Nothing son, just thoughts, that's all."

Over the next three weeks Mary and her companions, and in between the farm's needs, oversaw the packing of articles, which were not used much. These would be the first to be carried over to the manor on the four-wheeled trolley; she would, with the guile of Aunt Lillian, find homes for the said articles. Back and forth each day a little at a time they proceeded to organise and despatch pots and pans, bed clothing, and mostly themselves, until they set a date for the final move, which would involve some heavy lifting. This is where Hans became important to the whole operation.

Earlier, Jason had had a word with the refurbishment team who agreed to send two of his workforce over to assist once the date had been fixed, that date being the sixth of June. The barometer forecast was a dry day rising to fair, which made for an easier move than anticipated. Hans with the two-refurb men, extricated the wardrobes with smooth dexterity, and by one o'clock, they had completed the move. Jason rewarding the two contracted men handsomely, who doffed their caps and thanked the governor.

Henry felt a little sad on leaving his little room but his new surroundings meant he had elevated in to the roof space, giving him more area as a bed-sit-come-study. Just the ticket;

he could arrange the room to his own needs.

Jason had not only become a father but a very wise and understanding person, he would not forget the kindness shown to him and to Mary and Aunt Lillian, very few people would have been shown such consideration as they had. The old farmhouse would become a place for the employees to change their clothes, their break-time and bites, and things in general. Dotty would miss their banter.

The surroundings were very different. Dotty had her little moan but rolled up her sleeves with a determination to cook a meal of scrag-end lamb stew with spring greens, and a spotted dick to follow. She was invited to stay and celebrate the move.

The sun shone all day. Jason's mind was on haymaking. Hans moved Gyp's kennel to her new patch near the kitchen door where she had full view of the entire yard, plus plenty of lawn and paths through the privet hedges that encompassed the garden.

As Jason and his family sat round the oak table, the news over the radio couldn't have been more dramatic. The Allies had landed in France and gained a foothold on several beaches in Normandy.

"Poor devils." Dotty exclaimed. "I wonder how it must have been for them, you know, the unknown. Do you think the prisoners, the Germans, I mean, will be told of the landings, or do you think they have a secret wireless hidden somewhere on the compound?"

Dotty asked so many questions but she had lived through part of the First World War and knew about the slaughter. She had witnessed the homecoming of the troops, be-draggled and with injuries of gas and shell shock. "The truth was that none of this should have happened."

"Our politicians knew nothing of how to negotiate, that

was the trouble, and greed, I dare say"

"So, you recon you could have done better?" Jason said, pulling up his chair and relishing the aroma of the lamb stew she was about to serve.

Jason heaved himself out of bed. The mist had lifted, leaving a bright and sunny morning. He could see from the landing window that the cows already massed at Sweetacre gate to the yard and stalls, the hens cutting off, pigs were snorting and squealing. "Christ. A farmer's lot," he thought. "C'mon love rise and shine."

Mary sat up in bed. "What's the time?" she said, still drowsy.

"Well, one thing's for sure, we may be living in a Manor, but the work never stops." Jason pulled on his trousers and hopped over to the door, calling Henry to get up and let the cows in.

Henry had been assigned this job through the summer months. As he said he loved to get up early and feel the pleasure of the country air in his lungs, the love of the country pulling him closer and closer to his very being, something he'd never imagined when living in London. He pulled open the gate and the herd instantly followed one another into their chosen stall. It was uncanny that they all knew which stall was theirs, not one-stepped out of line. He next ran to the arks to let the hens out. On his way back he paused to see if anyone was about and watching his movements. He secretly had the urge to pop over to the ferret hutch to see if Hans had replied to Laura's letter, but he had sworn an oath and let the moment pass. It was their secret and one should never interfere.

When he entered, the Kitchen Dotty had arrived to begin breakfast. The farm had come alive and in the spate of an hour, there was so much to do. Next, the land army girls arrived, but Henry, maladroit in his haste to ready himself for the journey to Luton Tech, overlooked the collecting of the eggs.

The order from Jason that the radio should broadcast all day Dotty found most distracting, as there were items from the move still to be found homes. Mary had given her a list as to where these items should be placed, as later; she and Aunt Lillian were catching the bus into Leighton. Hopefully, to bargain hunt, plus a little shopping, if time allowed.

Meanwhile, Hans was to fix the motor horn loud-hailer to the wall outside the kitchen door, then go to Great Dinge where he would find Laura and Jenny cutting with scythe and sickle the boundaries around the field, prior to the mowing machine being hitched to the GM they would be ready for hay making the next day...weather permitting.

Hans's job was to rake the grass from the hedge into a swathe so that by the time he reached Great Dinge, the girls would be half way round. He soon caught up with them, and he offered to scythe while they followed him, taking it in turns to rake. He worked at twice the rate as they did, and once he got into rhythm, he made it look easy. Every now and then, he would take a breather and wipe his brow. The day was warm by now. As they stood close together, Laura and Hans's swapped glances, and he made a gesture with his hand that he'd replied to her letter, and that it was in the ferret hutch, under the brick.

Dotty had prepared some fish paste sandwiches and a flask of tea, not forgetting Hans's bottle of water. She then proceeded to give three blasts on the motor horn. It was surprising how far the sound carried. The girls and Hans were reminded it was time for their dinner break. Jason retired to his new study to sift through the days post. Aunt Lillian had arranged a new system for him. She had the filing cabinet set up with all the bills and invoices running in an A to Z fashion and this pleased Jason.

The Home Service was giving out intermittent bulletins on how the Allied Forces had breached the German defences. The Americans and British were gaining new ground, but the Canadians suffered greatly

"Poor souls," Dotty said with extreme sadness, her eyes watering as she peeled the last remaining onions. Soon there'll be new vegetables and spring cabbage, and these thoughts bucked her up no end.

Jason came out of his study to see Laura and Jenny enter the old farmhouse. He strode over to enquire how their work had progressed. As they sat eating their sandwiches and pouring out the tea, Laura, an inquisitive soul by nature, asked Jason "After the war is over have you any idea who'll be working on the farm, and what are your intentions on the old farmhouse, and what do you think you will do with the building?"

"A good question, Laura I haven't given it much thought as yet, let's wait till the war ends, see how the government intend to run the country or which government is in power, and their views on agriculture. I can tell you I will need a couple of hands to run this place. Henry recons if he passes his exams he'll move to wherever there's work on the subject he's studying, so I don't think he'll be around here for long.

"You was hoping he'd turn into a farm manager?"

"No, not really, Henry has his own agenda, and an articulate brain. Anything to do with academies and he's lost you."

"So, would I be right in thinking you would consider me to stay and work for you? I've no one else to bother about, my family are disinterested in me."

"Well let's wait and see how things work out, aye?"

CHAPTER THIRTY

HANS 'S REPLY

As the covered wagon collected Hans, so the girls were waiting, and washing their hands ready to be collected themselves. When Laura said to Jenny, "I won't' be a minute, if the wagon arrives ask them to wait." She took off across the yard, pulling on her blazer coat as she went. The farm was deserted. No people were on the allotments. She opened the gate to the orchard and slipped the catch on the hutch. Sure enough, the brown envelope lay under the brick. She quickly and deftly slid it into her inside pocket and ran back to where her companion was waiting. It was at that precise moment she felt the hairs on the back of her neck stand up, as Mary and Aunt Lillian walked arm in arm into the yard with just a split second to wave them goodbye as she clambered aboard the back of the wagon. "Phew!" she said, "That was close."

Jenny knew what she was talking about, but gave nothing away to the other girls who had been collected earlier. Laura couldn't wait to get to the hostel, her imagination-running wild as to what Hans had written. The girls piled out of the wagon, so Laura held back until they had all dispersed to their quarters, then she quietly tiptoed into the cloakroom where she sat silently, nervously contemplating opening the letter, her thoughts those of an excited teenager on her first date.

Her first impressions was of how carefully Hans had

constructed the letter in broken English, with a few exceptions of spelling. He'd endeavoured to write a reply of a nature to the extent of not being a love letter; it was quite evident he was missing his mother and father. He wrote on, expressing his concerns that the Allies had landed, or where his parents actually were, as he'd never received any mail since his interment, which Laura found very disturbing.

Laura couldn't understand why Hans never received any mail, unless his parents had been killed in the air raids. She knew the intensity of the raids in the build up to the landings, or they could have moved on, maybe to Hans's cousin whom he wrote about living a few kilometres away. He went on to describe how the living conditions at the camp were primitive, but they coped and are reasonably well. He also wrote of the welcome and hospitality of Mr Smith and all at the farm, and maybe after the war he would return to see the people whom he writes of with such deference and understanding, and Laura herself he would definitely correspond and keep in touch.

Laura could only describe the letter as being from a person whose mind was in a state of turmoil and at odds with the world, sometimes defensive but tempered with resignation of the inevitable. Hans concluded that he would love to continue with the present arrangement, something he found very amusing and if he was ever moved to a different part of the country he would endeavour to keep writing, even if it meant seducing the guard on the gate to post a letter to you; *It would mean, however, our association would be made public, and he would try his utmost to persuade the guard to keep it their secret, something that seemed insuperable, but he would try. He wrote that Laura should leave a forwarding address in the next letter assuming that a transfer was in the pipeline of if repatriation started earlier than once thought.*

Who knows what's in the mind of governments and military as we all live from one day to the next. I will be extremely happy for you to keep writing, as this alleviates all thoughts of war, a form of therapy, which I consider myself fortunate to have met you.

If for example return home and find that my parents are still at the Darmstadt smallholding or not, I have made up my mind to return to England and live my life out here. Laura felt an overwhelming urge to cry out "Yes!" she said it under her breath.

Jenny's call for her provoked an immediate reaction, joining her senses back to reality. She folded the letter and tucked it into her breast pocket to finish later.

"Are you going into town tonight?" Jenny asked. "Where are you?"

"Here in the cloak, just coming!" Laura hurried through the corridor and into the canteen to find most of the girls had eaten and left already for a night out to the Oriel cinema or pubs to pick up some unsuspecting airman who frequented the bars in Leighton. Sometimes it usually ended in a bout of fisticuffs but was the norm, all down to Benskins Draught Ale, so strong for the young heads. Laura felt the need to be alone, so she excused herself, and Jenny joined another party of girls who were just heading out.

Good she thought, and greedily ate some mince stew and mash potatoes before crashing down on the bunk bed, as each cubicle had its own wrap-around curtain for a little privacy. As she opened the letter for a second time, she became aware of someone near the bunk. A soft voice started to hum Vera Lynn's song The White Cliffs of Dover. It was Jenny who could not leave Laura on her own; she just had to know what was going on. Laura pulled the curtain back and grinned at Jenny, squeezed her hand and said, "Curiosity killed the cat."

They laughed their silly heads off, and she moved over to let Jenny lie beside her, while both read the letter.

With nobody else in the quarters, Laura was able to read Hans letter in her soft toned voice. When she read the last sentence, Jenny gave a sharp intake of breath.

"Does that mean he's returning for you?"

"I don't know, what do you think?"

"Well what else would he come back for, only you, surely. You'll certainly write to him, then you'll know once and for good he can't refuse?"

Supposition was flying in all directions, at this early stage they could only assume.

"Are you going to reply tonight I could help?" Jenny said. Anxious to know what Laura was thinking. Jenny couldn't wait. She fished in her locker for pen and paper.

"I'm not writing a long letter, Jenny," Laura said, "just a short note."

"Well, can't you write for an explanation, what he means about returning to England? Ask him if he intends to live at Claridges. I would."

"I'm sure you would," Laura said.

Jenny, so excited, prattled on. "I'll be your maid in waiting. I can see the headlines now in the local paper, Land Army girl falls in love with the enemy. No, with German airman prisoner of war."

"No. no, no. You've got it all wrong Jenny, there'll be no wedding or headlines, we do not know what will happen, not just yet, at any rate."

Jenny slipped her arm around Laura's waist and squeezed her. "You know, whatever the outcome of this so-called friendship of yours with Hans, in the end it all depends how he feels about you, nothing is that certain however you look at it." Jenny lay back on the bunk bed, and then said "Do you really love him, I mean love?"

CHAPTER THIRTY ONE

RAMIFICATIONS

Something wasn't quite fulfilling in Jason's life. He thought he had shown good judgement in what he had achieved, but the farm had come through the very worst of this period of time. Harvest, though moderate, had been retrieved, autumn beheld her glory. Jason spread his arms wide on the top rail of the gate to the orchard and allotments

Old Botty, the taxi driver, had taken advantage of Jason's gesture of giving the villagers a chance to dig for victory. He came towards Jason after digging out his crop of King Edward potatoes to lay and dry before storing for the winter months, they exchanged pleasantries about the weather, stood for a while chatting before heading off home pushing his wheelbarrow full of vegetables and garden tools, but not before he presented Jason with an autumn cabbage. Just as he was about to leave he dropped the barrow and said "Oh by the way, I quite forgot, as I came in to the allotments, this was lying on the path." He slid out the letter from his inside pocket and gave it to Jason; "I thought it must be yours, anyway, good-day to you, see you." he passed on his way whistling Rule Britannia.

Jason examined the letter with extreme curiosity and fingered it over to the address side. No name was written, it was unsealed.

***

"How could she?" Mary said, angst welling inside her. She handed the letter back to Jason who re-read the contents.

"Well, I suppose the inevitable was sure to happen, I'm partly to blame by throwing them together when they were spreading fertilizer. Dotty was right to criticize, she said no good would come mixing them like a pudding. Yea and I laughed at her."

"What will you do?" Mary asked

"We say nothing at the moment, just wait, and see."

"What I can't understand is why the letter was on the path in the first place."

Henry arrived home at the farm just as Laura and Jenny were leaving. Perched on the end seat of the waggon Laura gave Henry the thumbs up sign, Henry reciprocated. Clearly, she looked happy. The wagon drove off, the odour of petrol still lingering in the air. Gyp greeted him as usual with a couple of delighted woofs and a tail wag round his legs. He slumped into the chair and slapped his satchel down on to the refectory top. He sighed. "I'm fed up."

Jason and Mary eyed each other, wondering if something wasn't right with the boy.

"What now?" his mother asked.

"Well. I'm not old enough to join the forces, I'm not old enough to drink a pint of best bitter, I'm not anything at the moment. I worry of others having affairs, and getting away with it. It's not fair."

Jason, with raised eyebrows, looked again at Mary then at Henry "Are you being used for doing something you really don't want to do?" Jason asked.

"No," he replied, aware that he felt very insecure and out of his depth.

"You're not sure; can we be of any help?" Jason held the envelope in front of Henry. "Is it because of this?"

"You found out then." Henry showed bewilderment.

"Mr Bott found it on the path in front of the old ferret hutch, do you know about this?" Jason asked, waving it to and fro in front of Henry's face.

"I'm sworn to secrecy, I'm on oath." He answered.

"Since how long?"

"A couple of months, I think."

"How could she involve you?" Mary said with a dissatisfied shrug of the shoulders, you should not be burdened with such cloak and dagger stuff. I suppose you know what we are talking here?"

**

Hans sat on the end of the bunk bed wondering why there was no reply to his letter. Laura hadn't given any indication that anything was amiss; there was so much to write about. In his mind, Laura was the best thing to have happened to him. It was easy to be reticent but there was so much to learn about this a country. Hans had not given up on the idea about living in England, and it was no good for him to be anything other than retractile, quite the opposite, he would enrol himself into camp English class. Owing to illness, the camp Commander had been replaced by the second in command, who instantly hired a retired English professor to carry on with the Shakespearian play they were rehearsing. The professor would alternate from one camp to another offering Latin and English, a subject for the prisoners to alleviate any boredom or suffering, he was there to translate.

The months ahead would even be more beneficial to himself, as a proper drama group was formed which he participated in with much gusto. The professor had a command of German as well, which made learning about the play easier, so from Shakespeare's long list of classic's "Comedy of Errors" was right for them. The commander had chosen the central characters being mostly male, the female part being spoken by his wife. The professor had re-written and typed each character on a separate foolscap, i.e. Germanic underlined in English. He had gone to great length to help the prisoners understand the meaning of his work.

Plenty of volunteers came forward, so many; the professor had difficulty in retaining, and eliminating who he thought not good enough for a part. Hans had won the part of Old Solinus. He was proud of himself, but to be fair, and to others who failed, they would have another chance later, but would sit in on the rehearsals. Scores of foolscap were printed for them to follow the play and learn English at the same time.

Hans tried desperately to erase Laura from his mind, but for all his efforts he lay prone and none plus on his bunk. Studying the narrative and script, which the professor had distributed amongst his fellow thespians. Hans prepared and committed himself to learn William Shakespeare, but try as he may, Laura's face kept haunting him. He turned over on to his left side his side cheek cupped in his hand, trying in earnest to get her out of his mind. He fingered through the script until his eyelids closed and he slept soundly.

***

The alarm by Jason's bedside cabinet woke him at five thirty. The hall clock now standing by the front door, struck the half hour, its dulcet tone somewhat subdued as there were so many coves and twists and turns in the Manor leading to the front door and porch. Jason slid out of the new bed they had just purchased, a loud twang made him flinch as he stood up to go to the bathroom. Mary sat up with a start. A spring had sprung through the mattress.

"Well that's all we need right now, only a few weeks old and already damaged." Jason laughed his way to the bathroom.

"I'm glad you can see the funny side of it." She spluttered, it means I'll have to dig out the guarantee and receipt, do you know whcre we filed the invoices?"

Jason stood on the landing, his face covered in shaving soap, still giving little chuckles in between trying to shave.

Henry could here all of this as he propped himself up in bed and gazed out over the meadows; the herd waited patiently at Sweetacre Gate.

At the breakfast table, Jason said he'd made up his mind about Laura and Hans. "Henry," he said "Here, take the letter and replace it in the hutch. We'll say no more, let us all carry on as if nothing has happened, I don't want the farm to descend into a place of intrigue, not just yet."

Henry contemplated on revealing everything to Laura, but stopped short because of Jason's protracted piece of wisdom. An oath was an oath; the secret was still inside the farm boundary. If however, the tryst were to spread to the villager's all hell would be let loose. Jason in their eyes would be branded as bad as Laura for letting the association continue. So long as it remained just correspondence, what harm would there be? Better to let the whole thing die a death.

***

As the Allies drove deeper and deeper into France and the Netherlands, everybody couldn't wait for the Nazis to surrender and end this bloody war.

The girls gathered the apples, plums, and pears while Hans trundled the sack barrow to and fro to the loft for storage. Jason followed their every move. They suspected nothing, only Jason knew the truth about them; he gave them plenty of space while keeping a wary eye. This in turn caused Jason extreme displeasure and nervous tension, insomuch as to lay him to his bed through sheer exhaustion, the doctor prescribing complete rest, and a prescription of a bottle of medicine, iron tonic. Mary, Henry, and Alec would give out orders of the day; the daily planner was used to its full capacity.

The girls would carry much of the burden. Henry would take time out from Luton Tech on compassionate grounds, granted leave for two weeks to help his mother handle the farm management. Laura and Jenny would take over the milking, while Aunt Lillian, Mary and Dotty expedited everything else from shopping, cleaning, and just about everything else that needed doing, only to learn that Jason was an impatient patient forever knocking on the floor above the kitchen.

"What's going on?" he demanded, "Why am I being ignored?" Mary carried the tray with a hot mug of cocoa and a dry biscuit, which Dotty had baked the day before. "What's happening?" he enquired as Mary entered the bedroom.

"Oh shush now." She was about to inform him of how work was progressing, when Aunt Lillian called from the bottom of the staircase. "Alec's here, can he see Jason?" Mary had forewarned him that sometime during his recuperation he would be expected to receive somebody at some point about farm duties.

"What is it?" Mary called back.

"The Fordson tractor has seized up!"

Jason heard every word. "Christ, send him up. C'mon in

Alec, tell me the worst."

"Well we think the tractor has busted an oil ring in one of the cylinders. Hans says he could fix it if you'll let him. Anyway, how are you boss?" Alec was concerned about Jason.

"I'm alright, just don't want any fuss." He gave Mary a sideways glance.

She protested. "You know what the doctor said, rest!"

Jason sat propped up against the headboard and sipped his cocoa. He gently rested the mug on the tray.

"Well as I see it, we've got no option but to use the GM tractor for the milling and you'll have to unhitch the belt every time you want to use it for another job; let Hans strip the Fordson down and get to the problem. By that time I might be well enough to travel to Leighton with the Rover and purchase whatever he finds broken, from Browns Agri-implements, and while he's at it check all cylinders for defects."

"Do you think Hans is up to repairing the tractor?" Jason said, feeling very perplexed about the whole thing.

"I'm sure he can fix it, says he was always repairing his father's machines when they broke down. So he says."

Henry always wanted to ride the cycle that Jason rode. He was sent to the shop for aspirin as Jason was suffering a headache. Poor old Jason, what with fatigue, and the tractor problem, it was enough to give anyone a bad head. Gyp ran alongside Henry on the cycle, when he spotted Madge coming towards him on her cycle.

She waved him down. "Are you going AWOL from Tech?" she asked.

"No, we have a crisis at the farm, I've been granted leave to give assistance."

"What's the problem, can I help?"

"It's Jason, he must rest, doctors' orders. I've to hurry for aspirin from Ma Leeches, and I must return straight away. No time to chat." Henry could be a little discourteous sometimes.

"I'll come with you, I'm sure your mum needs some help?"

Madge was a peach of a girl, she always considered others first. They rode together back to the farm. "How's your studying coming along?" Madge asked.

"I have exams next month, I shall be swotting a lot, and not much time for anything I'm afraid."

"Won't this time off be an interference?" she asked.

"No, the tutor gave me a syllabus on my subject to complete before I return."

"You have a lot on your plate, why don't you let me help you with some of the chores. I'm sure you need some?"

Madge and Henry rode into the yard with Gyp running alongside. Mary saw them both as they propped their cycles under the hovel.

***

The Manor standing opposite the old farmhouse. She had a good view of the yard; she was able to see the comings and goings of the milk collection lorry, another lorry unloading feed to the mixing shed, the postman, and who would call next, none other than Gertrude.

"Ran into Dotty, told me about Jason, just thought I would pop in to see how things were with you and the farm, and how you are coping."

There was so much concern amongst the village people that Jason and Mary had to turn down most offers. It broke her heart, but she knew if too many were running about the place it meant a safety issue, and they couldn't afford that.

Mary was glad that Madge had cycled back with Henry, but first she made her ring her parents and explain where she was and why she was helping out. To have a young girl about the Manor lifted Mary's spirits.

She switched on the radio to listen to Workers Playtime, a live show coming direct from a factory in Luton, and she sang as she busied about the kitchen. Madge pitched in with Aunt Lillian to make the beds, some sheets needed washing. Jason's bed was first, he was sent to the bathroom while his bed was changed, griping, as he went.

"Why is everybody so happy and singing, nobody should be this happy in times like these, how can it be so?" he said grudgingly.

Alec made it his business to offer his services to Hans wherever possible. He was surprised at the speed he worked, when he last visited, Hans had actually removed the head off and exposed the cylinders.

Number three cylinder was the culprit with the oil ring showing to be broken.

"Gute, Gute, Gott Wohlwolen." He said. "It only remains for me to slide underneath and slacken off the main bearing nuts. If you can just hand me the spanner, Alec, I can push the piston up through the sleeve and we can remove the offending ring."

Alec stood back admiring Hans's tenacity, he'd always had reservations about POW.s, but Hans was quite unique inasmuch as he never once objected or feigned work whatever he was asked to carry out. He was resolute in his behaviour.

He would in future have second thoughts on Hans. Alec reported back to Jason that Hans had located the problem and showed him the broken ring.

"Crikey." That's all Jason could say.

After differences between Mary and himself Jason abandoned his sick bed and drove to Brown Agri Imp, as earlier, he had phoned the service department to see if they stocked the oil ring. They did indeed have the ring, and they enquired who was fitting the piece. After Jason explained, Brown Agri Imp became very interested in Hans accumulated knowledge of farm machinery, and how he earned a pfennig in Germany by repairing other breakdowns.

Jason drove the Rover under the hovel, retrieved the part from the passenger seat, and strode over to where Hans had just switched off the GM tractor. A mound of turnips and worzels had been sliced apart ready to mix with other variable foodstuff, while he'd been to Leighton. The cows would munch through this whilst being milked. Hans mind had been made up since he started work at the farm, now was the right time to approach Jason about his decision. When everything was taken into account the farm had just about coped, and would he consider that whatever he found back home in Germany after repatriation he would come back to England to work on his farm at Claridges, if need by him.

"I'll give you my answer when the war is finally over." Jason said, "The way the war is going, I shouldn't think it will be very long now."

Jason knew Hans would need an answer sometime. To be fair to him, Jason had made his mind up; Hans was a great asset, but not just yet. Laura was about to pursue him also over her recommendations of just how good she was about the farm. Jason would not worry over who should, or would not, be in his employ; as things stood, two very fine and opinionated people would come together at some time in the future. Jason would follow the couples swings, moods, and attitudes during the season to come.

AUTHORS NOTE

HANS & LAURA

After the war, ended Hans's association with Laura became publicly known throughout the community. Jason and Mary had no hesitation in agreeing to their tryst being recognised as a fact, their verdict was an emphatic yes, what anybody else thought did not really matter. Jason had the assurance from Hans that after his repatriation he would return to England and marry Laura. To live and work at Claridge farm. But, before his repatriation, he learned of his family's plight, via the Red Cross, of being wiped out by stray bombs that hit the homestead. He had no immediate relatives to go home for, so would stay in England, find lodgings somewhere in the village and work from there.

Jason had other ideas. Claridge farm's old house remained in reasonable habitable condition, made clear his idea to Laura and Hans that he would hire a contractor to clean and paint the interior if they would paint the exterior in their spare time of course, rent would be nominal, and stopped accordingly from their wages. A rent book would be provided. Jason also granted Hans time off if he wanted to return to Germany if only to satisfy himself that what had happened did happen. Everybody in the village, bar a few who did not approve, helped Laura with the wedding arrangements, the big question being would the Church of England allow the wedding to proceed. Hans's parents were

Lutheran, he also followed Lutheranism. The reverend Stefans had no objection, neither did the church.

Though shortages of food and clothing remained in England for some time, Hans was provided with a suit donated by Gertrude Wilson Green; her one time butler having left in a hurry, discarding it and it was still hanging in the wardrobe of his flat. It fitted Hans perfectly an alteration to the sleeves was the only adjustment to make.

Hans, although far from home, needed a witness, (best man). Laura's assumption of how easy it would be to marry Hans received a severe jolt. Jenny had agreed to maid of honour, but finding a best man from the inhabitants for Hans, that was a different matter. Hans however found a solution. He would apply for naturalization and become a British citizen. This way would soften the hearts of most of the village people into being more sympathetic to his plight. He needed desperately to be accepted by the locals. Feelings were running high, as the atrocities, which the Nazis inflicted on many Jews, were making headline news.

Hans decided to meet the challenge head on. One by one the prisoner of war camps closed down; so were the Land Army girls quarters shut, and remained empty till sold by auction. Jason's contribution to help Hans resulted in Hans giving details of his foot, chest, inside leg and waist measurements. With these Jason sojourned to Leighton for the day and purchased trousers, a leather jacket, two shirts, three pairs of socks, a boiler suit, and wellington boots all from a second hand stall on the Back Market. Restrictions began to relax as the months went by, the authorities turning a blind eye. Laura and Hans cohabited in the old farmhouse until the wedding day.

Bush burning was the order of the day planner; to commemorate his naturalization Hans pitched his old uniform on to the bonfire. Alec threw the cap up to the sky, but kept it as a memento, and they all cheered. Hans was free at last. A westerly wind blew the ignited remnants across Upper Dinge, gone forever. Hans found his best man in Alec, he had never ever been asked to be a best man in his entire life, although at first being very sceptical about the relationship, he now embraced the moment.

History had taught Alec not to hate or be critical of anyone. He loved both of them, for their honesty and integrity, above all their friendship.

Hans and Laura remained in Jason's employ for over four decades, and throughout those years they both mourned the passing of Alec, Dotty, Jason and Mary, and Aunt Lillian.

Mary outlived Jason by six years, during which time the Manor and the Old Farm House, the acreage to the farm, was sold. If Hans and Laura were still living their chance to purchase the Old Farm House would be on the understanding that whatever the house was valued at and was sold, the rent which they had paid over the years would be reimbursed from the proceeds of the asking price by the agents, and still they would live their life out in the Old Farm House, or with the monies to retire to wherever.

Hans in his infinite wisdom returned to Germany with Laura, as there were no children. Their lives weren't complicated. They made their way to Darmstadt where Hans would try to piece together what really happened to his family. They first visited the local library after they booked into a cheap local hostelry, a type of motel. It was cheap, but would facilitate their progress in search for the truth about his family. Darmstadt had changed beyond all recognition. Hans was troubled with his whereabouts, but one thing was certain, a glider caught his attention the sailplane had found a thermal; he pointed to the sky, pressed Laura's arm and smiled. He knew they were home.

The librarian was a charming woman in her late thirties. Her hair of chestnut brown was combed straight off the forehead and tied with a mauve ribbon into a bob. Her rimless glasses were thrust up and resting on her head. "Yes?" she said in perfect English, "Can I be of help?"

Hans and Laura gazed at the computer and sighed. "We are not used to this technology, never had the time." He said.

"Well, I am here to help. Tell me, do you live here in Darmstadt?" Hans replied, "I was born and lived here up until the war." "Well how can I be of assistance to you both?"

Hans reflected. "I don't know where to start, really. Before the war my family lived a kilometre or so to the west of Darmstadt on a homestead near the Glider-Drome. Rudy Maher was my father's name, my mother's Lidia."

"So you are trying to trace your family?"

"Ya, I was born at the homestead in nineteen twenty." At this point, she interrupted. "I think Mr Maher you should visit the Municipal Town Hall and ask for the Archive Department. It's in Dieburger Strabe. Turn right out of here, then right again, and you'll find the building at the end of the Bleichplatz.

"Thank you." He and Laura, holding hands, walked out of the building and the librarian followed to make sure they had listened correctly to her directions. She waved them goodbye.

They followed her directions to the letter. They passed through the revolving glass door and stepped into a magnificent marbled hall. The re building of Darmstadt was quite remarkable; Hans and Laura were noted by the receptionist, who beckoned them over.

"May I help you?" she said in good English.

Hans asked for the archivist and she directed them to the

stairs leading to the basement, to room thirty- two. Hans knocked lightly. They both waited.

"Come in!" a male voice answered.

They were met by a tall lean gentleman in his late fifties, bespectacled and dressed in a dark green velvet jacket and pink spotted bow tie, his appearance that of a man who had visited the Algarve or Costas just recently. He sported a greying goatee, his dress immaculate.

"What can I do for you?" he spoke in a soft baritone voice.

Hans and Laura were gestured to sit in a pair of high backed chairs upholstered in red fabric, plush and comfortable. He sat opposite, his hands clasped together and arms sprawled across the mahogany desk inlaid with a leather pad. He adjusted his bow tie. "Tell me, how I can assist you both?"

The archivist clicked his computer on while listening to Hans describing his family's history. In the middle eighties, computers were basic, but to monitor the job within the civic hall. To meet Hans needs the archivist asked him his father's full name.

"Rudi Van Maher....Your mother's?"

"Lydia Colette Maher, nee Blume." Replied Hans

"Ah, ah, that's good, as he keyed in the info, he asked." Do you know where their marriage took place?"

"Ya, right here in Darmstadt, at Concord Lutherans church." Is the church still intact?" Hans asked.

"The church took a direct hit, but has since been repaired, you should visit." He shifted his spectacles by their safety cord, on to his lapels, tampered with the computer once more, and said, "No, no, we would be better off checking through the archives manually." He replaced his glasses and said, "Come with me." He led them down a passageway and into a large room where oak pedestals were placed at spaced intervals. He chose one and asked them to remain.

He returned with a large hard backed file and opened it on the pedestal. He turned each page until he reached the letter M, and ran his forefinger down each column until he reached Maher. Hans squeezed Laura's hand and waited patiently.

"Ah, here we are, look, there."

He pointed at the wording. Rudi Van Maher and wife Lydia. Found their bodies burnt and lacerated in homestead after a stray bomb hit the property, and buried together in the grounds of Concord Lutherans Church. A tear rolled down the side of Hans's cheek.

"Danke you," he said, "You have been very helpful." The archivist shook hands and wished them well and good luck on their quest.

Hans had his bearings a bit straighter, now he knew the church would be in the Rhinestrade. As they entered through the Vorbau and Tor, the porch gate, a Lutheran Pastor met them walking towards his church. He greeted them with a smile and, knowing them not to be his regular flock, asked, "Could I be of help?"

The day had been long and warm for September. Hans decided to call it a day, but Laura insisted they press on until the sun finally set. The pastor duly rendered his services in such a manner that he forgo his teatime and placed himself at their disposal, and after listening to Hans's shortened version of why they were in Darmstadt, the pastor was delighted that the information they sought would be in the vestry, and cordially invited them in.

Hans remembered when as a boy he stood with his parents at Sunday evensong all those years ago, the east stained glass window still intact with the sun streaming in from the west oval window, throwing rays of gold, blues and greens. The pastor guided them to the vestry where he unlocked a cupboard and retrieved a large black leather bound type book. With renewed vigour and an urge to investigate further, Hans wanted to know where his parents were buried within the grounds. The pastor requested their names and once again, Hans followed the forefinger down each column.

The pastor gestured. "There we are, see? They lay buried at the Eastern end, plot ten.

Hans read the column as did Laura both gazing through watering eyes.

"Shall I accompany you?" the pastor asked

"Ya, if you can spare the time," Hans replied. They sauntered across the newly mown grass. The graves and headstones were kept neat but weatherworn, and in fair condition. The pastor approached and pointed to grave with a small marble scroll, with the inscription, "Bestowed with Dignity and Honour by the Town of Darmstadt, in memory of two wonderful people, Rudi and Lydia Maher. 1944."

The pastor left them to their sorrow, and Hans and Laura stood for quite some time with their heads bowed, occasionally looking up at the grandeur of the church. They both had the feeling of someone else standing close, but away a little so as not to invade their privacy. Holding each other's hand they turned and quietly walked towards the church's main door, the pastor welcomed them in with a serene reverence. He ushered them to a pew in front of the pulpit, and asked if they needed him anymore.

Hans replied "No" and thanked him for his kindness and understanding.

Meanwhile, the stranger who they noticed standing away

from them moved behind them, still keeping his distance. Being very patient, he sat down in the small annex, biding his time.

As Hans and Laura rose to leave, the pastor humbly requested them to return to the church on Sunday, as he would dedicate the evening service to his mother and father, a reunion service for Hans and Laura. To the congregation it was a homecoming for a long lost son of the diocese, and would Hans care to say something about his parents and how his life was spent in England? Even the pastor was eager to hear his story.

Hans agreed, but first they needed to return to the motel and eat and rest. The pastor shook their hands warmly and bade them farewell. "See you Sunday?"

Both of them needed time to reflect on the past few hours, they had achieved almost a miracle to find information so quickly.

As they walked to the annex the stranger stood up and begged his intrusion, he then introduced himself as Karl Wernerman, a reporter from the local paper. "The Darmstadt Press."

"How and why do you want to report on us?" Hans asked.

"Well, my name is Karl; you met my wife, the librarian. She told me she thought your being here and the information you were seeking, I should write a column. She put two and two together, and here I am reporting an interesting story, if you agree?"

Hans and Laura made their way back to the carpark and as they entered the car, Hans called to the reporter, "be at the Concord Lutheran Church Sunday night if you want my story!"

***

The congregation swelled to almost four times that of previous evensong, for the pews provided were overflowing. No doubt, the pastor had been busy in notifying his flock.

When Hans and Laura returned to the church, curious heads turned, their eagerness showing on everyone's face. Hans's mouth dried. He swallowed hard, expecting only a handful of people, and he and Laura were shown to their designated pew, they felt very honoured.

Hans scoured the congregation for the reporter; in fact, he was seated next to them; he held a small recording device and leaned over to ask Hans for his permission. Hans nodded in agreement for Karl to record his story. The last hymn was sung and the pastor moved to the green-carpeted aisle and introduced Hans to them.

An hour is a long time for anyone to hold an audience, never mind a person who has never addressed a crowded church before, but in his native tongue, Hans stuck to the storyline as best he could. Only once did he falter moment he reached the point of being told by his Air Kommandant that his mission was to kill one of his own people, that being Rudolph Von Hess. Murmurs surrounded the inner sanctum.

Many of the congregation were elderly; he suspected they had survived the Allied Forces push and the race for Berlin. Memories would have been ignited of those early days of the war and here they were enmeshed.

The smiles on their faces as Hans concluded, and introduced his wife Laura, and told how the villagers of Eggington had embraced him, and made him feel welcome within the community, given their friendship, and how he had become manager of the farm, his subsequent marriage to Laura, and the spirit they showed when bad times ruled, received tumultuous applause. Good times were here with peace.

Hans and Laura returned to England. Rose Cottage came up for sale, which they purchased and settled into for their retirement.

HENRY & MADGE

Henry's closeness to Madge became more noticeable by his friends and family. Their hope for the union would continue long after the war into something more tangible and lasting. His friendship with Jason never to wane on one's own volition and an ability to do things for yourself; was Jason's motto, and you become more self- satisfied.

Jason's wisdom was self- evident in which Henry tried not to placate himself; others would see him as a reliable member of the community. Henry's destiny had been governed, not by someone near, but someone far away who also thought he could become an artist but failed and took his revenge through antisemitism. Some artists, thought, preferred to shy away from the far left or far right political views; Henry was more liberal and politically correct, he intended to avoid implied prejudices.

After completing his studies at Luton Technical College and apprenticed with Dillimore & Wallis, the next decade beckoned, his military duties, i.e. National Service. His mother always said. "Dad gave his life for his country and freedom; keep this in mind, son, wherever you are, or whatever you are do." Henry joined the army R.E.M.E. and was stationed at Bulford camp where for two years he knuckled down to army life. He travelled to Italy and Canada, which broadened his mind and outlook towards different cultures. Many times, he received letters from Madge, mum and Aunt Lillian. Time flew by, the relationship with Madge revealed a serious meaning after returning to civilian life. The farm had move forward in mechanisation, new machinery had been purchased, a combine harvester, and a new seed drill stood side by side under the roof of a new building Jason had had built on the site of the allotments, which by now had fallen in to neglect. Hans and Laura lived happily in the old farmhouse. Most of the villagers accepted Hans as more of a local, than a foreigner.

Cricket resumed in the meadow, which Henry remembered as an evacuee sitting in the trailer. As they passed, the score- figures hung dejectedly askew.

Madge and Henry finally tied the knot, and were given a wing of the manor to live in until such times as to what Henry decided to do with his life. Would he resume his duties at Dillimore & Wallis, or pitch himself into farm life with Jason? Neither mum nor Jason would stand in his way, which ever he chose. The main thing for Henry was to sit down with the one hand he could not hurt anyone, Dillimore & Wallis were expecting him to resume his employ with them, in fact in his absence they had promoted him to a more senior role with the company, which he already knew of. On the other hand, Jason and his mum weren't getting any younger; they needed him as much as Dillimore &Wallis. There had to be a compromise. How was he to extricate himself from this dilemma!

It came out of the blue one day. A telephone call to the Manor for Henry just as he was preparing himself for work helping out on the farm until his mind was made up.

"Henry." The caller said, "Wallis speaking, Bad news, I'm afraid, Mr Dillimore passed away unexpectedly last night, leaving me in a bit of a quandary."

"I'm very sorry to hear that, but how does that affect me?"

"Well he was the head man as regards to finance of the business, as you well know, and I was just a supporting body with no clout as to how we run the firm, so as far as I know, this is the end of Dillimore & Wallis, I'm sorry to say."

The news couldn't have come at a better time for Henry, which was a relief. He knew now his path lay clear to immerse himself and his energy in the farm for his mum and Jason. In their heart of hearts, the family would engage as a unit.

"Don't despair." Jason had said, "If you want time off to further your career or a refresher course on whatever subject you choose, you are free at any time to pursue it." He chose art classes in all forms, such as watercolour, acrylic, and oil; there was little he didn't know but still so much to learn.

Baby Susannah had been born and she grew into a lovely fair-haired teenager. She had studied to a certain degree in the retail business and met her fiancée in the same trade, married and moved to the South coast to become manager of a large department store.

In Jason's will, if whosoever dies first the last shall inherit, until the farm, land, and chattels be sold on the open market, meant that Henry would inherit everything.

Madge and Henry moved to Petersfield, Hampshire, and purchased an Art and Craft studio. Madge supervised the craft side, and Henry the art, teaching on a one to one basis the technique of art, to budding artists. Their lives and work were so absorbing they both at times forgot who they were, where had all the years gone? They asked themselves.

One evening, tired and jaded, Henry switched on the television for no apparent reason other than to sit and relax. The programme was showing a viewing of the Antiques Road Show, and the presenter for the BBC, had just concluded an interview with owners of a mansion at Luton Hoo. Fascinated, Henry called Madge from the kitchen; they lived in a flat above the studio.

In full view on screen was a portrait of a Zulu Warrior in full ceremonial dress. The expert, addressing a well bosomed lady, asked her how she come by the portrait.

"Well, my husband and I purchased a farmhouse, which incidentally wasn't a listed property and had stood since William the IV we believe, so we gutted the interior only to find the picture wedged between two pieces of hardboard. We suspect it hung like a door as drought excluder. The whole door was painted emulsion white. We found some of the gold-lacquered frame showing on the edge, and prized away the boards only to find this."

"Hmm," the expert rubbed his chin. "I don't know the artist, but it's a striking portrait, and value? Hmm, I would put an estimate of fifty thousand pounds. Yes, it's that good."

Henry and Madge stood and looked at each other perplexed.

"Well I never," Madge said, "Shouldn't the portrait, I mean, wasn't it bequeathed to you?"

"Well I suppose, I knew at the time, I questioned myself that something wasn't quite right about the number of paintings listed."

"You still have correspondence?" Madge asked.

"I suppose so, think about it there might, but wait, how do we know it's the same painting, the presenter didn't name the artist."

"Well, why can't we contact Connaught's at Leighton to

see if litigation is possible," Madge yawned, "C'mon let's go to bed I'm tired."

They dreamed a dream. Had the Zulu eluded them?

Printed in Great Britain
by Amazon